CRUEL JOKE

K.A. MIHALICS

Dedication

This book is dedicated in loving memory of my Nana.
Her family was her greatest love and accomplishment, followed by slot
machines in Atlantic City and grocery shopping on Saturdays. There is
not a second, hour or day that goes by that I do not miss her.

1926 - 2014

"Cause I love you a bushel and a peck…"

"Shit too"

-Anna Bucher

"In the end, only three things matter: how much you loved, how gently you lived, and how gracefully you let go of things not meant for you."

-Buddha

Chapter 1 | Road Trip

The early summer sun was warm as it peered through my sunroof and shimmered through the tall, leafy trees while I drove up the NY Thruway. I had my mirrored aviators on and "Satellite" by Rise Against blaring from the speakers as I belted out the lyrics completely out of tune. My long, chestnut-brown hair was pulled back in a messy bun and pieces were flying freely around my face. I felt so relaxed and carefree as I kept with the afternoon traffic.

I was taking a trip to visit my best friend, Maggie Rowe, for her birthday. Maggie was twenty-seven and working as a veterinarian in upstate New York. It had been some time since I had made the three-and-a-half-hour drive to visit her. I hated this drive. To say it was boring was an understatement. I also never drove there in the winter. My car was terrible in the snow and she lived in the boonies. One time when I was leaving her house they had a dusting of snow and I nearly ended up in a ditch on the side of the road, trying to make it down the mountain. After that I told Maggie I would only visit her when snow wasn't an issue. Maggie, on the other hand, wouldn't think twice about driving fifteen hours across four states, so she would always visit me more. When she moved to Oneonta, New York to attend college, she decided to stay. Maggie loved Jersey and would always come back to visit her family—and me, of course. She always said that she would move back one day, but I was running out of patience waiting for that day to come.

It had been nine years since my best friend had left for college. Maggie wanted to be a veterinarian, so that meant years of school. I thought she would move back after graduating Cornell, but the veterinary clinic she had interned at offered her a full-time position. She gladly accepted. It was bittersweet. I was happy for Maggie and proud of all she had accomplished—she had worked so very hard and was doing what she loved—but at the same time she was too far away and I missed her dearly.

Maggie was two years older than I was. We had become best friends after I started to date her brother Masen. I'd met Masen in middle school, when everyone was going through that awkward voice-changing, overnight-acne, and growth-spurt stage. He had short dirty blond hair, baby blue eyes, and was tall and lanky. I always felt ordinary and out of place with my mousy brown hair, chocolate brown eyes, and fair skin. Not to mention I was short with no curves back then.

When freshman year started, everyone looked different. They all looked more confident, less awkward, a little more grown-up. On the first day of school I was walking off the bus with my cousin Alayna. I was four months older than she was, but she was also a freshman and we were very close growing up. Alayna and I were alike in many ways. We were both only children and both of our parents were divorced. We looked alike and you could see the family resemblance. We'd always had the same color hair, and thanks to hair dye we were both now a beautiful chestnut brown. I was taller, though, and she had hazel eyes. Alayna was always my partner in crime.

We just got back from spending the month of August at our aunt's beach house down the shore. Our sun-kissed skin showed our lazy days on the beach, soaking in the sun. Alayna was the sister I never had, and we could always count on each other. Of course, there were those moments where I just wanted to slap the shit out of her. The first day of school as freshmen was one of those moments.

Alayna and I were walking into school together when I saw Masen. He was cutting through a crowd of teenagers, all miserable and all dreading the ten months ahead. My mind went into overdrive and before I knew what I was doing I said "Whoa!" I stared at him with my mouth hanging open, practically drooling. The way Alayna looked at me told me I hadn't used my inside voice.

She asked me, "Who or what is *whoa*?"

I motioned with my head toward Masen, and my cousin asked, "Masen Rowe is *whoa*?" It was a little louder than I would have liked. Typical. There is nothing quiet about my family.

Praying that no one had overheard her, annoyed, I mouthed, *Shut the fuck up!*

She gave me a shocked, innocent look. I stormed away from her and went to find my homeroom. At that moment I was glad that we had different last names. Her father and my mother were brother and sister. My last name is Shaw and Alayna's is Bowen, which meant different homerooms.

After a brief but stressful search I found my new homeroom, walked in, and took a seat in the last aisle by the windows. I was gazing out the classroom windows, watching the birds soaring through the cloudless blue sky. I began daydreaming about the past summer and all the fun Alayna and I had had. I thought about what I would have been doing at that exact moment a week before. I would have been waking up to the sounds of the waves crashing, the seagulls squawking, and the smell of the salty ocean air. I never slept late at the beach house because it felt like a waste of my day. Even if it rained I would be up early reading on the covered deck off our bedroom, making the most of my time while I was there.

Someone laughed obnoxiously loud and brought me out of my daydream. Damn, I missed the beach. I looked around the room, seeing how everyone had changed. I'd spent the past three years sharing a homeroom with most of these people. Now, being in high school, everyone seemed a little more grown-up. I had also changed. I now had curves in all the right places and two good reasons to finally wear a bra. I was proud of the girls, even though they got a little help from my Victoria's Secret Bombshell Bra. I was taller, almost five-and-a-half feet. My hair was longer, and thanks to many hours spent on YouTube, Alayna and I were very good at applying makeup. Just as everyone was settling in, the last homeroom bell rang and in walked Masen Rowe.

He was hot, like OH MY GOD hot. I heard he'd spent the summer working for a landscaper around town. As I eyed him, noticing how tan and gorgeous he was, I thought of him mowing the lawn shirtless, sweat glistening off every single muscle of his body and dripping down the six-pack abs that my imagination swore he most definitely had. I started to get tingly in the pit of my stomach.

Masen took the seat across from me. He had clearly filled out in *all* the right places. He was taller, at least six feet now. His hair was longer and unkempt, and he had the most beautiful blue eyes that any straight girl or gay guy could get lost in. I knew I could. Then the tingly feeling in my stomach made me think of other things that involved Masen and being sweaty.

This was out of character for me, because I knew nothing when it came to sex or this tingly feeling that was traveling between my legs. I'd had my first kiss in fifth grade with a kid named Jay. It was both fun and stressful. We both had braces and I was worried that we were going to get stuck together. In her infinite parenting wisdom, my mom had told me it was more than possible, so it was all I could think about during that kiss. After that experience I stuck to holding hands and decided not to try it again until after I got my braces off. That was a long three years.

Just then, Masen looked over at me and we locked eyes. He looked as if he were seeing me for the first time. I couldn't help but smile and he smiled back. It was such a gorgeous smile. Then homeroom began, but that smile was all I could think about.

On the third day of school, Masen was waiting at my locker between classes. He asked me out and the rest was history.

Masen was a great guy. He was also my first for everything. Well, almost everything. We were inseparable from freshman year right up until we went to college. As college neared, Masen and I decided to go our separate ways. Trying to keep up a relationship while we were at different schools would have been difficult. Maggie was not happy about it, but with her being away at college herself, she understood our decision. Masen and I were a big part of each other's lives for a long time. Breaking up wasn't easy, but we swore to keep in touch. Plus, like it or not, having Maggie as my best friend meant Masen would always be in my life.

I was a half hour from Maggie's house when I noticed a sign that read "Hainsworth Farm Market ahead." It had a picture of an old blue pickup truck with a big tomato in the bed of it. I had promised Maggie that I would make her steak au poivre for her birthday dinner. I needed to get a couple things from the store, but if I could get them at a farm market instead it would save me some time.

I pulled into Hainsworth Farm Market. It was a quaint little place on the side of the road. There were a good amount of cars in the parking lot. The road was a busy one, so I'm sure the market did well. I parked my car and got out. When I walked in, I saw some people shopping. It was a nice little place with a great selection of fruits and vegetables. They even had milk, eggs, honey, and jams. There was a table with homemade pies, breads, muffins, and cookies too. I grabbed a bag of cookies, some stuff for a salad, and a bunch of fresh asparagus.

There was no price on the asparagus, so I walked up to a guy carrying a crate of strawberries from the back.

"Excuse me, can you tell me how much for the asparagus?" I asked. "There's no price listed."

He just stared at me. I didn't mind because he was really hot. Like deliciously hot. He seemed about six-two with a nice muscular build, messy, rusty brown hair, pale green eyes, and he looked like he hadn't shaved in a day or two. Not to mention he was sweaty and dirty in a hot kind of way that worked really well for him. My stomach got that old familiar tingle. Maybe I have a thing for sweaty guys?

As he stared at me, not saying a word, the seconds passed by and I had thoughts of doing some dirty things to him that left my panties damp. I cleared my throat and smiled. It seemed to snap him out of wherever he was. I was hoping he was having some equally dirty thoughts about me.

He smiled and then stammered, "Uh, yeah sure, let me check. Stay here. Don't move." Then he quickly walked out the back door still carrying the crate of strawberries.

A pretty but plain girl with long, straight, golden blond hair came around the corner. She wore a nametag that read *Amy* and said, with amusement in her voice, "Wow, that's a first."

Confused, I asked, "What's a first?"

She replied, "That speechless guy was my cousin, Jase. I've never seen a girl leave him at a loss for words before."

I wasn't sure what to say to that, so I just said "Oh, okay" and smiled. It seemed she thought I was a little embarrassed, but I was thinking that I left her hot cousin speechless and he left my panties damp.

She quickly changed the subject. "Hi, I'm Amy Ketley," she began. "Let me ring you up so you can be on your way. The bunch of asparagus is $3.49 a pound. Do you still want it?"

I told her I did. She rang up and bagged my groceries. I handed her some money, waited for my change, and started to leave.

Amy said, "Have a nice day, and come back again."

She was very pleasant and I responded with a generic "Thank you," and waved as I left. I walked back to my car, put the groceries in the trunk, and got into the driver's seat.

I backed out of the parking spot and was pulling onto the highway when I glanced at my rearview mirror. I noticed a guy walking out of the store who was now standing in the parking lot just staring at me. It was *the guy*, the really hot one, Jase. I pulled onto the road and headed for Maggie's, pondering if he came out looking for me. He did tell me to stay and not to move, after all. Was it as simple as he wanted to get me the price I had asked for or had my damp panties betrayed me? The girl Amy did say I left him speechless. I, Mckenzie Shaw, the most ordinary girl in the world, had left that hot country boy speechless. The thought put a smile on my face as I drove the rest of the way to Maggie's.

Chapter 2 | Happy Hour

Two Months Later

Here I was, driving all the way to upstate New York, again, to visit Maggie. It was the same boring drive as ever. The previous Sunday night I was lounging on my couch talking with her, having our weekly Sunday night phone call, when she asked me to visit her and I reluctantly agreed to it.

Maggie had met a guy and I could tell she was really into him. Every time we talked, she would mention Matt. Matt this and Matt that. He sounded… nice. He was twenty-seven, the same age as Maggie. He came from a big family and was the oldest of four sons. He went to college but didn't finish and almost got married, but that didn't work out either. I couldn't help but wonder if it was a pattern— committing to something but not following through? What was she getting herself into? I shouldn't have prejudged the guy. Who knows— he could be amazing. Then again, amazing could mean she would fall in love and stay upstate longer. Or even worse… forever!

"Ugh," I groaned loudly in my car.

I remembered her telling me that Matt worked on his family's farm. I couldn't picture Maggie dating a farm boy. Yes, she lived in the country; however, you can take the girl out of Jersey but you can't take the Jersey out of the girl. If she wanted to go shopping she would drive an hour and a half to the mall in Utica. She refused to give up Sephora, Macy's, or Express. Even after nine years upstate she still hated pumping her own gas, and had even paid people to pump it for her. Thinking about it, maybe this wouldn't be so bad after all.

Either way, she really wanted me to meet him, so I would try to be nice, although I was still a little leery. The last two guys she had dated since she'd moved there hadn't been worth my best friend's time. First there was "Larry the Loser." After him was "Garrett the Psycho." Both nicknames self-explanatory. Thankfully things fizzled out with both of them. Garrett took a little longer, being crazy and all, but at last it ended.

I told Maggie I would leave work early Thursday so I could make happy hour at the bar and meet the famous Matt Hainsworth. So there I was, two hours into my drive and preparing to meet country boy number three in my best friend's life. Disappointingly, but not surprisingly, it felt like déjà vu. I secretly hoped the saying "third time's the charm" wouldn't apply to this guy.

I pulled into Maggie's driveway and parked next to her Prius. She rented a small, two-bedroom cottage-style house from Old Man Dale, a farmer who lived up the road from her. Old Man Dale owned a couple hundred acres on the road Maggie lived on. She told me he'd started out with a small farm on a few acres, and when his neighbors put their properties up for sale he'd bought them, acquiring all the property around him. Some of the land had houses on it, which he rented out. The house Maggie rented was a charming little place, brick red with white shutters and a white porch. It was perfect for what she needed.

I grabbed my bags and walked up to the door. I knocked and then walked in, not waiting for a reply. "Maggs, I'm here!" I shouted, standing in the hallway.

As I put my bags down I was greeted by Susi, Maggie's calico cat. I bent down to pet her and she purred while rubbing against my leg. Maggie walked out of the kitchen, smiling. She said, "Hey Kenz, you made it. How was the drive up?"

I rolled my eyes as I stood up from petting Susi. "It was uneventful, as usual. Lots of trees, mountains, and the smell of cow shit in the air," I joked, mocking the country life she now lived. "What smells so good? Are you making nachos?" I could smell the zesty blend of Mexican seasonings and melting cheese filling the house.

"Of course I am," she said matter-of-factly. Maggie made the best nachos. Whenever I visited, she would make them every day—sometimes twice a day.

Just then the timer to the oven went off. Maggie beamed while she said, "Your timing is perfect! Grab two beers out of the fridge and sit down so we can eat." She placed the yummy nachos down on the table.

I opened our beers and took a slow pull of mine. It was exactly what I needed after the long drive. I was definitely going to need another one before heading over to the bar to meet country boy number three.

Maggie and I were just finishing up the nachos, talking about our week, when she asked, "Are you excited to meet Matt?"

Yup, it was time for my next beer.

I answered, "Oh sure! Almost as excited as I am for my yearly pap smear." I got up, walked to the fridge, and grabbed two more beers. I put one down in front of Maggie and opened the other for myself.

She looked at me with concern in her eyes and said, almost pleading, "He is really nice, Kenzie, and I hope you give him a chance."

I didn't want to ruin her mood and I could tell this meant a lot to her, so I relented and said, "Of course I will, but as your best friend I can't help but be cautious."

"I know," Maggie replied, lost in thought.

Not wanting to upset her any more, I said, "Let's clean up the nachos, or what's left of them, and get ready to head out." That perked her up.

Two hours later we were on the way to the bar, all decked out. Maggie straightened the natural wave in her caramel brown hair. I decided to curl my hair and was rocking long, loose curls that hung to the middle of my back. I did Maggie's makeup, which looked awesome. It complimented her skin and made the gray in her eyes stand out. I went with simple beiges on my eyes. I figured I stood out enough with my outfit. I had on my favorite electric blue pants from Express and a black, sleeveless T-shirt with a white Lynyrd Skynyrd logo on it. I finished it off with my black, five-inch peep toe heels.

Maggie wore a pair of low-waist jeans with a slouchy, belted tunic blouse. She was going to wear sandals, but I convinced her to wear a pair of cute wedges she had bought the summer before.

We pulled into the parking lot at the bar and Maggie and I both looked hot.

"I think I know why I never wore these wedges," she said, staring at her sore feet. "They looked cute in the store, but they're killing me," she griped as she tugged at her shoes.

Maggie looked a little nervous so I said, "We could always go back to your house, make more nachos, and open the bottle of wine I bought."

She laughed a nervous laugh and said, "Nachos and wine, huh? It sounds wrong." She stared out the car window for a moment and then said, "I really like this guy, Kenz. Things are so easy with him. He makes me so happy."

Right then it hit me. I realized I was screwed and my best friend was going to live in the boonies forever. "Okay, let's get this little meet-and-greet over with. I promise to behave, but if he's a dick or crazy, my promise is null and void."

Maggie grinned and said, "That seems fair. But he's not either. You'll see."

We got out of the car and walked into the bar. I looked around and the place was packed with a mixed crowd, from old grizzled farmers to new-age hipsters. Maggie scanned the room for Mr. Wonderful. She apparently spotted him and tugged on my arm to follow her. We walked up to a bar high table filled with a bunch of guys and a couple of girls. Maggie leaned into who I assumed was Matt and kissed him softly on the neck. His head whipped around, and as he realized it was Maggie he almost toppled his chair as he got to his feet. He wrapped his arms around her and kissed her passionately. They both smiled as their lips finally parted and they stared into each other's eyes. I began to feel like an ass just standing there, not knowing anyone, and trying not to stare at their private moment.

After a few awkward seconds had passed, I put my hand out and said, "Hi, I'm Kenzie Shaw, Maggie's best friend."

Regaining her senses, Maggie said, "Oh right, sorry about that Kenz. Matt, this is Mckenzie. Kenzie, this is Matt Hainsworth."

Matt shook my hand. "Nice to meet you, Mckenzie. I've heard so much about you. I feel like I already know you," he said, smiling.

I smiled back and said, "Please call me Kenzie. It's nice to meet you as well." I could have said I'd heard so much about him too, because I had, but I didn't feel like adding any more fuel to Maggie and Matt's already burning fire.

I was being a terrible friend. Was I jealous? Did I want a boyfriend? Nah, not right now. I was doing well at work. I was twenty-five and had just been promoted to senior consultant at RyLo Corporation. It was one of the top ten advertising agencies in the United States. There were four offices across the U.S. One in New Jersey, Illinois, Texas, and California. I, of course, worked in the Jersey office, in Parsippany. I poured my blood, sweat, and tears into work, so I didn' need any distractions at the moment. I didn't have time for dating, alone a relationship.

Why was I acting like this? Maybe I needed to get laid. It had awhile. Oh god, how long had it been? Oh my god, I didn' know. Maybe I should have been checking for cobwebs. I sm chuckled a little.

Maggie eyed me suspiciously.

"What?" I asked.

Maggie whispered, "What are you smirking abou you promised."

I smiled innocently. "I know. I was thinking ab spring cleaning."

"Sure you were," she said, giving me a side-ey'

Maggie brought her attention back to Matt. told her how incredible she looked. He did se' her. Matt then introduced me to the table of set of pale green eyes seemed oddly familiar.

Chapter 3 | Coincidence

I overheard one of the girls at the table say, "Jase, that's the girl from the market, the one with the New Jersey license plate." Of course I heard the word "Jersey" and looked over. It was the blond girl from the farm market that I had stopped at two months earlier on my way to visit Maggie. I thought her name might have been Amy. She was staring at me like she had just spotted Santa Claus. I looked at the guy sitting next to her, who she was speaking to. There were those pale green eyes, staring back at me and giving me the same look as Amy. Maybe they had a thing against Lynyrd Skynyrd or electric blue pants—or maybe the two worn together. I thought I looked really good, and aren't Lynyrd Skynyrd gods amongst country folk? Just then, as I was going over my outfit in my head, I realized why those es looked so familiar. It was the hot guy from the farm market. Oh it! I froze and my body instantly got warm as I stared back at him.

I'm not sure if Maggie overheard Amy or just saw the way they staring at me, but she whispered just loud enough for me to hear, e you met Amy and Jase before?"

ust as I was about to explain things, Matt said, "Everyone, this is e Shaw, Maggie's best friend from New Jersey." Matt looked at d, from left to right, he introduced me to the table of people. e, this is Susan, Luann, my cousin Amy, my brother Jase, my Casey, and my brother Cole. My other brother, Reid, who is in, might show up later."

ed at everyone and said, "Hello. Nice to meet you all."

at point everyone at the table started to exchange hushed nd then, as if on cue, turned to stare at me. The one girl,

Luann, made a very strange face. I couldn't tell if she was annoyed at something or just caught a whiff of a fart. I was seriously starting to get pissed off. This was the rudest bunch of assholes I had ever met. I was about five seconds from telling these people where the fuck they could go when Matt interrupted them.

Very annoyed, he leaned on the table and under his breath hissed, "What the hell are you all talking about? You're being rude!"

Maggie wasn't quite sure what was going on, but she seemed mortified. She looked at me and saw that I was clearly pissed off and mouthed *I'm sorry.*

The next thing I heard was laughing from the table of assholes and a loud "NO SHIT!" from Matt. He looked back over his shoulder at me and then to Maggie.

I was fucking lost. I looked at Maggie and she seemed as puzzled as I was. This was the strangest group of fucks I had ever been around. I was about to ask Maggie to take me back to her house and plead w' her to leave this place and never return when Matt walked over to 1 looked around his shoulder and saw that everyone was quietly s' at me.

Matt, with a shit-eating grin on his face, said to Maggie, ' do you remember me telling you about some girl that Jase stop talking about for over a month? He met her at the ' didn't get a chance to talk to her."

Maggie nodded her head yes and said, "The one · have thought he made up if it weren't for Amy seeing h

Matt said, "Yes, that one!" He said it really loud. had remembered. "It seems your best friend Kenzie ·

Matt and Maggie turned to look at me along v the table. Great, now everyone was staring at sucking big time. Tired of being pissed and re rudely said, "Well I'm so glad my presence } mystery, but can someone please get me a Ke

That snapped everyone out of their different voices mention getting me a drin'

I ended up with two Kettle One and first, I wasn't as pissed off anymore. ′

exactly what I needed. I was feeling really warm, which I first thought was from my drink, but every time I saw Jase shift or move out of the corner of my eye, my body reacted with want. It was as if I needed to be closer to him—though I thought it was best that I stayed standing with Maggie and Matt rather than sitting at the table. I felt like I was losing my mind.

I was still trying to make sense of everything that had happened. I thought back to the day I had seen Jase for the first time, all sweaty and scruffy. He cleaned up really well and was still hot. Plus the scruff on his face was still there, which I really liked. I couldn't really see his hair because he had a Yankees cap on. He might actually have been the hottest guy I had ever met. Just then he turned, looked at me with those beautiful pale green eyes, and smiled.

Shit, I was done for. I think his smile had just created an instant puddle between my legs. What was wrong with me? I needed to get a grip, and possibly new panties. Wait, no, definitely new panties. Fifteen minutes before, I was ready to walk out of the bar and never come back. Now I was sitting there wishing I'd packed my vibrator. I smiled a small smile and turned to Maggie. I desperately needed a distraction.

Maggie and I chatted for a little bit with Matt. He apologized for the awkwardness and whispers earlier. He was happy that they'd found out who the mystery girl was and that his brother wasn't as batshit crazy as he had thought. Matt was really nice and seemed genuine. I could see why Maggie was so smitten by him.

I tried not to look at Jase, who seemed to stare at me every chance got. Maybe he was afraid I was going to disappear again. The weird was, he never actually said anything to me—just stared and d. Every once in a while I would look at him and he would give smile, my stomach would clench, and my body would tingle. would happen if he actually touched me? Would I combust? Just to flames?

rned my attention to Casey, Matt's cousin. He was talking to r guys about a house that he and his father were building. at I gathered from the conversation, Casey and Amy were d sister. Casey worked for his father at Ketley Builders and

Amy worked at the Hainsworth Farm Market, which was owned by Matt's family. They seemed to be a close family, which was nice.

It also seemed that Matt and Luann's family were close as well. Luann's family owned a dairy farm. I tried not to stare at her when she talked. Ever since they had found out I was "the mystery girl" earlier, Luann would give me these really strange looks. I ignored her, but it was still early and I had just finished drink number two, not counting the beers I'd had at Maggie's. If she kept up with the looks, I might just have to slap the bitch. She clearly didn't like me. Good thing I didn't care.

Everyone was talking loudly and taking advantage of the happy hour specials. Bored with their conversations, I told Maggie I was going to check out the jukebox. I grabbed some money from my wristlet and made my way over to check out the selection of songs. Scrolling through, I was pleasantly surprised. Currently the jukebox was playing "Bottoms Up" by Brantley Gilbert. I really liked that song—enough to have it on my iPod. I have a very eclectic choice of music. It ranges from Johnny Cash to Paramore to Eminem. A little bit of everything.

I put five dollars in the jukebox, which gave me six songs. "Hmmm, what should I pick?" I said to no one in particular. I looked at my shirt, smiled, and made my choices.

"Sweet Home Alabama" by Lynyrd Skynyrd
"American Girl" by Tom Petty
"One More Night" by Maroon 5
"Cups" by Anna Kendrick
"Crazy Bitch" by Buckcherry
"Alone Together" by Fall Out Boy

Just as I entered my last choice, I felt someone behind me. Then I heard, "Alone Together, huh?"

I spun around and there he was. Jase was staring down at me with those beautiful pale green eyes of his. My breathing hitched and my heart skipped a beat. God, he was good-looking, and standing so close to me. I was mesmerized. My body felt so warm and tingly. This was bad.

Trying to shake whatever was going on with me, I said, "Excuse me, what did you say?" I clearly had no clue what he'd said or even if it was in English.

Jase laughed and said, "The last song you chose. It's a good one."

"Oh, right, 'Alone Together,'" I said. It was kind of ironic because we were actually alone together. Standing in front of the jukebox, looking into each other's eyes, not saying a word. The seconds ticked by. It was like a game: who was going to speak first?

Jase broke the silence and said, "I wanted to talk to you before, but you seemed pretty pissed about earlier and I thought I would give you some space. Sorry about that."

"Sure, don't worry about it," I said, trying to brush it off.

"Maybe we can start over." Jase stuck out his hand and said, "Jase Hainsworth. Nice to meet you."

I kept my eyes on him, peering up through my long lashes. He gave me a crooked smile that I'm sure was responsible for a lot of panty-dropping. I reached out and shook his hand, and right then and there I felt it. It was like nothing I had ever felt before. Like an electric current running through our hands, the touch sparking and heating up our skin.

My mind was swimming. I didn't understand what I was feeling. Was I imagining this? Did he feel it too? Jase looked down at our hands with a look of wonder on his face. All of this was making me slightly dizzy. His eyes, his smile. Him being so close and so delicious-looking. I thought my earlier question of combustion might actually play out right there, in that bar, in front of the jukebox. I quickly pulled my hand back and said, "I think I need another drink."

I started to walk toward the bar when Jase stopped me and said, "Let me get it for you," smiling at me. Damn that smile.

Still trying to pull myself together, I said, "That's okay, I got it."

"No, I insist," he quickly replied before walking away. I watched him as he left, making a mental note of his fine ass.

I walked back to Maggie and she was smiling. I asked, "Why are you smiling like that?"

She asked, "*And* just what were you two talking about?"

I rolled my eyes, called her an asshole, and waited for my drink.

Just then Jase walked up and handed it to me and said, "Here you go, Kettle One and cranberry."

I took it from him, trying not to make any kind of physical contact. I didn't feel like bursting into flames that night. I said, "Thank you."

He smiled and stood there right next to me. Maggie and Matt gave each other a stupid happy look that made me want to smack them both. Jase leaned in toward me. My heartbeat picked up as I noticed the lack of space between us. Awkwardly he asked, "So when do you go home?"

I responded with "Sunday morning," hoping the small talk was over.

He then asked, "Do you have plans tomorrow night?"

Before I even had a chance to think of an answer, Maggie stepped in and quickly said "Nope, none at all."

I glared at Maggie as she devilishly smiled at me and said, "Well, you don't."

Jase took the opportunity and said, "Great, would you like to do something?"

Floored that this was happening, I opened my mouth, ready to turn this hot piece of ass down, when my asshole of a best friend answered for me again and said, "She'd love to."

I whipped my head toward her and sharply said, "Maggie Fucking Rowe, I think I can answer for myself."

Maggie, clearly knowing she should have kept her mouth shut, apologetically said, "I'm sorry Kenz, but what do you have to lose? Just go out with him." She gave me a subtle look with a shrug of her shoulders, as if trying to give me the push I needed.

Why was she doing this? Now completely embarrassed, I started to think maybe it was better if she stayed upstate forever. That way she couldn't fuck with me. Frustrated, I turned and looked at Jase. He had a hopeful look on his face. I said, "Yeah, sure, apparently I'd love to."

Jase smiled that crooked smile and said, "Great. I'll pick you up at Maggie's at six."

Not thrilled with the way the night's events had played out, I knew I was in for a long night.

Chapter 4 | Dragging Ass

I woke up to water running and a god-awful clanking noise. My head was not happy with whatever Maggie was doing in the kitchen. I wished at the moment that she hadn't taken the day off. With one eye open, I peeked at my phone and saw it was one thirty in the afternoon. My head was pounding like a jackhammer. The Advil I had taken when I got up to pee earlier had apparently worn off. I had drunk way too much the night before. Given the circumstances, though, I think it was well deserved. My head told me otherwise.

I lay in bed trying to will myself to move. I was going over the events of the previous night and that's when it hit me. I sprung forward, which was clearly a mistake. I grabbed my head, hoping it would help stop the throbbing and dizziness. Not so much.

"Ugh," I moaned.

I heard a light tap on the door and then Maggie asked "You alive in there?"

Still annoyed at her for the night before, I snapped, "No. Go. Away."

Maggie laughed, opened the door, and walked in. "You don't look so good, Kenz. You need to get up. Remember, you have a *big* date tonight. Jase will be here in a couple of hours."

"No thanks to you! I blame you for this godforsaken headache," I said in the angriest tone I could muster.

I very slowly, very carefully lay back down. Maggie walked over and sat on the edge of the bed, trying not to jostle me. "Are you mad at me?" she asked, clearly worried.

I looked over at her and said, "Actually yes. You answered for me when Jase asked me out."

Sheepishly, Maggie responded with "You could have said no."

I eyed her and said, "Really? No clearly wasn't an option, because what did I have to lose? Sound familiar?"

"Oh right," she said, still sounding worried. "Sorry about that."

I wasn't convinced.

"I thought it would be good for you. It's been awhile since you've been on a date," Maggie said, a little too happily for my liking. "Plus, Matt told me that Jase was pissed that he didn't get a chance to talk to his mystery girl at the market that day. He thought he had lost his only chance."

I thought I noticed a small smirk on her face and my anger began to boil over again. "What the fuck is so funny now?" I demanded.

She raised her hands in mock surrender, laughed, and said, "Reid told Jase he was pussy-whipped by a chick who asked for a price check and he never even got her name."

Despite the constant pounding in my head, I couldn't help but laugh along with her at the comment.

Maggie stood as I sat up in bed. She said, "You look like shit. You need a shower and at least three cups of coffee."

I groaned loudly and said, "I really should be mad at you for my headache. If last night wasn't so fucked up, maybe I would have stopped at three drinks rather than having five."

Maggie laughed as she walked out of the bedroom, yelling back, "Don't forget the shots of tequila too."

I slowly swung my feet over the side of the bed and stood up. I seriously hated life right then. I shuffled out to the kitchen, and Maggie poured me a steaming cup of coffee and placed it on the table next to a bottle of Advil and a buttered roll. I sat down and reached for my coffee, holding it in front of my face and enjoying the aroma before taking a sip. It tasted amazing and was quite possibly the best cup of coffee I had ever had. Before I realized, it was all gone and I began to feel just a bit more human.

I quietly sat there eating while Maggie kindly refilled my cup with the sweet nectar of the gods. She walked over to me, put the cup on the table, and took a seat across from me. I grabbed the Advil, opened the top, and shook out four gel caps. Yes, four. I popped them in my mouth and washed them down with the coffee.

"So," I said, trying to recall the prior night's events through my fog, "nothing crazy happened last night, right?"

"By crazy are you referring to the part where you dropped your pants, mooned everyone, then ran around the bar giving random people lap dances as 'Crazy Bitch' played on the jukebox?" Maggie said with a devilish smile.

I felt the blood drain from my entire body. I must have turned white as snow because Maggie's eyes suddenly grew big and she said, "You don't look so good, Kenz. Are you okay?"

Mortified, I asked Maggie, "Please tell me you're kidding and none of that really happened."

Maggie cracked and up and said, "No, it didn't, but it would have been funny as shit if it did." As she carried on laughing—or in her case, cackling—I slowly felt the color return to my face. I wanted to be pissed at her for screwing with me, truly I did, but I had no energy to spare at the moment.

I threw the little bit of my buttered roll at her that I had left and said, "You're an asshole."

Maggie stopped laughing and said, "Seriously, nothing really happened. You were fine. He was fine. Except for..." She paused.

"Except for what?" I said loudly—maybe a bit too loudly for my hangover. "Stop fucking with me, Maggie. It's too goddamn early for this shit!"

"Actually, it's not early, Kenz," she corrected me. "It's almost two thirty in the afternoon."

"Whoop-dee-fucking-doo," I said as I rolled my eyes. "So glad you can tell time. Back to my question: except for what?" I asked again more sternly this time.

"Okay, fine," she said. "Except for you and Jase eye-fucking each other all night."

I stared at her blankly, trying to breathe while thinking back to the night before. As the fog started to clear I began to remember those pale green eyes, his crooked smile, and that fine ass. He did keep his distance from me after we spoke. But thinking back, he had kept his eyes on me all night long. Which meant I'd kept my eyes on him too. Oh my god, we did eye-fuck!

"What are you talking about?" I demanded, trying to conceal my sudden realization.

She smiled and said, "After you so graciously accepted Jase's offer to go out with him, you guys didn't really say much to each other the rest of the night. My guess is he was afraid you might change your mind, so he left you alone."

I smiled. "Maybe that's a good thing. If I'm lucky, he'll think I'm a bitch and cancel on me."

"Nah, I doubt you will get rid of him that easily. He called me earlier, since he didn't have your number. He wanted to see if you guys were still on for tonight," she replied with an exaggerated smile.

I sighed. "Let me guess: you told him yes?" I asked her.

Maggie somehow managed to smile even wider. "Let's just say you should probably get in the shower now, because with the way you look, you are going to need every second of every minute to get your ass ready," she said as she giggled.

I put my head on the table, not quite ready to get in the shower. I sat there trying to figure out how a night that was supposed be about Maggie and Matt had turned out to be about Jase and me. If I could shake the pounding in my head, maybe I would feel a little bit better about the night ahead.

Maggie interrupted my thoughts and said, "If you're worried about tonight, just think about the pros and cons. I think you'll find more pros."

I picked my head up off of the table. Maybe she had a point—although I'd never admit it to her. "Pros and cons, huh?" I said with a cocked head.

"Yes, pros and cons. Go get in the shower and think about it," she instructed me.

I did just that. I got up from the table, grabbed some clean clothes and my bag of toiletries, and headed for the bathroom.

I turned on the shower and let the bathroom fill up with steam. I got undressed and slipped into the steaming hot shower. The combination of coffee, food, Advil, and hot water was making me feel a little bit better. I started to wash my hair and thought about what Maggie had said, trying to weigh the pros and cons.

What were some of the pros of going out with Jase?

He was interested in me. I was *his* mystery girl from the market—someone he wondered about, even told people about. That pro put a smile on my face. It was just a date. One date. It had been a while since my last one, which was terrible. Jase was hot. Really hot. Those beautiful pale green eyes and killer smile. He was tall and had a nice body from what I could see with his clothes on. I wondered what his stomach felt like? Shit, I needed to focus. He looked deliciously good clean or dirty. God, I would like to make him dirty. Oh my god, it was time for the cons.

What were some of the cons? I hadn't a clue if he was single. Actually, come to think about it, I knew nothing about Jase other than his family owned a farm and he had three brothers. Did he work on the farm too? How old was he? Come to think of it, Jase wondering about me for over a month did seem a little strange. Oh my god, what if he was a crazy stalker or a psycho? Matt did say he was happy to find out that Jase wasn't as batshit crazy as he'd thought. So was he a little crazy? Great, just what I needed. Maybe weighing out the pros and cons wasn't such a good idea after all. Then again, the pros did outweigh the cons. Maybe this wouldn't be so bad.

I finished rinsing my hair, reached for the soap, lathered up my body, and made sure I scrubbed every inch. I grabbed my razor and made sure I was hair-free in every place that counted, just like making sure you have clean underwear on when you leave the house. After all, you never know what the day will bring. Not that I planned on anything happening, but a girl has to be prepared.

God knows I thought about Jase touching me, feeling me, caressing my skin, and grabbing my hair. Several of these thoughts crossed my mind just in the time that I showered. Good thing I was a girl who didn't have a problem taking care of her own needs—and did I have needs. Jase Hainsworth made me feel very needy. I wished I could give my body the release it craved, but time wasn't on my side at the moment.

I stepped out of the shower feeling like a new person. I dried off, put my hair up in a towel, and got dressed in yoga pants and a T-shirt. While walking back to the spare room I noticed a note Maggie had left on the counter for me. It read:

Kenz,
Ran to the store. Be back in a few. Text me if you need anything.
Ps. Jase said to dress comfortable.
Maggs

Dress comfortable, huh? I walked back to the spare room where my bags were, and rifled through my clothes, wondering what to wear. Maybe I should call Maggie and see what she suggests? Just then my cell phone began to vibrate and I saw Alayna's name on the screen.

"Hey," I said as I answered it.

"I assume you made it there in one piece," she said, skipping any sort of normal greeting. "You know you could've called someone to let them know if you made it there so they don't worry. How was the drive? How is Maggie? What are you guys doing? How was happy hour? What's Matt like?" Alayna asked as I withstood her machine-gun-like verbal assault. Her ability to rattle off endless questions without taking a single breath always impressed me.

This was typical of my cousin. She always talked way too much. Maybe I should have just let the call go to voice mail. Then again, maybe she could help me figure out what to wear.

"Which question would you like me to answer first?" I asked.

"All of them, of course—and don't leave out any juicy details," she insisted.

I sighed and said, "I will answer them all quickly, but I can't give you any juicy details. I have a date that I have to get ready for and I have very little time."

Yes, it had been awhile since I was on a date, but that must have shocked the shit out of my cousin because there were about five blissful seconds of silence before she screeched, "What!?! Did you say you're getting ready for a date? Do tell?"

"I can't get into it right now, but it's with Matt's brother, Jase. Do you remember me telling you about the hot guy I saw at the farm market the last time I visited Maggie?" I asked.

Alayna said, "Yeah, I think so."

"Well, it just so happens that Jase is that guy from the market. He was at the bar last night when Maggie and I met up with Matt," I said.

This was clearly taking my cousin time to process. I looked at my cell phone to see if the call had disconnected. Nope, still there. Then I noticed the time. Shit! I had an hour and a half before Jase arrived.

"Are you still there?" I asked Alayna.

"Yes! Yes, I'm still here. Wow, that's crazy. Small world! Tell me about him. What is he like? How old is he? What does he do?" she questioned, unleashing another verbal assault.

Running out of time and patience, I quickly summed it all up for her and said, "You're doing it again. I don't have time to answer all of your questions. Just know that I made it up here okay. Maggie's great but is a lovestruck asshole. Matt is nice and I hate that I like him. Happy hour was a shit show that ended with me agreeing to go on a date with Jase, who is still hot but I don't know much about him." Catching my breath, I wondered how she didn't constantly pass out talking like that.

"But…" Alayna quickly blurted out before I cut her off and said, "No more questions. I need to figure out what to wear on this date. Do you have any suggestions?"

Time was ticking away and I was no closer to getting ready.

"Please, Alayna, help me out," I pleaded with her.

"Grrrr!" I heard on the other end. Did she actually growl at me? "Fine," she huffed like a four-year-old being told to eat her broccoli. Clearly she was not happy she wasn't getting the juicy details she wanted. "What's the weather like up there? Did he say whether it was casual or dressy? I'm sure you overpacked, so what clothes did you bring?" she asked.

I rolled my eyes at the constant questions, glad she was miles away and unable to see me. "Maggie said to dress comfortable. It's hot out but not muggy like it is at home," I replied.

"Okay, comfortable is easy. Did you pack jean shorts?" she asked.

"Of course I did. I packed three pairs," I said.

"Do you have the strappy floral cami or the flowy navy peasant top with the cutouts on the shoulders?" Alayna asked, clearly enjoying helping me dress for the date.

I literally laughed out loud at how well my cousin knew my wardrobe and was glad that we were the same size and had the same taste in clothes. "I have both shirts," I said, knowing she was putting my outfit together in her head.

"Okay. Wear the flowy peasant top with whichever jean shorts make your ass look most amazing. And wear black strappy sandals if you brought a pair," Alayna said proudly.

"Thank you so much, I owe you!" I said, appreciating her fashion sense.

"Yes, you do owe me. You owe me all the juicy details. Now hurry up or you're going to be late! Have fun and be safe," she instructed. We said goodbye to each other and hung up.

I had to hurry because time was not on my side. I still had to blowout my hair and put on my makeup. I didn't have time to do it the way I would have liked, so I would have to keep it simple. Not that I should have cared what I looked like, right? I didn't even want to go on this date. Then it hit me: I was going out on a date with deliciously hot Jase. I started to get that tingly feeling in my stomach and I knew where that feeling was headed. Shit! My hands started to get sweaty and my heart started to pound. Fuck, I was nervous.

Chapter 5 | Redneck Picnic

I stared out the kitchen window closest to the driveway, waiting for Jase to arrive. I had just finished getting ready. Pressed for time, I'd decided to pin my hair up in a messy bun and kept my makeup light and fresh-looking. Maggie came home while I was getting ready and was now hovering around the kitchen, wiping down the counters for the fifth time. I wanted to tell her to stop after the third time, but my nerves were getting the best of me. Maybe we were both nervous. I looked at the clock on the microwave and saw that it was six on the dot.

My stomach dropped as I suddenly heard the gravel crunching in the driveway. I turned, looking back out the window, and saw a black Chevy Silverado pickup with a lift pulling in. Shit just got real. At least I knew he was punctual. That was one more for the pro column. I watched as he opened the door and stepped down from his truck.

It was like I had died and gone to redneck heaven. Jase looked good. Damn good. He was wearing a plaid, short-sleeved button-up shirt. The front was tucked into his jeans, which showed a fabric khaki-colored belt. I expected cowboy boots, but instead it looked like he was wearing a pair of Diesel sneakers. His rusty brown hair was a little longer than I remembered from the farm market, but still messy. I watched him run his fingers through it in an attempt to tame it. He still had the day-old scruff on his face, which I really liked.

He was just about to step onto the porch and out of view when he paused, took a deep breath, and stood there.

"What is he doing?" Maggie asked, scaring the shit out of me. She was also staring out the window over my shoulder.

"What are you doing? You scared the shit out me?" I whispered to her.

"I'm watching, just like you. Why are you whispering?" Maggie asked.

"Because the walls of this house are so damn thin you can hear a squirrel fart," I said.

We looked back at the window and he was gone. The sudden knock at the door made us both jump.

We looked at each other and then the front door. Maggie looked back at me and said, "We could just hang here, make nachos, and open that bottle of wine you brought."

I laughed a nervous laugh and said, "That sounds oddly familiar, Maggs, and I appreciate the offer, but I agreed to this so it's only fair that I go through with it."

Maggie smiled and said, "He's a nice, good-looking guy. Isn't there a little piece of you that actually wants to go out with him?"

Jase knocked again, saving me from answering her question.

Not able to prolong the inevitable, I sighed. "I should probably get that."

Maggie gave me a quick once-over and nodded her approval. I took a slow, deep, calming breath and walked over to the door. I opened it and saw him standing there, staring down at me. This time it was me who gave him the crooked smile as I looked up through my long lashes. I could have sworn I noticed his breathing hitch, but couldn't be sure.

It was I who spoke first. "Hi, sorry to keep you waiting."

He smiled back at me and said, "Don't worry about it. I'm just glad you answered the door. My brother Reid was betting you would cancel."

If he only knew the earlier conversation I'd had with Maggie. I smiled at his comment because I wasn't sure what to say.

He then asked, "Are you ready to go?"

I nodded, grabbed my wristlet, and quickly pulled the front door shut. I was relieved to have made it out of the house before Maggie could say something that may have either pissed me off or embarrassed me in front of Jase.

We were just reaching Jase's truck when I heard the window in the kitchen slide open. I looked over and saw Maggie with a big shit-eating grin on her face. She yelled out, "You two have a good time," and winked at me.

I smiled and waved at her, then continued to walk to the passenger side. I noticed there was a blue tarp covering the bed of the pickup. I was curious as to what was under it, but quickly dropped the thought when Jase opened the door for me.

Even though the truck had a lift, it wasn't too high, thankfully, and I was able to get into it without any problems. Jase shut my door, walked around to the driver's side, and got in. He looked over, smiled, and started the truck. I hung my arm out of the already open window and noticed for the first time what a beautiful day it was. Few clouds hung in the sky, and in the distance you could see a crescent moon peeking out.

We were both really quiet. The growl of the truck's engine was the only thing that could be heard as he backed out of the driveway. Wanting to break the ice, I gestured toward the truck's bed and asked, "What's under the blue tarp?"

"Ah, you noticed that, did you? It's a surprise. You'll have to wait and see," he said with a devilish smile.

I sat there beginning to obsess over the blue tarp. What kind of surprise requires it to be covered by a tarp in the first place? I'd seen way too many episodes of *CSI* and *Criminal Minds* and I knew what tarps were often used for. If I saw duct tape, zip ties, or rope, this girl was hitting the road running.

As I sat there pondering the surprise, Jase turned up the radio, which was playing "Cruise" by Florida Georgia Line. I started to quietly sing along, trying to calm my nerves. I wasn't sure if I was more nervous about being on the date or the possibility of being murdered, wrapped in the blue tarp, and dumped in some ditch along the country road. Maybe it was the lack of conversation that was adding to my nervousness. I stole a glance at Jase from the corner of my eye. He didn't look like a serial killer. He was too damn hot. It would be such a waste for him to sit in prison for life. Of course my death would be a bit inconvenient.

He was thrumming his long fingers on the steering wheel in time with the song. It ended and another began—one that I didn't recognize. I noticed his hands were a little rough, but strong-looking. I thought of them caressing my body, slowly sliding up my thigh, inch by inch, higher and higher. My body felt as if it was on fire. I was tingly all over. I started to fan myself.

Jase must have noticed and eyed me with a look of concern. "Are you okay?" he asked.

"Yeah, I'm good. Sometimes I get carsick, but I'll be okay," I reassured him.

If he only knew how I really felt. Just by wondering what his hands would feel like on my body was enough to make me break out in a sweat.

"Do you need me to pull over?" he asked, still concerned. He slowed the truck down and was staring at me with those pale green eyes of his. My body was going through an internal struggle. A big part of me wanted to say "pull over right now and fuck the shit out of me," but the smaller more responsible part of me decided against it.

"Nope, I'm good. Just fine," I responded quickly, before I lost the battle within my body.

Jase picked up speed again and continued down the country road. We drove for almost ten minutes in near silence, except for the saving grace of the radio. Spotting some sort of landmark, he let me know we were almost there. I looked around and there was nothing around but trees and farms. He slowed and turned onto a dirt road that was lined with trees for as far as I could see. Jase then stopped the truck and started to lean across the center console. His hand brushed against my leg as he leaned over. Oh my god, was he going for it already? No dinner. No drinks. Not one measly flower. As far as surprises went, this one took the cake. Then, as I began processing coherent thoughts again, I realized he wasn't reaching for me, he was reaching for the glove box. He took out a faded navy blue bandana which he then handed to me.

Puzzled, I looked at him and said, "And what am I supposed to do with this?"

Jase, sensing my apprehension, quickly said, "It's just a blind-fold—part of the surprise."

I must have given him a look like he had three heads, because he chuckled and said, "Trust me."

"Trust you? I barely know you!" I shot back. "You have a blue tarp covering a surprise in the back of your truck, and for all I know you're going to hack me up into tiny pieces!" I pointed out, getting annoyed.

Jase laughed hysterically loud and pounded on his steering wheel, as if what I had just said was the funniest thing he had ever heard. I sat there, staring out the windshield at nothing but a dirt road and trees, arms crossed and stewing. After a minute or two of him carrying on, he finally calmed down. He looked at me seriously and said my name.

"Kenzie."

My heart stopped. I think that was the first time I'd heard him say my name, and I loved the way he made it sound. With my arms still crossed, I turned my head toward him, staring into the depths of his pale green eyes.

"I have no intention of doing anything like that to you. I just want tonight to be perfect. Just trust me," he said.

Well holy hell, how could I say no to that? Unable to speak, I nodded yes and put the bandana over my eyes, tying it in place. I heard Jase put the truck in drive and we started down the dirt road again. It didn't seem long before we came to a stop and he turned off the truck. He asked me to stay put and insisted I not take off the blindfold. He got out of the truck, and within seconds I heard the tailgate drop. He must have hopped into the bed, because the truck started to shimmy. Then I heard the distinctive plastic crinkling of the tarp being moved around.

"Couple more minutes," he shouted.

I sat there wondering what the hell he was doing when I began to smell smoke followed by a familiar crackling sound.

A little worried and nervous, I thought about what he'd said and how he'd seemed sincere about not killing me. Dear god, if he did kill me I swore I was going to haunt Maggie for the rest of her life.

Just then the door to the truck opened. Jase said, "You can take off the blindfold now."

Relieved, I slid it off and saw Jase standing there with his hand out. In the other hand he held a single white daisy. From where I was sitting, we were the same height. He handed me the daisy. I raised it to my nose instinctively to smell the flower, even though it had no scent. "Thank you. Daisies are my favorite flower."

Jase smiled as I put my free hand in his. I felt the warmth and electricity flow between us again. Not wanting to make it obvious how I was affected by Jase's touch, I kept my gaze locked and allowed him to help me down.

I looked around, taking in my surroundings. We were at a clearing of trees in front of a beautiful large pond. I heard birds chirping, frogs croaking, and animals scurrying off in the woods. I followed Jase as he led me to the back of his truck. What I saw left me speechless. He had transformed the bed of the truck into the most romantic setting I had ever seen.

He'd laid a huge old seafoam-green quilt on the bed of the truck. There were at least ten pillows of different sizes and colors along the back, closest to the cab. On the roof he had lit a few white pillar candles, and on one side of the tailgate there lay a folded red-and-white crocheted blanket. On the other side was a bale of hay with a round tray on top of it, with a mason jar holding daisies and other wild flowers. I looked to the left several feet from his truck and saw a ring of rocks holding the fire that I had smelled. It had big old logs around it that made up seating, and next to one of the logs was a red cooler.

I was in awe. Here I was worried that he was going to kill me and cut me up into little pieces, yet *this* had been his plan all along. I stood there mesmerized, thinking that I was the luckiest girl alive. I slowly turned toward Jase and said with all sincerity, "This is the most beautiful, most romantic thing anyone has ever done for me. Thank you." I smiled and felt tears welling up but fought them off.

With the back of his hand he caressed my face and said, "You're very welcome," and smiled.

Noticing how quiet we both were, he asked, "How about some music?"

I nodded in agreement.

He walked back to the truck and turned on the radio. He left it low, more like background noise. He walked back over to me and said, "I made some sandwiches if you're hungry."

I wasn't hungry until he mentioned food. "I'm starving," I said with a shy smile.

Without asking, he picked me up by the waist and placed me on the tailgate. I was pleasantly taken by surprise. "I hope you like peanut butter and jelly, because it's the only thing I'm good at making," he laughed.

I smiled and told him I didn't mind. He went to the cooler, grabbed some napkins, bottles of water, sandwiches, and a container of what looked like fruit.

Jase hopped onto the tailgate next to me and handed me a sandwich and a napkin. He then opened my water, placing it next to me. "I thought water would be best after last night. How are you feeling, by the way?" he asked.

"I'm a little tired but I feel okay," I answered.

"I was worried that after last night you wouldn't be up for our date," he said, peeking over at me, laughing.

Great, he probably thought I was a lush. I rolled my eyes and said, "If you saw me four hours ago, I would not have used *okay* to describe how I was feeling."

Jase chuckled and we ate our sandwiches, making small talk. I was intrigued by him. He was way different from most guys. Besides being good-looking, he was very confident, smart, and went after what he wanted.

I found out that he and I were the same age. He worked at the farm and was going to school part time, finishing up his bachelor's degree. Then he told me about how his family had been farming forever. The farm was inherited by Jase's father, Robert, when his Grandpa Bill had passed away. It was never to be sold, but passed down through the generations. The land was enormous. Each Hainsworth was given five acres on their eighteenth birthday. The idea behind it was to keep the land in the family and the family close. Matt and Jase both had houses built on their properties not far from each other, with a pond separating the two. Reid and Cole, who were both still in college, worked on the farm part time. They lived at home with their parents, whose house was up the road from Matt and Jase.

He went on to tell me about how his parents, who were good, hard-working Christian people, believed in marrying young and popping out a bunch of kids. This led into why Matt had *almost* gotten married. When his brother was nineteen years old, he was engaged. Three months before the wedding he'd called it off, and was instantly the talk of the town. Jase said Matt had loved the girl, but wasn't in love with her. His parents were upset and his mom cried for what seemed like a month straight. She eventually accepted the fact that her son just wanted to be happy. After that ordeal, Matt swore to Jase that he would never go down that road again. On the five acres he was given, he made plans to build his own house with help from his uncle. And the rest was history.

I was shocked by this revelation but had a little more respect for Matt now. Jase said Matt's ordeal thankfully made his own situation a little easier on his parents. Curious about his *situation*, I listened intently as he told me about his and Luann's history. Jase and Luann's parents were best of friends, which meant their children grew up together. Jase and Luann where the same age, and when they were older they'd dated on and off. In their senior year of high school things got pretty serious, which was great in both of their parents' eyes. They pushed for the two of them to get married out of high school and they did, convinced it was the right thing to do. Luann had no plans to go to college and wanted to continue working at her family's dairy farm—unlike Jase, who wanted to further his education, wanting more for himself.

Jase and Luann got married at the end of the summer, right before Jase started college. They rented an apartment while Jase worked out plans to build a house on his five acres. He told me he'd loved Luann and thought that it was enough, but it wasn't. Four months into the marriage, it started to crumble. Jase said he and Luann both realized they wanted different things at that time in their lives. They felt that they had rushed into marriage, as young adults sometimes do, and the push from their parents hadn't helped. They separated and decided to divorce two months later. Now it made sense as to why she had given me those weird looks the night before. He told me he made the decision to get divorced when he realized he wanted more out of life. More than a good education, he wanted a life that didn't revolve around his family's farm. He wanted a career of his choice and didn't want to settle for a girl from the country.

With another failed relationship, his family was once again the talk of the town. Even though his parents were crushed by the failed marriage, they again, just wanted their son to be happy. Jase said the whispers around town were that the Hainsworth boys were heartbreakers. I had to laugh at that. He said Reid loved the label because it made him seem more like the bad guy, and girls always fell for the bad guy. On the other hand, his other brother Cole couldn't care less. I had yet to meet Reid, but he seemed cocky.

He asked how long Maggie and I had been friends, and I told him since high school. I explained that the beginning of my freshman year I'd started to date Maggie's brother, Masen. I told him that even after we'd broken up, Maggie and I had always remained the best of friends.

We made some more small talk about our pasts, but more about him than me. A familiar song came on—"Give Me Love" by Ed Sheeran.

I said, "I love this song."

With that being said, Jase hopped off the tailgate and smiled a crooked smile and said, "Dance with me."

There wasn't a question in his tone. He was telling me what he wanted and I was willing, without a second thought. He helped me down from the tailgate and we danced under the twilight sky. The fire roared and you could hear the crackle of the flames. Jase held me tight as he looked down at me, quietly singing along with the words of the song that he knew as well. I was awestruck. I felt every fiber of my body hum with want from being so close to him. Every so often he would spin me and I would giggle at the feeling of just letting go and being carefree.

As the song was ending, Jase dipped me back slowly. He watched my face and I stared up into his pale green eyes. My heart was pounding in my chest and I would have sworn he could hear it. Another song came on the radio and I had no clue what it was as he slowly stood me upright. As we were standing there holding each other, he ran his one hand up the side of my arm, still watching me. I felt the roughness of his hand as his touch left tingly trails along my skin. Jase slid his hand to the nape of my neck and pulled me toward him. I gave up the internal struggle I was having with my body as his lips pressed against mine. I let go of everything as he parted my mouth with his tongue. My body was on fire. If the night air was chilly, there was no way I could tell.

I was so lost in the moment that I didn't even notice that he had backed me up against his truck. Next thing I knew I was sitting on the tailgate again. Reluctantly, our lips parted and we were left staring into each other's eyes.

He cupped my face and slowly ran his thumb over my bottom lip. "Beautiful," he whispered.

I pleaded with myself not to give it up to this fine piece of ass, but I was sure as shit going to make out with him until the sun came up. Our lips once again found each other, picking up where we left off. Jase climbed onto the tailgate, lifted me up, and slid us back toward the pillows. We lay in the back of his truck, bodies entwined, kissing, feeling, and groping. It may have been hours, because the fire burned out, the sky was pitch dark, and the candles where half gone.

I couldn't get enough of him. I wanted more. No, *needed* more. I was about to say "fuck my morals" and suggest screwing right then and there when he suddenly stopped.

He pulled away, practically panting. He looked at me and said, "As much as I really want to fuck you right here and now, it's not gonna happen in the back of my truck. You deserve better than that."

My body surely didn't care at that point whether it was in the back of his truck, on the ground, or on top of the piano at the Waldorf Astoria. My mind and body were finally on the same page and *now* he decided to slam on the brakes.

All I could do was weakly nod and stutter, "O-Okay."

"It's really late. I should probably get you back to Maggie's," he said with an emotion I couldn't quite place.

The ride back to Maggie's seemed to go by much faster than the ride there. I'm not sure if it was because I wasn't so worried about being murdered and wrapped in a blue tarp, or because I was more focused on the night's events. My mind was on overload thinking about the way he had touched my skin, the way his tongue had parted my lips and danced with my tongue. Our quiet groans seemed to be embedded in my thoughts, and the way we connected was on a level that I wasn't entirely sure about.

Before I knew it, we reached Maggie's house. I looked over at Jase. He wore a mixed expression, a look of regret and anticipation. I think neither of us wanted the night to end.

"I had a great time," I said, shyly trying to act innocent. Ironic, knowing what we were doing thirty minutes before.

"Me too," he said, failing to hide the eagerness in his voice. "I want to see you tomorrow," he said with a tone that clearly gave me no other option but to agree.

Taken aback, I replied "Okay."

Okay seemed to be the word of the night for me.

Jase got out of the truck and walked around to my side. He opened my door and helped me down, watching my every move. He walked me up to Maggie's door and said, "I'll pick you up at six again. Wear something nice." I kissed him lightly on the lips, smiling as we parted. I wished him goodnight, went inside, and closed the door. A moment later I heard his truck start up and back out of the driveway.

I just stood there in the hallway, leaning against the wall, wondering what the fuck I had gotten myself into and how the fuck I was going to get myself out of it.

Chapter 6 | Going, Going, Gone

I woke up Saturday morning with a curious Maggie bouncing on my bed. I tried to pretend I was still sleeping, but she knew better.

"Get up! Get up!" she shouted and continued to bounce on the bed.

"What do you want?" I asked, not moving or opening my eyes, knowing that she wanted the details of the night before.

Maggie groaned, becoming impatient, and said, "I have been waiting all morning for Matt to leave so I can ask you about the date. Now, get up and spill."

I opened my eyes and saw Maggie with a huge smile on her face, dressed and ready for the day. Why did she have to get up so early?

"Come on, Kenz. Matt and I went to bed after midnight and you still weren't back yet," she said.

Knowing that I was going to lose the battle, I sat up in bed and began to tell her about the date. I told her about the blue tarp and the blindfold and how I thought he was going to kill me. Maggie laughed and said I needed to get out more and lay off the crime dramas. I went on to tell her how I was blown away by the thoughtfulness of what he had planned. I described the setup in detail, happily reliving it again in my mind. Speechless, it seemed Maggie was just as blown away as I was. I mentioned that we'd kissed, purposely downplaying the hours of intense tonsil hockey in the back of his truck. As I told her, I realized I absently touched my fingers tips to my lips, as if I could still feel his on mine. I cracked a small smile and sat there, lost in thought.

Still daydreaming, I felt an annoying nudge.

"Hello? Did you hear me?" she asked.

I looked at Maggie. "I'm sorry. What did you say?" I replied.

"How did you end things? Is he going to call you? Are you going to see him again?" she rambled, letting the questions tumble out.

"Actually, I never gave Jase my number. And we're going out again tonight. He's picking me up at six and told me to wear something nice," I answered, blushing at the possible continuation of yesterday.

"Oh. My. God. Really? Did you pack something nice to wear?" a shocked Maggie asked.

I laughed and said, "No. I don't think I have anything dressy."

Maggie stood, grabbed my blanket, and whipped it off of me in one quick motion.

"What the fuck are you doing?" I asked, annoyed.

"We have to go shopping. Get dressed. We're leaving in ten minutes," she said as she quickly left the room.

This is fucking fabulous, I thought to myself sarcastically. I grabbed my phone and saw it was nine thirty in the morning.

"Ugh!" I groaned. "It's too early and I haven't eaten anything or had coffee yet. And I need to take a shower!" I shouted in my most pathetic voice.

I heard her footsteps heading back toward my room. She popped her head in and began lecturing me. With a tone uncomfortably reminiscent of my mother, she explained that we had over an hour ride to the mall and could get coffee and donuts on the way. Then Maggie was gone again as I heard her footsteps walking away from my room. It seemed as though my shower would have to wait.

I sat up in bed, thinking about my impending date with Jase. Do I really want to do this? What am I expecting to get out of it? I know what my body wanted the night before, and I didn't think I could have the same self-control again. I took Maggie's previous advice and weighed the pros and cons in my head. The biggest pro and con were one and the same. I lived three-and-a-half hours away. Which meant I could comfortably go out with Jase knowing the distance wouldn't allow more than what this was—a casual date. Realizing this made me feel a little sad inside. I was thinking about the situation. If things were different then maybe, just maybe…

"Hey, you're not dressed," Maggie said, popping her head back through the doorway, bringing me out of my thoughts.

"Okay, I'm going, I'm going," I snapped.

Maggie left and I swung my legs around to the side of the bed, stretching as I stood. It took all of my willpower not to crawl back under the covers. Wary of another maternal lecture, I instead grabbed a pair of sweats and a T-shirt and continued to get ready.

While out running around in search of the perfect outfit, I explained to Maggie how Jase had told me about his divorce and Matt ending his engagement. She filled me in on some of the details and went on to tell me about their parents, Robert and Nancy Hainsworth. She said that Robert was very nice, hardworking, and told it like it is. Nancy was nice, as well. But it took her a while to warm up to you, especially if you were dating one of her sons. She told me that they were good people and were very involved in their church and community. I wondered if that was why their mother was so upset when Matt and Jase's relationships hadn't worked out. Maybe she was more worried about what people would say and think about them. Maggie went on to tell me that Robert and Nancy were still very close with their sons and, regrettably, involved in their daily lives.

We were walking to the next store when I remembered what Jase had said the night before about Matt's reluctance to get married. I wondered if Maggie knew that, but I didn't say anything. I changed the subject, knowing what I knew. Plus I didn't want to hear about Maggie wanting to marry Matt and stay in the boonies forever.

Finally after trying on anything and everything, I bought a cute, strapless, black-and-white striped tube dress. I also bought a pair of red ballet flats that I came across. I would have loved to have worn heels, but after the previous night's date and not knowing where we were going, I decided flats were probably a better choice. Maggie said she would lend me her red clutch to finish off my outfit. I was glad we went shopping and felt better about the night ahead, now having something really cute to wear. Once I'd paid for my things, we headed to the car and Maggie sped home. She wanted to give me enough time to get ready and I was grateful for that.

We pulled into Maggie's driveway a little after three in the afternoon. We jumped out of her car and ran to the house. Rushing inside, we practically ran over Susi. The poor cat was so scared she hissed, puffed out her tail, and sprinted down the hallway. Maggie and I couldn't help but laugh at our frantic behavior. With my purchases in hand, I headed to my room. I pulled the dress and the accessories from the bags and laid them out on the bed. I grabbed a towel and headed to the bathroom to take a quick shower.

I turned on the water, got undressed, and stepped in. It wasn't even hot enough yet but I didn't have the time to wait for it to heat up. I wanted to look hot for that night's date. It's funny how things can change in the matter of twenty-four hours. I needed to keep in mind that this was just another casual date—nothing more, nothing less. I washed my hair, grabbed the soap, and washed my body. I quickly but carefully shaved again, ridding my body of any day-old stubble. I thanked god for yesterday's attention to detail. I rinsed and stepped out of the shower, wrapping the towel around my body.

I walked back to my room to get ready. As soon as I walked in, I noticed my phone was blinking. I picked it up and saw I had two voicemails and three text messages from Alayna. Shit! She wanted details about the date and I didn't have time to give them to her. I wondered if I should call and tell her I had another date with Jase? Maybe I should just tell her it sucked, end of story. Either way she was going to ask questions. I decided calling and actually speaking with her would take too long, so I decided to text her back.

> Date went well. Going out again tonight. Bought an outfit. Can't talk, getting ready. Will give you all the details tomorrow. Pls don't be mad.

I wasn't sure if she would text me back or try to call me again. My phone vibrated before I even finished my thought. I looked and saw it was a text from Alayna. She said,

> Ok. You better. Send me a picture of your outfit. Remember you owe me details.

That was a first. She never let me off the hook that easy, but I couldn't give it any more thought. I needed to get my ass in gear.

I rifled through my bags, finding my strapless bra and matching thong, and put them on. I grabbed my makeup bag and laid my brushes out on the dresser, trying to figure out what to do with my eyes. I decided a dramatic look would be best.

I'd started working my magic when I heard the music turn on. A minute later Maggie walked into the bedroom. She had two glasses of wine, one for herself and one for me. She was a godsend when she wasn't fucking with my dating life. Then again, if she hadn't gotten involved, I wouldn't be getting ready for a second date. A second *casual* date, I corrected myself.

Maggie lounged on the bed, petting Susi. As we sipped wine and made small talk, I finished getting ready. I blew out my long, flowing brown hair, leaving it straight and hanging just past the middle of my back. I slipped into my new dress and put on my red ballet flats. Adding the last of my accessories, I took one final look at myself in the mirror. Damn, I was good. I looked hot and had twenty minutes to spare.

Maggie let out a low whistle and said, "You look amazing, Kenzie."

"Do you really think so?" I asked, nervous and needing some reassurance.

"Yes you do. The dress is simple but sexy, and your hair and makeup look flawless," she replied.

I smiled and thanked her. I finished the last sip of my wine and sprayed on some perfume. Then hurried to the bathroom to brush my teeth before Jase got there, knowing how punctual he was yesterday.

I paced by the kitchen window closest to the driveway. Maggie was leaning against the counter, sipping her glass of wine, when we heard a truck pull into the driveway. We both sprang toward the window, nearly running into each other. I carefully pushed the curtain aside, peeking out to see Jase's pickup truck. He stepped out, and the first thing I noticed was his black cowboy boots. I had to do a double take.

Maggie, also peeking through the curtain, said in a hushed tone, "Shit, he cleans up well."

I couldn't speak. I could only nod in agreement. He had on a crisp, white button-down shirt with the sleeves rolled up to his elbows and the top two buttons undone. It was tucked into a pair of charcoal gray, boot-cut chinos with a black leather belt. His hair was also cleaned up and trimmed. It was pushed back off his face, which was cleanly shaven. I was so glad I was able to see him before he saw me, because I was still speechless. My body was instantly on fire, remembering the events from the previous night.

As he walked his fine ass toward the front door, he looked over at the window we were peeking out from. I quickly let go of the curtain and we both ducked like five-year-olds, giggling at each other.

"Do you think he saw us?" I asked Maggie.

"Probably," she said, still giggling.

Jase knocked at the door. Not wanting to make him wait like I had the day before, I walked to the door, took a few calming breaths, and opened it. Looking up at him through my long lashes I smiled and said, "Hi."

Jase just stood there looking at me from head to toe, giving me the once-over. It took a minute but he finally said, "Wow, you look beautiful." He smiled that crooked, panty-dropping smile of his and asked, "Are you ready to go?"

I nodded, grabbed the red clutch Maggie had lent me, and we headed out. Jase reached and grabbed my hand as we walked to his truck. He opened the passenger door, helped me in, and then shut it behind me. As I watched him walk around the truck, I noticed Maggie waving from the same kitchen window we had both peeking through only minutes before. I gave my best friend a quick wave back as Jase got in the truck, and we were off on our date.

We pulled into the parking lot of a restaurant on the outskirts of town. We had to circle the lot twice until we found a spot. After Jase parked, we headed inside. The place was rather busy, with a modest line of patrons waiting to be seated. Hardly even acknowledging the line, Jase walked right up to the hostess. She must have known him, because they made small talk for a minute before she grabbed menus and showed us to our table. Ignoring the annoyed glances of the waiting patrons, the woman sat us toward the back where not too many people were dining. After we took our seats, the hostess handed us each a menu, smiled, and walked away.

As I glanced over the menu, I took a minute to look at my surroundings. I noticed the building we were in was an older place and wondered if it had once been a farmhouse. It was nicely decorated with a quaint and cozy feel. Jase looked up from his menu and asked if I wanted to share an appetizer. Since he was obviously familiar with the place, I told him I would trust his judgment. He also gave me a few recommendations for the entrees. By the time our waitress came over to greet us, we were ready to order.

Our dinners were amazing and I made a mental note to go back there again with Maggie someday soon. Jase and I sat there for an hour after we ate, just talking while drinking our wine and sharing dessert. I found that I liked to listen to him and hear his stories about college, his family, and especially the trouble he and his brothers would get into growing up. He asked me about myself, but I kept it vague, not wanting to give too much away. I felt the less he knew of me, the better off I was. Hell, he didn't even have my phone number, and I hoped he wouldn't ask for it. I was trying very hard to keep a clear head with everything that was going on. I had this gorgeous man who was into me sitting across the table, and after last night he knew I clearly felt the same about him. Whatever Jase and I had going on between us, it couldn't turn into anything more. I couldn't allow it to keep going, but the big question was, how far would I let it go?

Jase paid and we headed out to his truck. The night sky was clear and all the stars were out. I heard the distant sounds of the town as he walked me to the passenger side, again while holding my hand. He paused before opening the door, tilting my chin up with one finger, making me look into those pale green eyes. He leaned in and placed a gentle kiss on my lips. His lips felt so warm I fucking melted. Why couldn't he be a dick so I could cut this date short? But noooo, he had to be hot *and* interesting *and* smart. Did I mention really hot? Holding my gaze, Jase spoke four words: "Come home with me." Before my mind caught up with what he had just asked, my head nodded yes. I decided then and there to just take things as they came, no pun intended.

The ride to Jase's house was a quiet one. Trying to make the ride a little less awkward, he would point things out along the way. We passed the veterinary clinic where Maggie worked and his family's farm market where we first met. But no matter what he pointed out or what he said, I couldn't get my mind off of what we were going to do. *Maybe he just wants to have me over for coffee or a glass of wine and show me around his home.* I had to laugh at that thought. Who was I kidding? I saw the way he looked at me in the parking lot. I was pretty sure he was only interested in showing me one room in his house, and that wasn't the laundry room. Holy shit! I was going to have sex.

As I was trying to calm myself down, we turned off the road onto a long driveway hidden by trees. We pulled up to a log cabin with a porch, and up-lit trees in the front yard.

Jase parked the truck in front of a two-car garage, looked over at me, and said, "Here we are." He then opened the door and got out.

Feeling my nerves trying to get the best of me, I took a deep breath and opened the door. I turned in my seat to step out and Jase was already standing there. As he reached out his hand, I took it in mine and hopped down. We walked up to his house and I noticed how well kept it looked.

Jase opened the door, and as I stepped over the threshold it was like my world instantly changed. Standing in the foyer, he dropped his keys and wallet on the side table and closed the door. The house was dark except for the lights behind me that led upstairs. Jase turned around, and in two steps he was standing in front of me, staring at me the same way he had in the parking lot of the restaurant. We just stood there, looking at each other's eyes, searching for something—anything. Maybe he was waiting for me to make a move or ask him to take me home. Leaving wasn't an option, though. The thought of me leaving him at this moment was too much. So I did what any rational twenty-five-year-old girl would do, that hadn't had sex since god knows when, and a smoking hot guy was standing in front of her eyeing her up like his last meal: I attacked him. I dropped my clutch, which fell to the floor with a thud. I grabbed his face and fiercely kissed him with raw passion and aching desire. I was all tingly and I didn't think my body would allow me to stop, even if I wanted to.

Jase kissed me back just as fiercely, parting my lips with his tongue. I moaned with want, which only evoked something in him as he picked me up, slamming me against the wall. I wrapped my legs around him. He started to kiss my neck, slowly making his way past my collarbone.

He paused to look at me and said between shaky breaths, "We can stop. We don't have to do this if you don't want to."

It felt like it was now or never. I chose now. My morals had gone out the window and I wasn't sure when they would be back. Did I care? Nope.

I grabbed him by his hair, pulling him back to my lips. He carried me upstairs to his bedroom, not taking his mouth off mine until he placed me on the edge of the bed. Jase worked on the buttons of his shirt as I quickly unbuckled his belt and pants. I slid them over his ass and down his legs, noticing he was commando. Damn! I was grateful for the strapless tube dress I had chosen to wear, as Jase frantically slid it off of me. I even more frantically unfastened my bra before he laid me down on his bed with only my thong on.

He stood in front of me and I eyed his tan, muscular body. My eyes roamed his broad shoulders, full pecs, and chiseled stomach. My eyes caught sight of the subtle trail of hair that led from his navel down past the well-defined V in his lower abdomen. Jase's impressive manhood stood very much ready and waiting. I wanted to reach out and touch him. He looked me up and down almost as if he was wondering where to start. With one finger he grabbed the delicate fabric of my thong and tugged hard and quick, ripping it off of my body.

If I wasn't wet before, I was Niagara Falls now. Throwing aside the scraps of what a moment before had been my thong, Jase climbed on top of me, pressing his very hard shaft against me. He claimed my mouth with his as we felt one another, getting familiar with each other's bodies. I was consumed by a feeling that I had never felt before. Our bodies meshed together as one and the connection I felt with Jase was on a level like no other. We spent hours in his bed and on the floor before we finally ended up in the shower. Exhausted, we crashed naked in his bed as the first rays of the sun started to peek through the trees. As if on cue, an obnoxious rooster crowed in the distance.

I woke to the sun blaring through his bedroom window and the smell of fresh coffee brewing. Whoever invented coffee pots with automatic timers was a genius. Lying in a strange bed, I thought about the things that Jase and I had done the night before. Dear god, it was amazing! *Goodbye, cobwebs*, I thought to myself, smiling. Who would have thought I would have had sex with some guy after only two dates? I looked over at Jase, who was lying on his stomach, peacefully sleeping. I gently picked up the edge of the blanket, checking out his ass. Yup, just as nice as I remembered.

Giggling quietly to myself and now craving a nice hot cup of coffee, I decided to slip out of bed. I grabbed Jase's white button-down shirt that was lying on the floor and put it on, not bothering to button it. I walked down the stairs and looked around at the house, noticing everything I hadn't noticed before. It was nicely decorated for a single guy. When I got to the first floor I realized I had no idea where the kitchen was, so I followed my nose. I walked down the hallway, turned the corner, and found the kitchen. "Bingo," I said to no one in particular.

I went straight to the coffee pot and reached for the cabinet above it. I was searching for a mug when a woman's voice stopped me.

"Excuse me, but what do *you* think you're doing?" the woman said, her tone laced with equal parts surprise and disgust.

Startled, I forced myself to slowly turn around. I saw a woman in her mid-fifties carrying a container of muffins and a basket of eggs. She had features similar to Matt and had short, dirty blond hair styled in a pixie cut. She stared at me with shock and annoyance, taking in the half-naked girl before her. I realized just then that I had nothing else on but Jase's white dress shirt, and it wasn't even buttoned. I quickly grabbed the shirt, wrapping it around myself as best I could. Oh please let this be a cleaning person.

"What are you doing in *my* son's house?" she demanded.

Yup, definitely his mother. Shit.

She put the muffins and eggs on the table and walked over to me, crossing her arms in a defiant stance. If she started to tap her foot I was going to make a run for it. Call me chicken but this was supposed to be casual, with no involvement or meeting of parental figures. I was starting to regret the previous night just a teensy, tiny bit.

Holding onto Jase's shirt with one hand and extending the other, I said, "Hi, I'm Mckenzie Shaw, a friend of Jase's." I was so embarrassed. I felt my cheeks flush and my stomach drop. I thought if she only knew what that hand had done to her son the night before, she wouldn't shake it. Oh my god, did I just think that? I was a horrible, horrible person. *Rein it in, Kenz,* I thought to myself.

Jase's mom wasn't having it. Either she had an idea as to what I might have done with that hand or was just pissed at my presence in general. I'm sure my being half-naked and wandering around her son's house surely didn't help. She glanced down at my hand and then back up at me. It was pretty clear she had no interest in exchanging niceties. I was really trying to be nice until she said, "I don't really give a damn as to who you are, and it's pretty clear *what* you have been doing. Now, I'd appreciate it if you would remove your trashy self from my son's home immediately!" Her tone went from angry to irate and her face was getting redder by the second.

I stood there stunned, trying to process what had just happened. What the fuck? Wondering if I had said something offensive, I began to replay our brief exchange in my mind. Then I thought, *This is Jase's house, and he's a grown-ass man.* If he wanted to bring a girl home and fuck her sideways on the roof of his house while singing "Macho Man" by the Village People, he could. Who was she to be angry? I could understand if she was embarrassed, but to tell me to leave and call me trashy! Oh hell no. Now I was pissed! Fuck being nice.

Trying to keep in mind that this was someone's mom and not some bitch at a bar, I did my best to curb my attitude. "I'm sorry, but did you just call me trashy?" I hissed.

She opened her mouth to say something, but before she had a chance to answer I cut her off.

"You know nothing about me. For your information, I am not trash. I'm far from it. I'm sorry that you had to see me like this, but if I had known Jase's mommy was coming over, I would have worn something more appropriate. Now, if you'll excuse me, I'll go get your son." Not waiting to see how she felt about my statement, I turned on my heel and stormed off down the hallway toward the stairs. With each step I was regretting this casual date more and more.

I opened the bedroom door and saw that Jase was still sleeping. I walked over to the bed and placed my hand on his shoulder and shook him awake.

He opened his eyes and rolled onto his side. Cracking a smile, he said, "Good morning, beautiful."

My body started to tingle as I looked at him. Flashes of us fucking like jackrabbits entered my mind and I almost forgot why I was so pissed.

"You look good in my shirt. Why don't you take it off and come back to bed," he said with a devilish smile as he pulled back the covers.

Good god, he was so hot. I could only stare at his naked body. Jase smiled anxiously as he watched me take off his shirt and throw it to the floor. His smile changed to a look of confusion when I walked over to the end of the bed to pick up my bra and dress. Remembering that my thong had been sacrificed for the cause, I guessed I was going commando. *Maybe I should take the remaining scraps and tie it to his mother's car antenna if she wants to see trash.*

As I started to put my clothes on, Jase asked, "What are you doing?"

"Apparently your mother doesn't think I look good in your shirt. She is quite pissed and was very rude to me. Oh, did I mention she called me trash?" I said as I pulled up my dress.

"Shit," was all he said as he fell back against the pillow, rubbing his face with his hands. Jase sat up, swung his legs over the side of the bed, and stood. He walked over to his dresser. While I did admire his fine ass and naked body, I was still pissed.

With his back to me he opened a drawer, grabbed a pair of sweatpants, and slipped them on. I watched this as if it was in slow motion, noticing each muscle as he moved or flexed.

Jase turned and looked at me. "Just so I know, what did you do or say to piss her off?" he asked, as if I was responsible for this somehow.

What. The. Fuck.

Did I just hear him right?

"Excuse me? What did *I* do or say to piss her off? You're kidding, right? I didn't do or say anything. I walked downstairs to get coffee and she was in your kitchen. She was rude when she spoke to me, even when I tried to be nice, and she called me trash!" I said, now getting really angry.

"You must have done something, because my mom wouldn't act that way," Jase said, clearly getting annoyed that I was putting this all on his mom.

I put my hands on my hips. "Really? Okay then. How about you go fuck yourself," I said, giving up on the conversation and the momma's boy standing in front on me. I stomped over to get my shoes when Jase grabbed my arm and stopped me. I looked up at him and saw he was conflicted.

He said, "Look, I'm not sure what happened but don't leave. Stay here while I go talk to her." He let go of me and walked out of the bedroom, heading downstairs.

He isn't sure what happened? I fucking told him what happened. Stay here my ass. I grabbed my ballet flats and slipped them on. I was done. I needed to call Maggie and have her pick me up. I looked around the room for my clutch. I remembered I had dropped it in the foyer last night. Shit. *God, I wish I could forget last night.*

I saw a phone on the nightstand. I picked it up and dialed Maggie's number. On the third ring she picked up.

"Hello?" she said, half-asleep.

"Maggs, its Kenzie. Is Matt there?" I whispered into the phone.

"Kenzie? What's wrong? Are you okay?" she responded as I got her attention.

"I'm fine. I promise," I assured her. "Is Matt there?" I asked again.

"No he's not here, do you need me to call him?" Maggie asked with concern in her voice.

"No, don't call him. Listen to me. I need you to pick me up at Jase's immediately. Don't ask. I'll explain in the car. I'm going to start walking so pick me up at the end of the driveway. And hurry up!" I said and hung up the phone.

I tiptoed down the stairs without making a noise. I overheard hushed voices coming from the kitchen. I wasn't sure how that conversation was going and I really didn't care. I saw my clutch on the side table in the foyer. Jase must have picked it up and put it there at some point. I walked to the door and opened it slowly, praying I didn't make a sound. I slipped out and carefully closed it quietly behind me.

I saw an older, silver Ford Explorer in the driveway parked next to Jase's truck. I assumed it was his mother's. As I walked past it, I wished I had found my thong so I could have tied it to her antenna. I walked the walk of shame down the driveway, not once looking back. Walking away from him wasn't easy. Even though he didn't believe me, Jase was different; we connected. Then I thought how great the previous night was, but it had only led to shit in the morning. I guess nothing good can come from a one-night stand. Vowing to never make that mistake again, I waited at the end of the long driveway for my best friend.

I saw Maggie's Prius heading toward me as she pulled onto the shoulder and I quickly hopped in. She made an illegal U-turn in the middle of the road and headed back to her house.

She took one look at me and asked if I was okay. I nodded yes as I held back the tears that threatened to spill over. As I struggled to regain my composure, I briefly told Maggie what had happened with Jase's mother and him not believing me. I told her it was a huge mistake and I regretted the night before, knowing that nothing could ever come of Jase and me. I explained to Maggie that as soon as we got back to her house I was going to pack up my things and head home. Under no circumstances was she to give Jase my number. I wanted to go home and forget this ever happened, regardless of what I had felt with him.

When we reached Maggie's house, I ran through it like a whirlwind. I grabbed my stuff and threw it in my bags. Susi was so startled that she ran under the bed and refused to come out. I heard Maggie's phone ringing off the hook but thankfully she didn't answer it. I had my shit packed and in the car in under ten minutes. I hugged Maggie and said goodbye. I apologized for leaving so abruptly and promised I would call her as soon as I got home.

I knew Maggie might feel some repercussions from my actions, but she could see how mad and hurt I was. After she picked me up she had listened to me vent and not once did she try to talk me out of leaving or chastise me for walking out on Jase. She was a great friend, and for that I owed her big time, but it was time for me to go home and get back to reality.

Chapter 7 | Favor

It was seven o'clock on Friday night and I was still at work. It had been three months since I'd visited Maggie, which had ended horribly. I had spoken to her after I got home that afternoon, and apparently Jase was the one calling her when we were packing my bags. He ended up driving to her house when she didn't answer her phone. Thankfully I had left minutes earlier and avoided seeing him. Maggie had said he was worried when he couldn't find me. She explained to him that I had called her asking to be picked up, and how she had driven right over. She said his mood changed when he heard this and he seemed to be slightly annoyed that I had left his house the way I had. Jase wanted to talk to me about what had happened, but she told him that I had left to go home, which only added to his annoyance. He apparently went off about everything that had happened that morning, but Maggie told him she wouldn't get involved. When he asked for my number, she refused.

Defeated and out of options, Jase left her house, but an hour later Matt showed up looking for answers. He said that Jase was hurt when I left like I did, without even talking to him or saying goodbye. Maggie explained to him that she didn't want to get involved and that they should stay out of it. Begrudgingly, Matt agreed. I could tell by the sound of Maggie's voice that she seemed unsure if and how this was going to affect her and Matt. The Hainsworth family was very close, and it seemed that if one was mad or hurt, they all were. I apologized profusely to Maggie, but she wouldn't hear any of it and told me not be sorry.

Since then I hadn't seen Maggie, but we still talked every Sunday. Things between her and Matt were a little awkward at first but were getting better. She never brought up Jase again, for which I was grateful. Did I think about him? Sure—I would be lying if I said I didn't. He was often in my thoughts and dreams. I didn't think I could ever forget the connection he and I had and the way my body had reacted to his touch. I wondered if I would ever find anything like that again.

That is why I buried myself in my work. If I kept my mind busy, I thought about him less. My boss thought I was dedicated, which I was, but I was more desperate to keep the thoughts of Jase Hainsworth at bay.

Exhausted and not able to create one more PowerPoint slide, I decided it was time to pack up and head home. I stood up from my desk and stretched my back after what seemed like hours of not moving from my chair. I looked around the office and noticed that I was the last person there. Twenty-five years old with no life—yup, that was me.

I was dreading the walk to my car in the bitter November cold. At least traffic at this hour wouldn't be an issue. I was logging off my laptop when my phone started to vibrate. I looked at the screen and saw it was Masen. Curious as to why he was calling, I answered the phone. "Hello," I said.

"Hey stranger. How are you?" he asked. I wasn't fooled. Masen and I were still close and we kept in touch, but him calling me out of the blue on a Friday night was odd. He must have called for a specific reason.

"Okay, spill. What's going on?" I asked.

"You know me too well," he chuckled.

"I should. We dated for four years, remember?" I pointed out. "Or did you forget?"

"I could never forget that," he said. We were quiet for a couple seconds.

"So why the phone call? What's up?" I asked again, curious to find out.

"I need a favor. A *huge* favor," he said, sounding desperate.

"Sure, anything. Is everything okay?" I questioned, a little worried.

"I'm fine, but I need you to come with me to Maggie's tomorrow," he answered.

Shit.

"I can't this weekend. I have plans," I quickly replied.

He laughed and said, "Come on, Kenz. I know you don't any have plans. You're a workaholic."

Shit.

I pinched the bridge of my nose. He knew me all too well. "Maybe I have a date," I told him, trying to sound convincing but failing miserably.

"Mckenzie Shaw, when was the last time you went out on a date?" he asked.

Ouch. That stung a little. Maybe I should hang up on him and blame it on poor signal strength. I smiled slyly as I considered it.

What was I going to do? I didn't want to go to Maggie's. I wondered why he was going up there, though she did mention to me last Sunday that she was having people over the following weekend. Plus she had also asked Masen a couple times to visit her recently but he had been too busy.

What if I went to Maggie's with Masen and Jase was there? What would happen?

I'm sure he's over it. I mean, it's been three months. Time heals all wounds, right?

"So you'll come with me, right?" he asked.

"You're not giving me much notice here, Masen. Why are you going exactly?" I questioned.

"Maggie has been hounding me to visit, but I've been swamped with work. My plans fell through and my weekend is now free and clear. I know she is having people over and I thought who better to crash her plans but her two favorite people," he responded proudly. Clearly he had given this some thought.

Taking my silence as a yes, Masen said, "I'll pick you up at five. I have some running around to do before we leave."

Making one last-ditch effort to weasel out of it.

I said, "What if they get snow? You know I won't drive up there in the snow. Also, I have a meeting first thing Monday morning and I can't afford to get stuck at Maggie's." I crossed my fingers, hoping he would let me off the hook and go without me.

"I'll drive, so don't worry about that. Plus I just had new tires put on the Pilot. It's a beast," he said proudly.

Damn Honda and their quality car-making abilities.

Conceding to his request, I said, "Fine, I'll go with you. See you at five."

"Great! See you tomorrow," he said before hanging up.

How did I get myself into these situations?

Feeling exhausted, I grabbed my laptop, put it in my messenger bag, and threw on my winter jacket. I made the short walk to the parking garage and sadly noticed my car was the only one left. It seemed so eerie at that time of night. I could hear the wind howling, and every step I took echoed as I walked toward my car. I unlocked the door as I approached and quickly jumped in. There was something about being alone in a parking garage that scared me. I guess that's what I got for watching the movie *Candyman* when I was little. I was scarred for life. If I left at a normal hour, it wouldn't be an issue. I seriously needed to do more with my time rather than working every waking minute.

I started my car and left work, making the lonely forty-minute commute home. During my drive, I couldn't help but think about my life. I was going to be twenty-six in a couple months, and what did I have to show for it? I did have a house, a car, and money saved, but I never went out or treated myself. Most of my friends were in serious relationships or even engaged. Alayna always came over when she was bored because she knew I was usually home.

My dating life was still nonexistent since my last date—and look how that went. Before that, I couldn't remember the last actual date I had been on. Oh wait, yes I could. It was a blind date with a guy named Marc. I met him at a Chinese restaurant. We sat at a table, in front of a mirrored wall, which his back was to. Marc then proceeded to pick his nose, examined his findings, and ate it while hiding behind his menu. He must not have noticed the mirrored wall—or maybe he forgot—but either way I could see his reflection. I was so disgusted that I got up and walked out before he'd finished his snack and put his menu down.

Now I knew why I couldn't remember my last date before Jase: because I'd tried so very hard to forget about it. *Maybe I should just give up dating and become a nun.* Then again, that probably wouldn't work. I liked sex too much. When I was having it, that is, and I was pretty sure vibrators were frowned upon in a convent. I sighed as I turned up the music to drown out my thoughts for the rest of the ride.

Once I got home I had a few glasses of wine and tried to unwind from the hectic week I'd had, yet again. I did some laundry and packed my clothes for the trip upstate. Even though I was only going for one night, I still overpacked. I knew Masen was going to give me shit for bringing my duffel bag rather than an overnight bag, but he would have to deal with it.

Lying in bed, I was going through my mental checklist to make sure I hadn't forgotten anything. My mind inevitably started to drift to Jase. I tried to convince myself that everyone would be over what had happened between Jase and me months ago. I wondered if I should tell Masen about it but decided against it. Last thing I needed was his opinion on what I should or shouldn't have done. Plus I don't think he would've wanted to hear about the hot country guy that I fucked after knowing him for only two days. God, I hoped the next day wouldn't be a clusterfuck. I shut my eyes, welcoming sleep, and hoping Jase wouldn't be in my dreams.

The next day I woke midmorning, feeling refreshed. I had slept like a rock and didn't remember dreaming at all. I had to get some stuff done before Masen picked me up, so I decided to get my day started. I checked my phone and saw I had three text messages—two the previous night from Alayna and one that morning from Masen. Alayna's first text was a picture of her with our friends at a bar in Hoboken saying, "Wish you were here." The second one was a picture of Alayna with a gorgeous guy saying, "I take that back. More for me."

I rolled my eyes and gave my phone the finger. I knew she couldn't see my reaction or gesture, but it made me feel better. I texted her back, calling her an asshole, and told her I was going to Maggie's that night with Masen and that I would be back the next day. I was sure she would have a million and one questions when she read that, so I decided it might be best to ignore her texts and calls. I moved on to Masen's text:

> Change of plans. Picking you up at 3. We'll grab dinner at the diner in Roscoe on our way up there.

Great. I better get my ass in gear. I texted Masen back:

> Ok. I'll be ready.

I quickly threw on a sweat outfit and tied my bedhead hair into a messy bun. I headed out to run some errands. When I got home I had little time to shower and get ready, but I made it happen. It seemed I was always rushing around for someone else. Maybe I needed to make time for myself. But first things first: I had to do this favor for Masen. I didn't totally mind, because I got to see my best friend, but I could have used a little more notice. That's Masen for you—always doing stuff last minute.

Given the circumstances of recent events, I made sure I looked good. I was not walking into the unknown looking haggard. I had to look good, but I also wanted to be comfortable on the ride to Maggie's.

I stood in front of the mirror, checking myself out. I blew out my hair and left it straight, hanging down to the middle of my back. I kept my makeup simple. If I fell asleep on the ride there, I didn't want to deal with makeup smudges. I put on an olive-green, open-knit, off-the-shoulder sweater with a white tank top underneath. I had on my favorite low-waist skinny jeans that made my ass look amazing. Last but not least, I wore my knee-high black wedge biker boots that had buckles and straps and screamed *badass*. I checked myself in the mirror one last time. I was missing something. I reached into my closet, grabbed a black scarf, and wrapped it loosely around my neck. I checked myself one last time in the mirror. I looked good. I looked like Tara from *Sons of Anarchy* after she went biker bitch but before she went all mom.

I checked the time and noticed it was after three o'clock. I should have known Masen would be late. He was hardly ever on time. Just then I heard beeping outside and figured it was my ride. I looked out of my bedroom window and saw Masen getting out of his SUV, opening the hatch. I grabbed my stuff and headed down the stairs, shutting off all of the lights and locking up the house.

Masen met me on the sidewalk and gave me a hug. "Looking good, Kenz," he said, flashing his beautiful smile at me.

"You don't look so bad yourself, Rowe," I replied as I punched him in the shoulder, teasing him like I'd done for years.

Just then he noticed my bag, frowned, and shook his head. "Seriously, Kenzie? A fucking duffel bag? We're only staying overnight," he said, shocked that I'd packed so much.

I put my duffel bag down, tilted my head, crossed my arms, and said, "Masen Rowe, I'll take my duffel bag and walk my sweet ass back into my house and you can go to Maggie's without me. Or you can just deal with my overpacking issues and leave me alone. Plus, it's not like you're a pack mule and you're carrying my shit all the way there."

Masen sighed and shook his head, annoyed. He picked up my bag, turned, and walked toward the SUV without saying another word. He put my bag in the back, closed the hatch, and then we both got into his SUV. I could tell that he was stewing a little but I ignored it. I asked him some questions about his parents and work and soon my packing indiscretions were forgotten.

Masen and I talked the whole drive, catching up on each other's lives—his more so than mine, since not much was going on in my life. Masen talked about work, mainly. He was a history teacher at the high school we'd graduated from. He also coached the basketball team there. He loved his job and always had great stories. I had no doubt that he had the high school girls' full attention in his classes—although the girls probably paid more attention to the teacher rather than the history lesson itself. Masen had always been attractive and could have been a Calvin Klein underwear model in my eyes.

We were a little over two hours into the ride when Masen was talking football and boring the hell out of me. I glanced at the approaching sign and saw it said "Roscoe 5 miles." My stomach instantly started to rumble. Ten minutes later we got off the highway at exit ninety-four and headed toward the Roscoe Diner. Thankfully it was less than a mile from the exit. It was not only convenient, but they had great food.

An hour later and full from dinner, Masen and I got back on the highway. Being so stuffed, it was only a matter of time before I fell asleep. I knew we had at least another hour and a half ahead of us, so I reclined my seat, turned on my side, and used my winter coat as a pillow. Masen laughed to himself. He knew me well enough to realize he had just lost his copilot. I closed my eyes and surrendered to the food-induced slumber.

Chapter 8 | Surprise

I woke to Masen shaking my shoulder. "Wake up, sleepy head, we're almost there," he said.

A little groggy, I put my seat in the upright position and peered out the window. We passed through a blinking red traffic light, which meant we were about ten minutes from Maggie's. I took notice of how dark it was and it made me miss the comfort of streetlights. The trees were highlighted by the moon, high in the night sky, and the millions of stars made for a beautiful backdrop. With very few cars on the road in this area, the darkness was broken up only by the headlights of the SUV.

We were getting closer, so I flipped down the visor to fix my makeup and brush my hair. For being in a car for hours, plus taking a nap, I still looked pretty good. Masen started to slow down. I flipped up my visor as he pulled in behind Maggie's Prius and parked.

I looked left and right, scanning the cars and trucks parked along the road and in her driveway. My heart stopped as I noticed one in particular. I'd recognize the bed of that pickup truck anywhere. It was Jase's. He was here. Shit. *Okay, Kenz, put your big girl pants on and let's do this,* I thought to myself. The pep talk wasn't working as well as I would have liked. I felt frozen in my seat, unable to move. After all the times I had thought and dreamt about Jase, I was finally going to see him again. My body began to tremble.

Just then my door swung open. I jumped and screeched, startling Masen, who had opened my door.

"What the fuck is wrong with you?" he asked.

I hadn't even noticed he had gotten out. "Nothing!" I snapped back. "I just woke up ten minutes ago. I'm a little out of it, give a girl a break," I said as I got out.

I heard Masen mumble something under his breath, but I couldn't make it out. I put my coat over my shoulders as we walked toward Maggie's front door. It was freezing outside and there was a slight gust of wind that sent shivers through my body. At least I could blame my trembling on the cold and not on my nerves.

When we got up to the front door, Masen looked at me and asked, "Do we knock or just walk in?"

"You're her brother and I'm her best friend. I don't think we need to knock."

He shrugged his shoulders, accepting my reasoning. As he reached for the knob, the door opened and standing there was a guy who looked just like Jase's brother Cole. Except this guy was more muscular and oozed arrogance as he looked me up and down, totally ignoring Masen. He must have been the other twin, Reid.

"Why hello, beautiful. I've never met you before. And you are?" he asked, never taking his eyes off of me.

I rolled my eyes and looked over at Masen, who was trying to keep his cool. I saw the way he clenched and unclenched his jaw, which meant he was probably five seconds away from punching Reid.

I looked back at the arrogant jackass leaning in the doorway. I smiled and kindly said, "I'm a friend of Maggie's, and this," gesturing to Masen, "is her brother."

"Come on in, then," Reid said as he turned and strolled back into the house.

Masen and I walked in and shut the door. We took off our coats and hung them on the hooks in the hallway. We walked toward the voices in the kitchen. That is when I heard Reid say, "Maggs, why didn't you tell me you had a really hot friend?"

This was going to be interesting.

I peeked up at Masen, looking down at me. "Seems you have an admirer and we haven't even been here five minutes," he said, not looking too thrilled. If he only knew the story with Jase and me.

Keeping that to myself, I gave a weak chuckle as we turned the corner into the kitchen.

"Who are you talking about?" Maggie asked Reid.

No one had noticed our presence until he nodded his head in our direction and said, "Your friend over there."

The few people that were paying attention to Reid, including Maggie, turned and looked toward Masen and me.

"Surprise!" I said.

Maggie did a double take and looked at us, clearly in shock. "No fucking way! You guys are here!" she shouted as she ran over and bear-hugged us. "I can't believe it," she said, finally letting go of us. Maggie was ecstatic. She looked up at Masen and said, "I thought you couldn't make it because you had plans."

"They fell through, so I asked Kenzie to take the ride with me," Masen explained.

Maggie turned to everyone in the kitchen and loudly said, "Everyone, this is my brother Masen. Masen, this is everyone."

I had a feeling that my best friend had a good buzz going on. She continued: "And this is my bestie, Mckenzie, but you can call her Kenzie. Some of you met her a couple months ago," she said as she swayed just a little.

Yup, she was going to be shitfaced before the night was out.

We waved hello to everyone, and as I looked around the kitchen I saw some familiar faces staring back at me.

I couldn't help but feel like I was being judged. I smiled and turned to Maggie. I whispered to her, "Is it okay that I'm here, after what happened with Jase?"

Maggie looked at me like I had three heads. "Of course it's okay. That's over and done with. No worries," she said, trying to make me feel more at ease.

Maybe I was being just a bit paranoid. Maggie said not to worry, so I wouldn't worry. After our introductions, Masen said he was going to get our bags from his SUV.

In a low voice I asked curiously, "Was that Reid who told you we were here?"

Maggie rolled her eyes. "Yes, that's Reid. He can be an ass but he's a good guy. It's strange how he and Cole are twins but polar opposites. Reid is loud and confident, whereas Cole is quiet and reserved," she said.

I definitely saw the differences, even though they were twins.

"But watch out—he thinks you're hot and I'm sure that will piss Jase off."

Concerned, I asked, "Why would it piss Jase off?"

With both of her hands, she grabbed my shoulders and looked me square in the eyes. Very seriously she said, "Because you're the one that walked away. No girl has ever walked away from a Hainsworth boy. Ever. They're like crack in this town. They're hot, educated, three out of four are single, and their family has money." Maggie continued, "Plus that cocky little shit loves to annoy his brothers. Once Reid finds out you're *that* girl, expect the ball-busting to begin."

Great, just what I needed. And she said I didn't have anything to worry about. "I don't plan on hooking up with Reid or anyone from up here," I explained as I shrugged Maggie's hands off my shoulders. I would not be making that mistake again.

"Cheer up, Kenz. Have a drink and just relax," she said happily.

Maybe if I had a couple of drinks I would be as oblivious as she was.

"Did someone say they needed drinks?"

Maggie and I turned and saw Reid wearing a sly smile on his face, walking toward us carrying three beers. As he stopped in front of us, I felt an arm sling over my shoulder. I looked up and it was Masen, and he was looking at Reid.

"Thanks for the beer, man," Masen said as he grabbed one with his free hand, not taking his arm off me.

The smile on Reid's face disappeared and you could feel the tension building. Through gritted teeth and with a slight twitch of his head, Reid said, "Anytime… man." He handed Maggie and I the other two beers and walked away in a huff.

Maggie looked at Masen and muttered, "You better behave yourself, little brother."

Masen smiled at his sister and said one word, "Always," as he winked at her.

I looked up at Masen and asked, "Protective much?"

He responded with a gentle squeeze and a smile.

Maggie, Masen, and I were chatting about the drive up when I realized I hadn't seen Jase or Matt. I did recognize their cousins, Amy and Casey, and some people that Maggie worked with. Reid was talking with some girls I didn't know. Just as I was about to ask Maggie where Jase and Matt were, Casey reached for the back door. As he opened it, in came Matt first, carrying two cases of beer, then Jase carrying a few of pizza boxes.

My heart stopped yet again. At the rate I was going, I'd be dead before the night was over. Matt and Jase were still hysterically laughing as they put the beer and pizza down on the counter.

Maggie walked over and noticed that Matt's pants were all dirty and wet. "What happened?" she asked him, worried.

Matt was still hysterically laughing so Jase answered Maggie, still chuckling himself. "He's okay, Maggs. He slipped on the runner getting out of the truck and fell on his ass."

Getting a grip on himself, Matt said, "Really, I'm okay. Just a little dirty, that's all."

"Good," she said as she grabbed his hand and tugged him to follow her. "I want you to meet someone."

I watched Jase talking with Reid and the girls while Casey put the beer in the fridge. Everyone else was already digging into the pizza.

Maggie, with Matt in tow, stopped in front of Masen, who still had his arm around my shoulders. Matt was whispering something into Maggie's ear when she interrupted him and said, "Matt, this is my brother Masen. Masen, this is my boyfriend Matt Hainsworth."

Matt looked at Masen, smiled, and stuck his hand out.

Masen did the same. "Nice to meet you, Matt. I've heard so much about you. Sorry I didn't come up sooner, but things have been hectic back home," Masen said.

"No worries. Nice to meet you as well," Matt replied.

That's when Matt turned his attention to me. I saw his smile falter just a little, and I was sure no one else noticed it, but I did. Then I saw his eyes wander from me, to Masen's arm draped over my shoulder, then back to Masen. Suddenly my anxiety was at an all-time high.

Matt and Masen dropped the handshake and Maggie gestured to me and said, "Matt, you remember Kenzie?"

With a tight smile and a slight nod of his head, Matt said, "Of course, how could I forget?"

Not wanting to add to the tension in the small house, I kept my response short and sweet. I smiled and said, "Good to see you again Matt."

His reply was even shorter. "Likewise."

Matt turned his attention back to my best friend. Maggie explained to Matt that Masen's plans for the weekend had fallen through, so he'd decided to take the trip up here and had dragged me along with him.

"That's a nice surprise, guys. I just ran out with my brother, Jase, to get beer and pizza. You remember Jase, right Kenzie?" Matt asked, smirking at me.

I noticed Maggie's eyes widen and her mouth pop open in shock, but thank goodness Masen was clueless.

The anxiety was gone, replaced with anger, and I was trying very hard to keep my cool. If Matt kept this shit up, I would release my inner bitch.

"Yes, I remember him," was all I said, with no emotion in my voice. I'd be dammed if I'd give him the satisfaction.

"Great—help yourselves to some pizza and beer."

Maggie quickly excused herself and pulled Matt into the hallway. I knew that would not be a pleasant conversation.

"He seems really nice," Masen said, watching them walk away.

"Yup," was my only response.

I looked across the kitchen and saw Reid talking to Jase. I was hoping and praying that he wasn't mentioning me. Seemed my prayers weren't answered, because as Reid turned to look my way, Jase's head snapped up and he stared directly at me. He then looked at Masen, who still had his arm around my shoulders. Fuck! Could this night get any worse? Was this how things were going to be when I visited from now on?

So I did the first thing that came to mind: I chugged my beer.

Masen eyed me suspiciously. "Since when do you chug beer?" he questioned.

"I think I'm going to make it my thing when I come to Maggie's," I said, finishing the last of it.

"You want another one?" he asked, seemingly confused.

"Yup," was all I said.

"You're quite the talker since we got here," he said, laughing.

I smiled and said "Yup" again.

He shook his head and walked into the danger zone, the kitchen. Not wanting to face Jase, I walked into the living room and took a seat on the window bench.

I stared out the window, looking at all the stars and the moon. I felt something cold and hard tap my shoulder. I turned in the seat to grab the bottle of beer and said, "Thanks, Rowe." But when I looked up, it wasn't Masen. It was Jase's beautiful pale green eyes peering down at me.

My heart stopped, my stomach dropped, and my body began to hum. He was so close to me and I was having flashbacks of our last night together. My breath hitched and he took notice. His eyes darted to my lips. Then he looked me over as I sat there feeling completely submissive to him.

"Sorry to disappoint. Maggie was talking with your *boyfriend*, so me being the gentleman that I am, I offered to bring you your beer. And here I am," he said, thick with sarcasm.

"You really shouldn't assume things, Jase. Oh, and thanks for the beer," I hissed back at him.

Taking a sip, I turned and looked out the window. This time, instead of the stars and moon, all I saw was his reflection standing behind me. I could see he was seething.

"So that's it? That's all you have to say?" he retorted angrily.

Trying my best not to turn and look at him, I continued to stare at his reflection and said, "What would you like me to say? Are you expecting an apology? *It* was a mistake. *It* shouldn't have happened. I don't know what I was thinking. I wish I could take it all back, but I can't."

This infuriated Jase. He bent down next to my ear and said in a gruff voice, "Really? A mistake, huh? It didn't seem like a mistake when my mouth was on that sweet pussy of yours as you moaned and wiggled on my face. I don't recall you screaming out 'This is a mistake' while we were fucking. No, you were screaming my fucking name, wanting every inch I gave you. You were awfully greedy that night, but I didn't mind."

I could feel a sly smile creeping onto his face as he threw the memories of that night back at me. He was so close that I could feel his breath just inches from my neck.

Jase took a deep breath and continued. "You know you ruined me. You walked out and I haven't been the same since. You're in my thoughts and my fucking dreams. Just when I think I can move past it, you show up here. And with Maggie's brother! Are you two back together? Here I thought we had something. I know you felt it too, Kenzie. Just admit it."

The way he said my name, as if he were claiming me, made me tremble, and I was sure he could see it. There was too much truth laced in his words.

Slowly, I took a long sip from my beer. I stood and looked up at him through my lashes. I could see the anger, hurt, and hope as he stood inches from me. I was not willing to let him hold onto that hope. Hope wouldn't get either of us anywhere but more hurt. I was really pissed at that point, but I didn't want to make a scene. I needed to keep it together.

In a hushed voice, I spat back at him, "I am here because Maggie's *my* best friend, and if you don't like it, then tough shit. Know this: I am not sorry for walking out on you. Your mom treated me like shit, called me trash, and told me to leave," I hissed. "I explained to you what happened, yet you thought I said or did something to piss her off. So yes, I left. Did you ever think maybe she was out of line? Maybe she woke up on the wrong side of the hay bale. Or maybe you should tell your mommy to call first before dropping shit off. You want me to admit to a feeling that you feel, but I can't admit to something that isn't there," I said, finishing my rant.

His eyes widened with my last words, and I could see the hope fade and only the pain and anger remained. I wanted to take back the words as soon as I had spoken them, but it was the only way. Nothing could ever become of us and we needed a clean break, even if it ended like this. Jase slowly backed away, staring in disbelief, and then turned and walked out of the room.

As soon as he disappeared from my view, I chugged the rest of my beer and placed the empty bottle on the coffee table. I sat back down on window bench and stared off into the night sky. As I sat there, I thought the only way to get through the night was to drink enough so I wouldn't remember a thing. I couldn't shake the image of his eyes as I thought about the last words I had said to Jase. I felt my eyes begin to moisten. I couldn't get emotional—not here, not now.

I brought my knees up to my chest and hugged them tight.

"Are you okay?" I heard someone say.

Startled, I whipped my head around to see Amy, Jase's cousin. "Umm, yeah, I'm okay," I said, wondering if she had overhead Jase and me moments before.

She smiled and looked out of the window. "Pretty, isn't it?" Amy said.

She must have noticed my puzzled expression as she began to answer my unasked question.

"The night sky—when it's clear like this, it's so pretty. I love to look at all of the stars in the sky. They say you can hardly see the stars at night from the city. Is that true?"

Did this girl ever leave the country? I was under the impression that everyone from Jase's family hated me, and here she was asking me about stars.

It took me a moment to reply. "I can see stars when I'm home, but not nearly as many as I can see here."

Satisfied with my answer, she smiled and looked back out the window.

We were quiet for a minute or two and I was wondering if she had anything else to say when she broke the silence.

"The day Jase first met you at the market, I saw the way he was with you and again the day at the bar. I also couldn't help but notice how you were with him as well. He told me about how great the picnic went and how happy he was when you agreed to go out with him again." She turned to face me and continued. "I apologize, but I heard what you said before, that you felt nothing. I know it's none of my business, and you seem like a nice person, but why would you say that? It seemed that you had feelings for Jase."

I wanted to be pissed, but when I looked at her I saw no sarcasm or judgment—just a girl asking a question. I quickly thought of what to say. I couldn't tell her how I really felt. She could possibly tell Jase, and I surely didn't need that.

I decided to keep it simple. I smiled a weak smile at her and said, "Sometimes things aren't meant to be."

"Oh. Sorry. I didn't mean to pry," she apologized, worried that maybe she had overstepped.

"It's okay. I can see you care for your cousin. You had a question and you asked it. No harm, no foul," I quickly replied, trying to lighten the mood.

Amy nodded her head in agreement. "Do you need anything?" she asked, as Masen and Maggie were walking into the living room.

I shook my head, smiled, and said, "No. I'm good. Thanks."

Amy smiled back, turned, and left the room.

Masen and Maggie were in deep conversation as they approached me.

"Kenz, what was the name of the snake I got Masen for his birthday?" Maggie demanded.

Were they seriously discussing this?

"I told you what his name was," Masen said, frustrated that his sister didn't believe him.

"Shut up, Masen. Let her answer," Maggie snapped.

Jesus, this was getting annoying. It was going to be a long night.

I eyed both of their beers. I looked at them and barked, "Ralph. The stupid snake was named Ralph. He somehow got out of the aquarium and you never found him."

"See? I told you," Masen said proudly.

I shook my head at them both. They clearly didn't need me for this conversation. I stood and took both of their beers and walked away, toward the hallway. I heard them both say, "Hey!" in unison as I grabbed my coat and went outside for some fresh air.

After thirty seconds of standing outside, I realized it was way too cold. The wind was blowing and I watched the leaves swirling around the driveway. I started to drink the beers I'd hijacked from Maggie and Masen. I stood on the front steps of Maggie's house, wondering how the rest of the night would pan out. I hoped no one else would question me. Just then I saw a shooting star. I'm not a superstitious person, but given what had happened so far that night, I figured making a wish couldn't hurt.

I closed my eyes and silently wished for no more bullshit with Jase that night. I opened my eyes and finished one of the beers. I heard the crunch of leaves to the left of me.

"What did you wish for?" someone asked.

I didn't have to look to know who it was. I could hear the disgust in his voice. It was Matt. Fucking great. Maybe I should have gone broader with my wish, to cover all of the Hainsworth family.

I didn't respond to his question and decided to ignore him. I guess he didn't appreciate my silence, because he walked up and stood directly in front of me. I had no choice but to look at him. I really wanted to act like a three-year-old, close my eyes, and stick my tongue out, but I thought better of it.

"I saw the shooting star too. So what did you wish for?" Matt asked again.

I took a long, deep breath before replying. "If you tell someone what you wish for, it won't come true," I said, trying to be cordial.

As I eyed Matt, I could see he was not happy with me. Plus, I knew Maggie had probably given him a piece of her mind earlier for the way he had acted.

He laughed and said, "That's what they say, but my wish has to do with you so maybe you can help it come true."

I looked at him warily. Given his tone, I could only see this conversation going south and my inner bitch was preparing.

"Well, do you want to hear it or not?" he asked, trying to bait me.

I wondered how bad it would be to dick-kick my best friend's boyfriend with a houseful of his family and friends inside.

"Enlighten me," was all I said as I sipped my beer, acting as if his presence didn't faze me.

"I wished that my brother would no longer be hung up on some stupid city bitch that used him and hung him out to dry," he hissed, waiting for a reaction.

I silently counted down—*Ten, nine, eight, seven, six, five, four, three, two, motherfucking one*—before I replied. "Really, that's what you wished for? Who do you think you are, the big bad brother? I can give two shits what you think. You want to know why?" Without giving him a chance to answer, I continued: "Because you're an ignorant fuck that sticks his nose where it doesn't belong. What happened between Jase and me is between Jase and me. I don't believe you were there while we were fucking, so as far as I'm concerned your opinions are meaningless. Maybe you should let Jase handle his own life situations rather than his mommy or big brother trying to do it for him."

I think I shocked the shit out of him, because he had nothing to say.

I took a sip of beer, glared at Matt, and said, "I think it would be in your best interest to stay clear of me for the rest of the night."

On that note, I turned on my heel and walked inside, leaving Matt to stew. Fuck him. I needed another beer.

I walked inside, hung my coat on the hook in the hallway, and headed toward the kitchen. I turned the corner, put my empty beer bottles on the counter, and saw Maggie was pouring shots of tequila. Perfect timing. I wanted to get shitfaced and forget this night had ever existed, and that was exactly what I planned to do.

Masen saw me walk in and handed me a shot. I put the shot glass to my lips and threw it back. I could feel the sharp taste burn my throat on the way down and the warmth of it as it settled in my belly. I slammed the empty glass onto the counter and said, "Another please."

Maggie looked at me and said, "You're not gonna blame me for feeling like shit tomorrow, right?"

"Nope. Now pour me another shot," I told her, and she did. After three more shots I was feeling great and didn't have a care in the world.

My body was numb as I walked over to the fridge to get a beer and saw a guy and girl making out against the counter. I opened the fridge and reached in to get a beer when I heard the girl moan. Seriously? I must have lost my filter after the fourth shot because without thinking, I said rudely, "Maybe you two should get a room," as I closed the door to the fridge.

The guy turned to look at me, and as soon as I saw those pale green eyes, I saw red.

It was Jase making out with a girl who looked as easy as a TV Guide crossword. I was pissed. What a piece of shit! He said I'd ruined him. He didn't look too ruined to me. A sly smile crept across his face and I got the sense that he'd wanted me to see this.

I was more than pissed, I was furious. I smiled a wicked smile back at Jase. I stared into his green eyes and said, "Just remember, Jase—if you bring her back home, don't forget to tell your mommy that you have a friend staying. Otherwise she might take the trash out for you." As I walked away, I overheard the girl asking Jase what that was about and him telling her to just ignore me. I hoped they did.

I chose to ignore every Hainsworth in the house with the exception of Amy. She was really nice. Technically Amy wasn't a Hainsworth, she was a Ketley, but they were still family. From what I could tell, no one else knew about tonight's drama and I wanted to keep it that way. Amy did overhear Jase and me, but didn't seem to be bothered by it—unlike Matt. I wasn't going to tell Maggie what Matt had said and how much of a dick he was to me. I didn't want to be the cause of a fight between them. I also knew she really liked him, and I could only hope that in time Matt would get over the bullshit—even though he would forever be on my shit list.

The rest of the night and into the early morning were uneventful compared to earlier. Maggie, Masen, Amy, and I drank, sang, and danced obnoxiously. I was kind of surprised at Amy, but after a couple drinks the country girl loosened up. Matt kept his distance and seemed short with Maggie when she would talk or try to include him in our shenanigans. I noticed Jase watching me on more than one occasion but was too drunk to care about his or anyone's feelings.

It was almost two in the morning when people started to leave. Surprisingly, Jase was still there—especially since the chick he was sucking face with had left a little while before.

Amy and I were picking up around the house while some of the others were cleaning up the kitchen. Just as we were finishing up, a drunken Masen walked over to me with a childish grin on his face. I knew I was in trouble. Dropping the empty beer can, I put my hands out in front of me, gesturing for him to stop whatever it was he planned on doing.

"Masen Rowe," I said in a pleading voice as I backed away from him. "What are you doing?" I asked, slurring my words a little bit.

"It's late, Kenz, time to go to bed." Then in two big strides Masen was in front of me. Before I knew it he was tossing me over his shoulder as he carried me off to the spare room. I couldn't help but laugh, as did Maggie. I yelled at him to put me down, smacking his back, but it was no use.

Out of the corner of my eye I saw Reid and Casey holding Jase back, and if looks could kill, Masen would be dead. Jase was clearly furious. It should have felt good, giving Jase a taste of his own medicine, but it didn't. Maggie yelled goodnight to us as Masen walked into the spare room. He kicked the door closed with his foot and plopped me on the bed.

"What the fuck was that all about, Masen?" I asked.

Masen laughed and said, "I overheard Reid talking to Jason about you."

"You mean Jase," I corrected him.

"Jason, Jase, does it matter?"

I couldn't help but chuckle at his seriousness.

"Anyway, I heard Reid tell *Jase* that you were real cute and had nice ass. *Jase* was eyeing you like a piece of meat. I didn't like it, so I decided it was bedtime for you," Masen confessed.

"What are you, a caveman?" I asked him.

"If I was, I would have clubbed you and dragged you by your hair. You would have surely beaten my ass for that."

Masen and I laughed together at his comment.

"But seriously, Kenz—we may not be together anymore, but I still care about you," he said as he sat next to me on the bed.

I put my head on his shoulder and gave him a big hug and thanked him.

Masen and I were having a bonding moment when I heard loud voices, and then heard a door slam. Masen and I both jumped.

"What the fuck was that?" Masen questioned.

I had an idea what *that* was about. He was just about to go check when Maggie cracked the door of the spare room and asked "You two need anything?"

"Nope, we're good. Is everything okay?" I asked her.

"Yup, all is fine. See you when you wake up," she quickly replied as she closed the door.

Masen and I kicked off our shoes and pulled up the blanket as we lay down. We didn't even have the energy to get changed. Although we weren't together, Masen and I were good friends and sharing a bed in our drunken state didn't even bother us. I closed my eyes and felt the room spinning. I had drunk way too much, and I knew a hangover was inevitable. I hoped that the spinning would stop, and before I knew it, I was asleep.

Next thing I knew, Masen was nudging me awake. I felt like complete shit and probably looked like it too. Masen seemed in better shape than I was, which was probably good, since he would be driving. It was beginning to snow and we needed to get on the road. I begrudgingly crawled out of bed and changed into something more comfortable for the ride home.

When I walked into the kitchen, I was disappointed to see that there was no coffee made. Susi also looked disappointed, meowing by her empty food bowl. I assumed Maggie was still in bed, and I had a feeling that she would be spending most of her day there. I grabbed the cat food from the cabinet and poured some into the cat's bowl. I heard Masen carrying our bags outside, mumbling to himself about how heavy mine was. I guess there was no time to make coffee.

I had begun writing Maggie a note when I heard Masen shouting from outside, "Hurry up!"

I quickly finished scribbling my note and hurried out the door. Five minutes into the drive, I was sound asleep.

When Masen dropped me off, we said our goodbyes and I shuffled to my door. I dumped my bag in the hallway and marched up the stairs to my room. Thinking about the shape my best friend was most likely in, I decided to give Maggie a quick call. It rang several times before eventually going to voice mail. I guessed she was still sleeping.

I collapsed on my bed and wondered how things would be going forward. If Maggie was going to stay upstate, then I could only hope that one day we could all move past this. Or better yet, maybe my best friend would eventually move back home and I wouldn't have to deal with this shit ever again. Although that would mean never seeing Jase ever again. That thought made me sad, but I couldn't allow it to take root in my heart. Feeling stressed and hungover, I drifted to sleep, hoping everything would work itself out.

Chapter 9 | Roommate

I was at the grocery store doing some shopping when I got a weird text from Maggie. She asked if I would be home later to talk. I wasn't sure why I needed to be home to talk, since I only had a cell phone and not a house phone, but whatever. I replied to her text, saying I would be home after four o'clock when I was done running around. Strangely, she didn't text back.

It had been six days since Masen and I had left Maggie's. I had tried to call my best friend a couple of times, but I only got her voice mail. I would text her, and she would reply saying she couldn't talk or that she was busy and would call me later. Maggie never called. I hoped everything was okay, and after the weird text I got, I was a little worried. Sunday was our day to talk, not Saturday. I was tempted to call Masen to see if he knew anything, but decided against it. I didn't want him to worry about his sister, especially if there was nothing to worry about. I decided it was best to wait and talk to her myself.

It was a little after five o'clock and I was pacing my living room. I must have checked my cell phone at least seven times. No missed calls and no text messages. I read over the previous text messages between us, and she never mentioned what time she would be calling.

I was checking my phone for the eighth time when it began to vibrate. It was about time she called. I felt relieved, but it was short-lived. It turned out to be Alayna calling, not Maggie. I sighed and answered the call, "Hello."

"Hey, what are you doing? Do you want to get dinner and drinks?" Alayna asked.

"I can't, not tonight," I replied, rolling my eyes as I braced myself for her twenty questions.

"Why not? It's Saturday and you said you had no plans. You told me you needed to get out more, so why can't you come out tonight? Wait, did you meet a really hot guy at the grocery store and have a date again? Maybe that's your thing—meeting hot guys near the produce," Alayna said, laughing at her dig.

She was right. I did want to get out more rather than being a workaholic, but I couldn't help but feel like something was wrong with Maggie. Annoyed, I responded, "I'm so glad you find humor in my dating fuckups," knowing she was referring to Jase. I heard her laugh a little, and then I continued: "I can't go out because Maggie is supposed to be calling me. I haven't talked to her since last weekend. I didn't even get a chance to say goodbye since she was sleeping when I left."

"I thought you guys talked on Sundays?" Alayna asked, puzzled.

"We do. I reached out to her all week. I wanted to make sure everything was okay." Frustrated, I sighed. "This isn't like her. And now I'm waiting for her to call, but she never said what time."

"You're right, that doesn't sound like Maggie," she said, agreeing with me. At least I wasn't the only one who thought it was odd.

I heard a knock at the door as Alayna asked, "Do you want me to pick up a pizza and some beer? I can stop by Redbox and see if they have anything good."

"Hold on one second, someone is at my door," I told her. I walked across the house to see who it was.

As I opened it, I found my best friend standing there looking like shit with her cat Susi in her hand. What. The. Fuck. Shocked and taken aback, I realized I was still on the phone with Alayna.

"Umm, yeah, I'm gonna have to pass on the pizza, Maggie's here," I said into the phone.

"Did you just say Maggie is—"

I cut her off and quickly said, "Yes, she's here, and I'm not sure why. Let me call you back."

She agreed and we hung up.

I opened the screen door and said, "Hey, Maggs, what are you doing here?"

She forced a smile and handed me the carrier that Susi was in. Then she picked up the litter box that was on the porch, came inside, and closed the door. Things just got interesting.

I put the cat carrier down and let Susi out. I walked over to Maggie, took the litter box from her, and put it in the bathroom. When I walked back into the living room, Maggie was still standing in the same spot I had left her but her head was in her hands and she was sobbing. What had happened that brought her to my door like this? I went up to her and gave her a big hug. My heart broke for my best friend. In all the years I had known Maggie, I had never seen her so upset. We made our way to the couch and sat down. After a few minutes and several tissues, Maggie began to explain how she'd ended up at my house.

Everything had been great between her and Matt until the night Masen and I had shown up for her party. When Matt saw me there with Masen's arm around my shoulders, he thought it was a slap in the face to his brother. As I suspected, Maggie wasn't happy about the remark Matt had made to me about Jase. She had pulled Matt aside and told him to cut the shit. She explained to Matt that Masen and I were just friends, nothing more. Also, she reminded him that they had agreed to stay out of the issues between Jase and me. Matt had still seemed annoyed, but reluctantly told her she was right. Relieved, she thought it was over and done with, but apparently it wasn't.

Matt found out that Jase had confronted me in the living room. He didn't know what was said, but it was clear that Jase was pissed. It was made worse when he saw Masen with his arm around me. Matt tried to explain to his brother that Masen and I weren't together and that we were just good friends. Jase didn't care—he already knew our history, and none of that made a difference in his eyes.

Just when I thought she was finished retelling the drama of the previous weekend, Maggie looked at me and asked, "What happened between you and Matt Saturday night?"

Shit! She knew. But just how much did she know? *Do I tell her everything?* I didn't plan on telling Maggie what Matt had said to me outside. I didn't want to cause any more trouble for her and Matt, but it seemed a little too late for that now. Maggie wanted to know and I was going to have to tell her.

I grabbed her hand, held it tight as we sat facing each other, and began to tell her. "I went outside to get some fresh air. Well, really I just needed to get away from Jase. While standing on the porch steps, I saw a shooting star. I wished on it, hoping for some dumb luck. I didn't realize it, but Matt was also outside and must have seen the shooting star too." I paused. "Are you sure you really want to know?" I asked her.

She nodded yes, looking so exhausted and hurt.

I continued. "Matt must have guessed what I was doing, and when he surprised me he asked what I had wished for. I tried to ignore him because I didn't want to add to his mood. I could tell by the tone of his voice that he was angry. He went on to tell me that he also made a wish, and that maybe I could help his come true, since it involved me. Then he explained his wish."

I took a deep breath and repeated to Maggie what Matt had said. "He told me he'd wished that his brother would no longer be hung up on some stupid city bitch that had used him and hung him out to dry."

Maggie's eyes went wide and she gasped at Matt's words to me. I let go of her hand and balled mine into fists. Recounting his words really pissed me off. I should have just dick-kicked him when I had the chance.

I could see Maggie's mood change from hurt to angry. I thought of the pain I was putting my best friend through, and my knuckles started to turn white from my own anger. "I'm so sorry, Maggie. You ended up in the middle of all of this and it's not fair to you," I choked out.

"It's not your fault, Kenz," she said. "Matt was wrong. He's very close with Jase, and seeing his brother messed up over you hasn't been easy on him, but that's no excuse for his actions."

Maggie stood and started pacing the floor. I unclenched my fists, trying to get some of the feeling back in my hands.

"Matt was pissed after he saw Masen carry you off to bed that night. We got into an argument over it. He felt that you were purposely flaunting yourself and Masen in Jase's face. I tried to explain to him that you and Masen where just having fun and you would never be malicious like that. I also mentioned to him that when you first got to my house, you cared enough to ask if Jase would be okay with you being there. As usual, Matt was too stubborn to listen. He left that night with his brothers and didn't call me until Monday. I think he finally realized that I did nothing wrong and that I wouldn't make the first move to call," she told me.

I was in shock and couldn't believe what had happened. This whole thing between Jase and I was affecting too many people. I felt so guilty. Maggie stopped pacing and leaned her back against the wall, looking down at me. She continued with her story.

"When Matt called me Monday, he asked to come over and talk. I could hear the worry in his voice. I was still mad at how he acted, but agreed to talk with him.

"When he walked into the house, he looked like shit. He started by apologizing for the way he had acted. He explained to me how he should have just stayed out of it and let Jase handle things on his own. But he never saw his brother this way with any girl. Not even Luann. And that worried him. He understood that he should have only been there for Jase to vent to him, instead of intervening. I was confused as to what he meant by intervening. Matt must have thought you told me about your run-in with him, and that's why I didn't call him after the party. But as far as I knew he only made that one comment to you when you first got to my house. I was curious, and felt as if there was more to the story, so I let him keep talking," Maggie said.

She took a deep breath, let it out, and continued.

"That's when he told me he needed to apologize to you for being so mean and calling you a stupid bitch."

Maggie walked back to the couch and sat down next to me. "Why didn't you tell me what happened, Kenzie?" she asked.

"I didn't want you and Matt to argue because of me. I know when I left the last time things were a little rocky between you and Matt, and I didn't want that to happen again. I know how much you care about him and I didn't want to mess that up for you," I choked out.

Maggie grabbed my hand and looked me in the eyes. "Mckenzie Shaw, you are my best friend and no one is to talk to you like that. Do you understand me?" Maggie said as we both started to cry.

I think we both felt a little better getting everything out in the open.

Susi must have felt left out, because she walked up to us and started to rub and purr against my leg. We wiped our tears as I picked up Susi and started to pet her. Then it hit me: I had been so caught up with Maggie showing up out of the blue that I didn't get a chance to ask why she had Susi with her.

"Maggs, since when do you bring Susi with you when you visit?" I asked, puzzled.

A conflicted Maggie looked up at the ceiling as if it held the answers she needed. "I left," was all she said.

Confused, I said, "I know you did. You're here. But why do you have Susi with you?"

Maggie turned and looked at me. "I left upstate. After I found out what Matt said to you, I was furious. I care about him—hell, I think I'm in love with him—but he was wrong and acted like an asshole. What he said to you was the last straw. I couldn't accept it. I told him to get out and that I didn't want to see him again," she said proudly, sticking up for the both of us. She continued: "I went into work Tuesday and gave them notice that Friday would be my last day. I felt bad about the short notice, but I told them I had some personal things to deal with that I could only handle back home. I also stopped by Old Man Dale's place, paid him the rent for this month, and told him I would be out by Friday. When I got home Tuesday night I called one of those storage container places, ordered a moving container to be delivered, packed up my shit, and here I am."

I'm not sure what my face looked like, but it must have been funny because Maggie started to laugh.

"I guess you didn't expect that when you opened your front door, huh?" Maggie asked.

"Not at all. So, umm, where are you going to stay?" I asked her, still shocked.

"Well… I was wondering if I could stay with you. I could go back home and stay with my parents, but I've been on my own for so long. I'm not sure how I feel about moving back home. I'm sure Masen would take me in, but then I would have to deal with his bachelor lifestyle and I don't think I want to know what goes on there. Since you have four bedrooms and only use one, maybe you can spare one for me? It would only be for a little while—until I find a job and get settled," Maggie blurted out, trying to convince me.

"Of course you can stay with me!" I beamed. "Stay as long as you like, roommate."

I couldn't believe it. My best friend had moved back to Jersey. I wished the circumstances were different, but regardless, Maggie was back and I was ecstatic. We talked a little more about what had happened and decided to put it behind us. We were not going to think or speak about either of the Hainsworth boys that had taken a piece of our hearts. We knew that chapter of our lives was officially done and it was time for us to move on. Change was good and we both needed it.

Chapter 10 | Bar-Hopping

It had almost been a year since Maggie and Susi had moved in with me. I swore to myself that I would make some changes, and I did. I learned to balance work and life, and excelled at both.

I started to date again, but stayed away from guys at the grocery store. I didn't need to give Alayna a reason to poke fun at me any more than she did already.

Maggie had taken a couple weeks to unwind after moving in. She wanted to spend time with her family and adjust to a busier life after living in the country. She settled in rather quickly, enjoying the gas attendants pumping her gas, three malls in a ten-mile radius, and giving people the finger when they cut her off. She got a job at a veterinary clinic nearby and also started volunteering at the local animal shelter. Life was good for both of us.

Since Maggie and I lived together, we didn't have to make weekly phone calls to catch up on each other's lives. We saw each other almost daily but we were both busy with our own jobs. That left us the weekends to unwind and hang out. Sometimes we would go down the shore, and others we would go into Hoboken or Manhattan. We were always on the go. I was no longer a boring workaholic. I had places to be and people to meet.

Speaking of meeting people, that is just what Maggie, Alayna, and I were going to do. As we walked up Washington Street in Hoboken, there was a charge in the fall air. There were so many people out enjoying their Saturday night before the days began to grow shorter. I loved Hoboken. It was a lively town that had an eclectic variety of bars and restaurants. We were hanging out with some old friends at a bar on First Street, celebrating Alayna's promotion at work. We then headed to another bar to meet up with Ryan, a guy I was seeing from work.

Ryan had mentioned to me that he would be in Hoboken at a tavern, hanging out with some friends, and suggested we stop by. He was a nice guy—both good-looking and smart. He had the clean-cut corporate look, with intense dark chocolate eyes and dirty blond hair. He was tall, with a surfer's body that was lean and muscular. The best part was that Ryan was very easy to be with. No pressures, no expectations.

Along our bar-hopping adventure, Alayna and I listened to Maggie tell us about a guy she met while volunteering at the shelter in town. They had gone on a handful of dates and she thought it was going well. Maggie said that during their last date the guy suggested going to Cape May for a weekend getaway. She wasn't sure what to do, because it felt as if it might be too soon. I had seen this look before in my best friend's eyes. She wasn't sure what to do with this guy. He seemed to want more than she was willing to give.

This was a pattern we had created. While enjoying ourselves out there in the dating world, some guys would want more of a commitment. Then, before you knew it, we would cut ties. Maybe it was because we didn't want to get too close, or maybe it was because none of them lived up to the same kind of connection that we'd had with Matt or Jase. Either way, it was easier to keep it casual because that meant it would be effortless to walk away. That was why things worked with Ryan and me. The past three months with him had been easy, and I was more than okay with that.

We came up to the tavern Ryan was at with his friends. The place was buzzing with people and the outside patio along the brick sidewalk was packed. I began to wonder if we would be able to find him. We went inside and looked around, but no Ryan. We started to walk alongside the beautiful wooden bar when a set of arms wrapped around my waist, pulling me into them. I recognized the scent of his body wash and immediately knew it was Ryan. He nuzzled his face into the crook of my neck, sparing a few kisses before pulling away. I turned around, taking him in. God, he was a great guy. I stood up on the tips of my toes, wrapped my arms around his neck, and gave him a deep, passionate kiss.

Being with Ryan was fun. At work we would flirt, but no one knew we were seeing each other. Like me, he was also a senior consultant, but on a different account. He'd started with RyLo three months ago and I remembered the first time I saw him. Hooray for eye candy! I had noticed how good-looking he was—particularly how good he looked in a suit. I also noticed the way his eyes fell on me as he scanned the faces of his new peers.

The first two weeks, Ryan shadowed me. We would often have lunch together and talk. By his third week he was on his own, but he would still ask me to lunch or to grab coffee with him. Sometimes I would go, sometimes I wouldn't. I wasn't playing hard to get or anything; I was just busy. I had no intention of having an office romance, so I was a little taken aback when he asked me out two months after he'd started.

The first couple of times I turned him down. Then the last time he asked, he said he liked me but also said that he wasn't looking for anything serious. He thought it would be nice to just simply get a drink or dinner sometime. Thinking that might work, I caved and agreed to meet up with him for drinks after work one night. We had a great time, which led to another date. Before either of us knew it, we were spending more time together.

Bringing me back to reality, I felt a smack on my back and heard Alayna shout, "Enough already!" over the voices of the bar. "Go get a room," she added, shaking her head in mock disapproval.

Ryan and I pulled away from each other, smirking and laughing at her comment.

"Don't worry, Alayna. Some of the guys I'm hanging out with are single," Ryan said.

Alayna perked up. "Really? Where are these single men you speak of?" she asked, eyes wide and looking around.

Ryan chuckled and pointed to the end of the bar against the wall. One of his friends saw Ryan point toward them so he raised his hand and waved at us.

"Hey, I have to run to the bathroom. Why don't you guys go introduce yourselves. I'll be right there," Ryan told us. He gave me a quick kiss on the lips, turned, and walked toward the bathroom.

I watched Ryan walk away, vanishing into the crowd of people, and then felt a hand grab my wrist a little too tight. When I saw it was Maggie's hand I looked up at her and said, "What the fuck, Maggs?" as I tried to pull away.

She wasn't looking at me and I heard Alayna whisper, "Who is that?"

Confused as to what was going on with my best friend and wondering who my cousin was talking about, I followed the direction of Maggie's eyes.

It was as an instant gut punch. I started to tremble and my knees almost gave out as I saw those pale green eyes piercing my soul. The connection that I had been missing for almost a year was immediately back again as I locked eyes with Jase. He was watching me. I could tell he was enjoying my reaction by the sly smile on his face. I had no words. I couldn't even move. How long had he been standing there? What was he doing here? I felt Maggie's grip on my wrist tighten even more.

I know it was only a couple of seconds, but it felt like hours as we stood there. I think Jase saw I was too shocked to make the first move, so he walked toward me. With each step he took, my body began to hum with desire for him. The memories of us together flooded my mind. All the feelings that I had buried down deep in my soul, hoping never to feel again, began to resurface.

He stopped and stood in front of me and said, "Mckenzie Shaw. I never thought I would see you again." Then he smiled that damn panty-dropping smile of his. I watched his eyes look me up and down until they stopped at my lips.

Was this really happening? I felt the overwhelming need to reach out and touch him. I wanted him to crush his lips against mine. My stomach got tingly and I knew that feeling would only travel south.

I heard my cousin's voice and it helped bring me back to my senses. I had no idea what she actually said, but it was enough to shake the haze of feelings I was having.

"Jase… how are you?" was all I was able to mutter out.

Maggie was completely still and I heard Alayna gasp when she realized who the gorgeous guy was standing before me. Jase looked the same as when I had seen him at Maggie's house the last time, when I had shattered his heart.

"I'm good. It seems you're doing well yourself," he said, with a hint of sarcasm as he quickly glanced toward the direction of the bathrooms.

Shit. He must have seen Ryan and me.

Looking past me, his eyes landed on Maggie. "Hi Maggs," Jase said nonchalantly, as if there were no hard feelings.

"Hello, Jase," was all Maggie replied, with a hint of indifference in her voice.

Jase then looked at Alayna. It seemed as though he was going to introduce himself to her when some rude asshole cut in between us. I was thankful for the momentary reprieve until the asshole leaned in toward Jase, and over the noise of the bar crowd I heard him shout, "Where have you been? We've got to go. We're gonna be late." The asshole glanced over his shoulder to see who Jase had been talking to.

Just when I thought it couldn't get any worse, it did.

When I saw his face, I felt my blood pressure rise as Maggie tugged on my arm. It was Matt. How could this be? They were both here? Was there some kind of cruel and fucked-up celestial event going on? Were planets aligning somewhere in the universe that made this night fucked up for Maggie and me. I looked at her and she was clearly taken aback by seeing Matt, but she kept it together.

A wide-eyed Maggie looked at us and mouthed *Let's go* as she pulled us away, not looking back at either of them. Maggie had me in tow toward the bar, where Ryan's friends were. I couldn't help but watch a shocked Matt stand there stone-cold still while the sly smile slowly fell from Jase's handsome face. When I finally looked away from the two brothers, I heard Jase shout, "It was good to see you again, Kenzie."

I didn't look back. I couldn't. I felt like I might break if I did. Once again I was walking away from him, and it was torture.

We made our way through the crowd of people to the end of the bar. Ryan's friends were there to greet us. Thank god for Alayna, because she introduced the three of us. Maggie and I could barely speak as we exchanged names and niceties.

Alayna whispered in my ear, "Holy shit, that was awkward, but damn that country boy *is* good-looking."

I could only roll my eyes at her. Leave it to Alayna to make a comment like that at a time like this.

"Relax a little, they left," Alayna told me.

I didn't think I could relax while my mind was going a mile a minute, asking myself questions that I had no answers for.

I felt an arm wrap around my waist and I jumped.

"Hey, you okay? Are you trembling?"

I looked up and my heart sank. It was Ryan. For a split second I had hoped it was Jase. Once again I pushed those feelings away. I mustered what was left of my resolve and smiled up at him. "I'm okay. I'm just a little chilly is all."

Ryan rubbed my arms with his hands to warm me up while his friends ordered us drinks. I barely paid attention to the conversations going on. I looked at Maggie and she looked like I felt. Both of our minds were somewhere else. I stood there staring out the open doors of the patio, wondering if that would be the last time I would see Jase.

Chapter 11 | Worst Day Ever

I was at my desk at work preparing for my three o'clock meeting with my client, Rivers Enterprises, who were based out of Manhattan, New York. My boss wanted to make some last-minute changes to our presentation, so I was scrambling to get them done. I had a little over an hour to make it happen. Today was not my day.

I got a flat on my way to work and had to wait forty-five minutes for roadside assistance to come and change it. I would have changed it myself, but it was freezing outside. I also didn't think my five-inch platform heels and fitted black-and-white peplum dress would be conducive to changing a tire. Once I finally got into work I had three back-to-back calls, and then with those last-minute changes I couldn't even take a lunch. To say I was stressing was an understatement. I couldn't even concentrate because there were people down the aisle from my cubicle arguing over color choices used in a flowchart. Seriously? I so wanted to stand up and tell them to shut the fuck up. Since I needed this job, I decided that wouldn't be prudent and kept my mouth shut.

I was trying really hard to be calm and work through the distractions when Ryan plopped his ass on my desk.

"Hey beautiful," he whispered to me.

I looked up at him, gave him a tight smile, and said, "Hey yourself."

I looked back to my screen and continued to work when he asked, "Busy?" "

Yup," is all I said, not taking my eyes off of the PowerPoint slide.

I guess Ryan noticed he wasn't going to get much of a conversation out of me at that rate. He pulled my chair away from my desk and spun me around so I had no choice but to look at him.

"Ryan! What are you doing? I have to get this finished for my meeting!" I said quietly through gritted teeth, gesturing to my laptop.

"We need to talk. Can you give me five minutes?" he said. I let out a big huff and gave in to his request. Besides, I thought maybe a few minutes away from my desk would be good for me.

"You have five minutes, no more," I said in my most serious tone. Ryan smirked and said, "Yes ma'am."

I got up from my chair and walked away from my desk, following him into the stairwell. That was where we would talk privately about us while we were at work. Only one other person at work knew about Ryan and me, my manager Ben, who was also a good friend. I was there to work, not to be part of office gossip.

Once in the stairwell, Ryan looked around to make sure no one was coming up or down the stairs. He seemed a little nervous and I wondered what he needed to talk to me about.

"I know you're busy so I'll make this quick," Ryan paused. "I'm not sure how to say this."

Curious and concerned as to where this was going, I asked, "What is it, Ryan? Are you okay?"

He let out a big sigh and said, "I've been thinking about us. We've been seeing each other for a little over three months now. Next week is Thanksgiving and I was hoping you would come with me to my parents' house for dinner. We can make a long weekend out of it."

What. The. Fuck.

Is he really dropping this shit on me now? He wants me to meet his parents. Holy shit! He wants to get serious. Breathe, Kenzie, breathe.

"Ryan, I don't know," I stuttered. "I'm not sure if I'm ready for that. I'd have to think about it," I replied to his proposal.

Ryan stood there looking down at nothing in particular, chewing on his lip, and said, "Sure, think about it and let me know."

I could tell it wasn't the answer he wanted. I knew it was a big deal for him to take the next step, but all I could think about was the pie chart I still had to update.

"I have to go finish my presentation. We'll talk later," I told him as I turned. I opened the door to the stairwell and walked back to my desk. Ryan didn't follow me.

It was go time. Our clients from Rivers Enterprises arrived and were being escorted by our assistant to the conference room. I had made the necessary changes and finalized everything with Ben and our big boss with minutes to spare. Ben and I were walking to meet them when Ryan stopped me down the hall from the conference room.

"Kenzie, I need to talk with you real quick," Ryan pleaded.

I looked at Ben, who looked at both of us and said, "You have two minutes," and walked on without me. Out of the corner of my eye, I could see our assistant walking with the clients and showing them into the conference room.

Already frustrated at Ryan's timing that day, I asked him sharply, "What is it now Ryan?"

"Kenz, I'm sorry about before. I shouldn't have asked you that in a stairwell at work. I get it if you're not ready. It's okay. I don't want you to feel pressured." Ryan instinctively reached out his hand only to pull it back, knowing we couldn't have an intimate moment like that in the hallway at work.

I felt a little better about his earlier question, but I knew he was already in too deep and I wanted out. I gave Ryan a weak smile and said, "We'll talk later, I have to run." I walked away from Ryan toward the conference room.

Ben was patiently standing outside the door waiting for me. "Everyone's inside. We're waiting on you," Ben said.

"Sorry, Ben, it won't happen again," I reassured him. I hurried into the meeting with Ben following me, not making eye contact with anyone.

I took my seat, turning my chair toward the big boss who sat at the head of the large table. I grabbed my pen and readied my notepad. The big boss started with his usual speech and welcomed our clients. Rivers had been a client of ours for five years. It was the first account I was put on when I started at RyLo. Since I was on the account this whole time with no complaints, I figured I had been doing something right. I had a great rapport with their team, but recently they had shuffled some people around. I was no longer working with the same contacts and I wondered who I would be dealing with going forward.

When the big boss was done, it was the clients' turn. Joe Manna was the head guy at Rivers. Word around the office was that our big boss and Mr. Manna went way back. That meant it was highly visible and that all eyes were on this particular account. It was closely watched to make sure it was handled appropriately. No one wanted to piss off the big boss or his buddy. Mr. Manna said the usual spiel that I'd heard many times before. I took notes on what his company was looking for in the upcoming year. I was an avid note taker. The more I knew the better.

Mr. Manna began to introduce the new team that we would be working with. I wrote down their names and what they would be handling. "…and last but not least, the newest member to our company and team is Jase Hainsworth," Mr. Manna said, wrapping up his introductions.

My body went numb, my heart began to race, and I couldn't move. Did I hear him right? Was my mind playing tricks on me? I sat there frozen in my seat with my pen on my notepad with only the letters *J-a-* written out. I couldn't think. *What do I do?* I had to see if it was him. It couldn't be, right? What were the fucking chances? *I'm sure there are plenty of guys named Jase Hainsworth out there. Right?*

I took a deep breath, trying to ready myself for what I might see. I slowly turned my chair, forcing myself to look down the large table. It was those familiar pale green eyes. Motherfucker, it was him. It was Jase, with that panty-dropping smile looking back at me.

Fuck my life. This was the worst day ever! I couldn't read his face. He seemed shocked, but nowhere near as shocked as I was. He wouldn't be, though, right? I was sure the whole time he had known it was me while I was oblivious to being in the same room as he was. He probably saw me in the hallway talking to Ryan as they were brought into the conference room. Then he saw me walk in and take my seat, watching and waiting for me to notice him.

Fuck.

My breathing hitched and I started to panic. I had to get out of the room, but I couldn't leave. I did the only thing that I could do, which was turn away and try to concentrate on the meeting.

I heard Ben start to speak as our assistant handed out the presentation to everyone around the table. The lights dimmed and the projector showed the slides I had been working on. I knew them all by heart. That was a good thing, because at that moment the last thing I could do was pay attention to what Ben was going over. Then it hit me: I was going to be working with Jase. He was going to be in my life whether I wanted him to be or not. I could have fainted right there. I must be the butt of some cruel joke.

The rest of the meeting was a blur. I was pretty much catatonic in my seat while Ben presented to our client. I was grateful the lights were dimmed so I could sort through the fucked-up situation in my head without anyone noticing. I wondered if Jase could be stalking me. But the more I thought about it, the less sense it made. I had never told him about my job or what I did. I had made sure I was vague about my life, knowing nothing would come out of our time together. Also, I had been pretty adamant with Maggie about not giving Jase any information about me, so I was sure she hadn't. Just to be on the safe side, as soon as the meeting was over I was going to call my best friend and drill her.

Our meeting concluded and I had barely taken any notes. Fucking fabulous.

We exchanged business cards, *thank you*s, and handshakes. I tried my best to stay away from Jase, but I should have known from past experiences that it could only last so long. Everyone was filing out of the conference room. Our assistant was escorting the clients back to the lobby. I stayed near Ben because I thought it would be safer. Boy, was I wrong.

Jase must have been waiting for me outside the door. He caught me by the elbow as soon as I walked into the hallway. My body was an instant traitor as soon as he touched me. The need and want I felt echoed the rise and fall of my lungs demanding their next breath. I got caught up in his eyes and I swear I could see the want there too.

"Mckenzie Shaw, we meet again," Jase said, smiling that sly smile of his.

I wanted to slap that shit off of his face.

"Do you have a minute?" he said, staring at me with those pale green eyes.

My body went numb and I felt the urge to push him up against the wall and have him take me right then and there.

Shit, this is not good. My thoughts were betraying me. Ben, who was walking beside me, overheard Jase and seemed a little puzzled. He probably wondered how Jase and I knew each other. I smiled a tight smile and told Ben I would meet him back by his desk. He gave me a nod and continued down the hallway.

Turning all of my attention to Jase, I noticed that his hair was a little shorter and he was disappointingly clean-shaven. I missed the day-or-two-old scruff. He was wearing a charcoal-gray suit that was clearly tailored to fit his physique perfectly, a white button-down shirt, and a black tie with white stripes. Damn, he looked good. Too good.

Control yourself, Kenzie, I thought to myself.

"Jase Hainsworth. It seems we will be working together, so let's try to keep it civil, shall we?" I told him.

I should have turned and walked away. I wanted to, but I didn't. I was still caught up in his eyes and my body was on fire from being so close to him. His stare held me in place as much as his hand on my elbow. Realizing this, I quickly shook it off.

Jase laughed a little. "You're feisty. That's one of the things I find so endearing about you," he said.

Endearing? He finds me fucking endearing? He must be the most frustrating man in the world.

"Great. So glad you like my personality," I said in my best snarky tone.

"Oh, I like more than your personality, Kenzie,"

Shit. Shit. Shit. He was getting under my skin in a wet-panties kind of way. I needed to end this conversation, and quickly.

I looked up and down the hallway to make sure we were alone. In a low, stern voice I said, "Cut the shit, Jase. What do you want?"

"You," was the only thing he said.

That one word stole the breath from my lungs. I stood there frozen as he studied my face very carefully. Realizing I hadn't taken another breath, I gasped and he zeroed in on my lips. God, I wanted that man. I had never stopped wanting him. The feelings that I had folded up, stuffed in a box, and stored far from my heart were now unleashed and raw at the surface. I wanted to grab him by his suit jacket, push him back into the conference room, and fuck him silly on the goddamn table.

My traitorous thoughts left me speechless. He looked back into my eyes, leaned in close to my ear, and said, "Seems the feeling is mutual." He glanced back at me one last time before walking away.

I stood there paralyzed. Just like that, he fucking walked away from me. My heart constricted. I had to brace myself against the wall as I watched him leave, never once turning around. What was wrong with me? Why did I feel this way?

As soon as Jase was out of my sight I hurried back to my desk, grabbed my cell phone, and walked to an empty office near my cubicle. I locked the door and dialed Maggie's number, praying she wasn't in surgery. It rang and rang, then went to voice mail. Fuck my life! I then called her work number. I never called her there, but it was an emergency. The receptionist picked up, and when I asked for Maggie Rowe she said she had left for the day. I didn't even say thank you or goodbye; I just hung up on her.

Shit.

My chest was getting tight. I thought I was starting to have a panic attack. I focused on trying to calm my breathing.

My phone vibrated in my hand, making me jump and screech at the same time. I was on edge. The way I was acting, you would have thought I'd just murdered someone. My phone vibrated again, and when I looked at the screen I saw it was Maggie. I felt relief as I swiped the screen to answer her call.

"Maggie fucking Rowe, where are you? Are you sitting down?" I demanded.

That must have taken her by surprise. "Kenz, are you okay?" she asked, sounding worried.

"No, I'm not fucking okay," I said in a hushed voice, trying to keep my level of flipping out to a minimum.

"Shit, you know. I'm sorry, Kenz. I planned to tell you about Matt but I wasn't sure how," Maggie groaned.

"What are you talking about, Maggs? What did you plan to tell me about Matt?" I asked sharply, a little shocked.

"Wait, you don't know? Why are you so upset then?" Maggie asked, confused.

"Why am I upset?" I snapped. "Because I had the worst day ever!" I began to hysterically rant: "I got a flat on my way to work. I had back-to-back calls. Ben had me make last-minute changes to the presentation for our meeting. Ryan asked me to meet his parents and take our relationship to the next level, while in a stairwell. Oh yeah, let's not forget the part where I go to my meeting only to find out that my client hired Jase fucking Hainsworth and I will be working with him. Fucking great, right? Now I call you to vent and find out you have something to tell me about Matt." I was now pacing the floor of the empty office.

I took a deep breath, trying to calm myself down. My best friend was quiet.

I stopped pacing and took another deep breath. "I'm sorry, Maggs. I shouldn't have snapped at you like that," I said, apologizing.

"It's fine, really, Kenz. You had a really shitty day, and I should have told you about Matt already."

"Yes, you should have. Now spill. What's the deal with Matt?" I asked curiously, starting to pace again.

Maggie took a weary breath and said, "The week after we saw Matt and Jase at the bar in Hoboken, he started to call and text me. After three weeks, and thirty-something voicemails and text messages, I finally gave in and called him back. He apologized profusely for what had happened between us and also for what happened with you two. He told me that he regretted everything and wanted a second chance, but under one condition."

"What was the condition?" I asked.

"That we start out slow, hanging out when he is in Jersey. He also told me he would like to talk to you about what happened."

"Wait, what? What do you mean when he is in Jersey?" I asked, confused.

"Oh, I guess you don't know. Jase lives in Hoboken now and works in the city. He goes upstate every other weekend to visit his family and help out with the farm. The weekends he is in Jersey, Matt comes down and stays with him. Sometimes Reid, Cole, or Casey come too," she told me.

I couldn't believe it. "Wow, this day just keeps getting better and better," I said, floored at the revelation.

"Sorry I didn't tell you sooner, Kenz. First I wanted to see where things were going with Matt. Everything has been going so well, it was a matter of figuring out how to tell you. Matt will be down this weekend and asked to take me out on our first date. He also asked if you would be home so he could talk to you. Being that today is Thursday, it only left me with two more days to break the news, so I was going to tell you. I swear," Maggie said, sounding guilty.

I stopped pacing and sat on the desk, pinching the bridge of my nose. *How do things like this happen to me?* If there was anything I was sure of after the day's events, it was that I needed a drink. What was I talking about? I needed several.

"Okay, okay. So let me get this straight, and if there is anything I missed *or* you missed, please jump in: Jase moved to Hoboken and works in the city for my client, and you're talking to Matt again, who comes down and visits Jase every other weekend," I asked, hoping I'd covered all the bases.

"Yup, I swear no other surprises," my best friend promised.

"Good, because I don't think I can take any more today," I said, feeling relieved. "I better get back to work. We'll talk more tonight," I told her.

We said our goodbyes and hung up.

I was heading back to my desk when I decided to pop into Ben's office. I walked in and shut the door. He was just getting off a call and eyed me suspiciously. I collapsed in one of his chairs, mentally exhausted from the day.

"Are you okay, Kenz? You were fine when we left the meeting and now you look like shit. What happened?" Ben asked.

"You mean what didn't happen," I corrected him. "I wanted to let you know that I will probably be in late tomorrow, or maybe I'll just take a personal day. I plan on drinking heavily tonight and I'm not sure what condition I'll be in when I wake up," I told my boss.

"Interesting. I appreciate you telling me ahead of time. What brought this on?" Ben asked, laughing.

"Do you have an hour?" I replied.

He nodded.

So I went back—way back—to when I had first met Jase, and told Ben everything that had led up to the day's events. I did, however, leave out the intimate parts between Jase and me.

After two and a half hours, I think I summed up the story of my fucked-up life pretty well. Ben commented at how interesting it was, which I didn't find as funny as he did. It felt good to talk to someone other than Maggie or Alayna about it. Ben was understanding and told me to come in late or take the day off. He said with all that had happened, he was impressed that he had never seen my work falter. It was probably best that Ben knew, especially now that I would be working with Jase on such a closely watched account.

I left Ben's office feeling better. I walked back to my desk, shut down my laptop, and gathered my things. I saw a note on my desk from Ryan saying he had stopped by. Great, I forgot I had to deal with him too.

I remembered when life was boring, and boring seemed better at the moment. I wondered if things would be normal again, because the craziness that lurked around every corner of my life was getting old.

Chapter 12 | And it Begins...

I woke up with a slight headache and saw it was ten o'clock in the morning. The night before, I had told Maggie and Alayna about my day from hell, start to finish. Maggie couldn't believe my luck and Alayna was speechless—a rare event. They both agreed that the cure to my fucked-up day was lots of alcohol, which I welcomed. So that's what we did: we ordered pizza, drank, and talked all night long. Before passing out I remembered to text Ben around two in the morning, letting him know that I was definitely taking a personal day. I couldn't even remember the last time I had called out of work.

Next to my alarm clock was my cell phone, which was blinking. I grabbed it and saw I had a text message. It was from Ben, telling me to enjoy my day and to remember to put my Out-of-Office on.

Crap, I should probably hurry up and do that before it gets any later. Ugh. I realized I had left my laptop bag downstairs in the living room.

I reluctantly got out of bed, stretched as I stood, and almost stepped on Susi's tail. Damn cat, always hiding under my bed. I dragged my ass downstairs to get my laptop and saw Alayna passed out on the couch. I guessed she wasn't making it into work either. I walked over and shook her shoulder, trying to wake her, but all she did was moan and turn over.

Crap.

I shook her shoulder a little harder and shouted her name.

"What the fuck, Kenz? No need to shout. I have a screaming headache and I'm trying to sleep," she said without opening her eyes.

I grinned and chuckled at her. A hungover Alayna was funny to me.

"Did you call out of work?" I asked, worried she would get in trouble.

"Yes, I did. Now please leave me alone," she said, pulling the blanket over her head.

"You do realize there's another bedroom rather than sleeping on the couch," I told her.

Alayna didn't care, she just ignored me. I chuckled again, grabbed my laptop bag, and went back up the stairs.

I walked over to my bed, stepping over Susi, who was sprawled out across the floor. I sat down, sliding back under the covers and tucking myself in. I opened my laptop and powered it on. I signed into my work email, turned on my Out-of-Office, and put Ben as my contact. With that taken care of I could go back to sleep—and hopefully when I woke up, this annoying headache would be gone. Just as I was about to shut it down, my laptop pinged to notify me that I had a new email. I was going to ignore it, since I had taken the day off, but of course I didn't. Big mistake!

There were several emails in my inbox, but the one that stood out from the rest was sent from Jase Hainsworth.

"Fuck my life!" I shouted up at my bedroom ceiling.

"Shut the fuck up! *I'm trying* to sleep," Alayna shouted back.

Ignoring her, which was no easy task, I looked back at the screen. The subject line read "Looking forward to working with you."

Shit. Do I open it? Maybe I should just delete it? What if it's an email related to the account? What if he's just being a dick?

The mental debate was overwhelming and making what was an annoying headache into something worse. I heard someone walking up the stairs to my bedroom. I expected Alayna but was shocked to see Maggie when she opened my door.

"What the hell is all the shouting about?" she asked, walking over and plopping down on my bed.

I guessed she didn't go to work either.

"Remind me to never drink tequila again," she grumbled, rubbing her forehead and looking a little pale.

"You say that every time, but continue to buy that shit. Then you make us do shots with you," I explained to her.

I started to feel queasy at the thought of the previous night's tequila shots. I was glad I had stopped at two because Maggie and Alayna seemed to be worse off than I was, for a change.

"I guess you called out too, huh?" I asked her.

"Hell yeah. I told them I had food poisoning and couldn't come in," Maggie said.

"More like alcohol poisoning," I told her.

We were definitely a sad bunch this morning.

"Are you going to tell me why you were shouting?" she asked again.

"Oh yeah, about that," I said, turning my laptop so she could see the screen. She looked down, and I knew by her eyes bugging out that she saw his name.

"Holy Shit!" Maggie screeched.

"Seriously, what the fuck is going on up there?" we heard Alayna shout.

Maggie and I both ignored my cousin's question.

"Are you going to open it?" Maggie asked, still wide-eyed.

"I guess I have to," I replied to her.

The next thing I knew, Alayna was walking into my bedroom holding her head. She must have been part ninja, because I hadn't even heard her come up the stairs. "Jesus, why are you guys so damn loud?" Alayna complained as she walked over to my bed and lay down.

It started to feel a little cramped, but I was thankful for my king-sized bed at that moment.

I pointed to my laptop screen.

Alayna leaned in, squinting at the screen. "Oh fuck! He emailed you? He's a persistent little fuck, isn't he? Are you going to read it? Can I read it?" Alayna asked me.

"That's what Maggie and I were just talking about. I thought of deleting it, but what if it's really work-related?" I said.

"You should read it—or better yet, we should read it together," Maggie suggested.

"That's a good idea," I said, grabbing my laptop as Alayna and Maggie situated themselves on either side of me.

I inhaled a deep breath, mentally bracing myself for the contents of Jase's email. I slowly moved the pointer over and double-clicked on it. The email opened and the three of us silently read his words.

From: Jase Hainsworth
Sent: Friday, November 14, 2014 8:07 AM
To: Shaw, Mckenzie
Subject: Looking forward to working with you

Good Morning Mckenzie,

It was a pleasure meeting you. I look forward to working closely with you on this project. I wanted to touch base to discuss the action items from yesterday's meeting. It was a lot to take in I'm sure, and it may be prudent for us to go through everything more thoroughly. I would love to bounce some ideas off of you that might pique your interest.

I spoke with Mr. Manna and he expressed how competent you are and how well you have handled our business in the past. He felt that you and I would work well together to continue these efforts, and I hope to prove him right.

If you could let me know when you have some free time so we can set up a meeting, that would be great. I would love to jump on this right away.

Sincerely,

Jase Hainsworth
Consultant, Rivers Enterprises

I could only shake my head in disbelief. It read like an introductory email, but knowing Jase and the history we shared, it had hidden innuendos. I must have read it ten times before I shut my laptop. I noticed Maggie and Alayna were oddly quiet. They looked at me, clearly waiting for my reaction. I had nothing.

My phone started to vibrate on my nightstand. I looked and saw Ryan's name on the screen. Great, I still had to deal with him. How had my life become so complicated in less than twenty-four hours?

I grabbed my phone and swiped the screen to answer the call. "Hello," I said.

"Hey, you okay?" Ryan asked, concerned. Then he continued: "I ran into Ben. He said you weren't feeling good and called out."

Thank god for Ben covering my ass. I'd have to remember to thank him. "Yeah, it was a rough night," I replied, while Alayna and Maggie giggled to themselves. I swatted at them and mouthed *Stop*. "I'm better now, though. Look, we need to talk. Are you free after work?" I asked him.

Ryan was silent for a few seconds before asking, "Does this talk have to do with our conversation in the stairwell?"

"I don't want to get into it on the phone, Ryan. I'd rather talk in person," I told him.

"Just answer the question, Mckenzie," Ryan said, beginning to sound impatient. I didn't want to do it over the phone, but he wasn't leaving me much of a choice.

I got up from my bed and started to pace the floor. Both Maggie and Alayna were watching me and whispering to each other. My life felt like it was straight out of a Lifetime movie.

"Well, Kenz? Answer me," Ryan demanded.

"Fine. I didn't want to do this over the phone, but yes—it does have to do with the conversation in the stairwell."

I took a deep breath, debating whether this was really what I wanted to do. I knew that I liked Ryan, but I didn't see a future in us. We enjoyed each other's company and had a good time together, but we didn't have a connection. I only had that with one other person: Jase. I had to break it off with Ryan. There was no avoiding it.

"Ryan... You want more and I don't. You told me to forget what you said in the stairwell, but if I did that, it would be selfish of me and unfair to you. I don't want to do that to you. I can't do this anymore," I told him in an even tone.

"So that's it? Just like that?" he said, sounding defeated.

I felt bad and I wasn't sure what else to say. "I have to go. I'm late for a meeting. Bye, Mckenzie," Ryan said, and disconnected the call.

I stopped pacing and tossed my phone on the nightstand. I looked over at Maggie and Alayna, who were wide-eyed, staring at me.

All they needed was a bucket of popcorn and some Sour Patch Kids, and they would have looked like they were watching a movie.

"Since when did my life become so complicated?" I asked them. "My life was so simple," I stated.

"Don't forget boring," Alayna chimed in.

I gave my cousin a nasty look and said, "I thought you had a headache. Maybe you should go home—like now."

"Fuck, no. This is way too interesting," Alayna said, smiling proudly at getting under my skin.

I rolled my eyes, and then plopped on my bed and stared at my ceiling. This shit was not helping my headache. "When and why did my life decide to take a left at complicated rather than continue straight on simple?" I asked no one in particular.

"Maybe it's the universe trying to tell you something," Maggie said.

Alayna and I both looked at Maggie like she had three heads.

"No more tequila for you, Maggs. That shit is fucking with your mind," Alayna said.

"No, seriously, think about it. When did your life get complicated? Ever since you met Jase! Every time you think he is out of your life, you two cross paths. It's like the universe is pushing you two together," Maggie explained.

"Wow, that is some deep shit," said Alayna.

"That is ridiculous, Maggs," I scoffed.

"Maybe it is, maybe it isn't. But it does make sense," Maggie replied.

First I'd had to deal with Jase's email and then I'd had to break things off with Ryan. Now my best friend thought she'd figured out the mysteries of the universe and how they related to my love life. It was all too much to handle at the moment. I figured it was time to kick Alayna and Maggie out of my room and try to get some more sleep.

"All right, the both of you, out! I've had my fill of bullshit for the morning and I need to go back to bed," I told them, pointing toward my bedroom door.

They both stood, Maggie rolling her eyes and Alayna mumbling something under her breath about me waking her up.

Maggie was following Alayna out of my room when she stopped at the door. "Kenz, remember Matt is coming over tomorrow," she said.

"Oh right, your first date, take two," I said, laughing to myself, but Maggie didn't find it as funny. I could tell she was really looking forward to their take-two date.

"He wants to talk to you and apologize. Will you be around tomorrow so you two can talk?" Maggie asked, sounding curious but with apprehension in her voice.

Did I really want to see Matt? Did I really want to hear his apology? Maggie was my best friend, and if she could give him a second chance then why couldn't I?

"Fine. But if he ever starts shit with me again, I will most definitely dick-kick him without a second thought. You can tell him I said that too," I told her.

"Thanks, Kenz. This means a lot to me," Maggie said as she closed my bedroom door.

I turned on my side and pulled the blankets up, getting comfortable in my big bed. I lay there feeling unsure of my life. It was only the day before that I'd had control and things were going well for me. Then BAM! Jase Hainsworth popped back into my life, and I had a feeling he wouldn't be popping out anytime soon. It seemed he was staying for good, and walking away wasn't an option this time. I had to figure out how I was going to make it work with him.

Maybe he and I could do a take two and try again as friends. Would that work? We could only try and find out. It would be hard shaking his hand, looking into his pale green eyes, and seeing his panty-dropping smile. Who was I kidding? It would be damn near impossible being around that piece of hot, country-now-corporate ass. I couldn't even handle being within ten feet of him.

"Ugh," I groaned loudly into my pillow.

What if Maggie was right about the universe and its pushing Jase and me together? I wondered what other fucked-up shit could happen to me.

Chapter 13 | Apology

I was putting my clothes away when I heard a knock on my bedroom door. Maggie strolled in, looking amazing. She had spent the past two hours primping herself for her date with Matt. I could tell by the smile on her face that she was really excited but also a little nervous.

When we ran into Jase and Matt in Hoboken, my best friend's life changed. That chance encounter triggered both her and Matt's emotions for one another again. Matt began reaching out to Maggie and she tried her hardest to ignore his calls and texts. She questioned whether it was fate bringing them back together. I wondered when Maggie had become so philosophical. Eventually she gave in and tonight was their first date, take two.

This also meant that Matt wanted to talk to me, and I wasn't entirely sure how I felt about that. Part of me thought it was the right thing to do, but an even bigger part wanted to look Matt in the eyes and tell him to fuck off.

As good as that might feel, it wouldn't help Maggie in any way. I still felt bad about her being in the middle of all my drama with Jase. If I hadn't met him, maybe none of this would have happened. Then again, if none of it would have happened, my best friend would still be in upstate New York and not living here with me.

I looked at Maggie and smiled. I spun my finger in the air, motioning for her to spin around. She smiled back and began to slowly turn. She was wearing a burgundy sweater dress with a cowl neck that showed just enough cleavage, black patterned tights, and matching knee-high boots. Her hair was pinned up in a messy bun.

As she finished her twirl I said, "You look great, Maggs."

"Are you sure? Do the boots look okay with this dress, or should I wear an ankle boot instead? Maybe I should change my whole outfit," she rambled on, doubting herself.

"Seriously, you look amazing," I reassured her. "Hold on," I said, and walked over to my jewelry box.

I took out some bangle bracelets that I thought would look nice with her outfit. I handed them to her and watched as she slid them onto her wrist.

"Now your outfit is complete," I told her, smiling at her again.

Maggie had mentioned the day before that Matt had made reservations for seven o'clock, which meant he would arrive shortly to pick her up.

"I'm a nervous wreck," Maggie said.

"Maybe we should have a drink before he gets here," I suggested. "But no tequila!" I told her.

Maggie eagerly nodded in agreement, so I ushered her downstairs and into the kitchen to make us both drinks. She grabbed the glasses and some ice. I grabbed the Kettle One and cranberry juice.

I made our drinks and handed one to Maggie, lifted my glass, and said, "To your first date, take two. I hope it's better the second time around."

Maggie smirked as we clanked our glasses and drank to my toast. We stood in the kitchen talking and finishing our drinks. It must have helped, because Maggie seemed a little more at ease.

There was a knock at the door. Maggie looked at me with panic in her eyes. "Do you really think I look okay?" she asked.

I put my drink down, walked over to her, and put both my hands on her shoulders, giving them a reassuring squeeze. "Maggie Rowe, you look beautiful, so stop worrying. Remember, he's seen you naked. Do you really think he gives a fuck what you're wearing?"

She laughed a little at that. "You're right. I'm not sure why I'm so nervous," she said.

"You're nervous because he means a lot to you. Now shut the fuck up, you hot bitch. I'll answer the door, you go freshen up," I directed Maggie as I spun her around and lightly shoved her toward her bedroom.

There was another knock so I walked toward the door, taking my time. I could have put a little pep in my step, but I remembered how much of a dick Matt had been to me. I figured a few extra seconds waiting in the cold November air wouldn't hurt. I finally reached the door, opened it, and there stood Matt with a bouquet of white daisies. My immediate thought was *asshole*. Maggie loved red roses and sunflowers. Since they had dated before, he should have known that, so I wasn't quite sure why he'd gotten daisies.

"Matt, won't you come in," I said to him.

He smiled at me and walked into my house as I closed the door behind him.

I caught him looking around, taking in the scenery. He saw me watching him closely and I'm sure the look on my face was not a welcoming one.

He cleared his throat and said, "You have a very nice house, Kenzie."

"Not bad for a stupid city bitch, huh?" was my response.

From the shocked look on Matt's face, he was clearly taken aback. I'm not sure if he expected me to be cordial just because he wanted to apologize. He needed to learn it wasn't going to be that simple. Seconds ticked by and he started to fidget with the bouquet of white daises. I could tell the shock was wearing off. He was about to speak, and at that moment I wasn't sure if I was ready to listen to his apology.

Seeing him standing there brought back memories of how rude and mean he was that night at Maggie's party. I felt my fists clench as I started to get angry. Maybe I could avoid the conversation altogether. I started to take a step backwards. "I'll get Maggie for you," I said and started to walk away.

"Kenzie, wait, do you have a minute?" Matt finally asked, and reached out his hand, gesturing me to not to leave.

I looked at him and could see he was a little nervous, which made me feel better. Maybe I should have danced around, circling him and chanting. He would probably think I was crazy as fuck, but he would definitely think twice before speaking to me again.

Then Matt did something completely unexpected: he handed me the bouquet of white daisies. "These are for you. Consider them a peace offering," he told me with timid smile.

Instead of taking the flowers, I crossed my arms. He wanted to talk so we were going to talk, but I'd never once said I had to be nice about it. "A fucking peace offering?" I questioned, pissed at his choice of words.

Matt's eyes darted from left to right, searching for a way out of the hole he had started to dig for himself. I enjoyed seeing the asshole squirm.

"Last I checked, we weren't at war. You were a dick to me and my best friend. A repeat offender, I might add. You stuck your nose in shit where it didn't belong," I stated bluntly.

I heard the bedroom door creak and I'm sure Maggie was listening intently, and probably wishing for another drink. I know Matt wanted to apologize, but I wasn't about to make that shit easy for him.

"You're right, I'm sorry. Bad choice of words." Matt took a deep breath and continued: "I was an asshole to you, Kenzie, and I'm truly sorry. I didn't realize how wrong I was until it was too late. I shouldn't have gotten involved in what was going on with you and Jase. If you will hear me out, just know that this isn't me wanting to rehash the past. I want you to understand where I was coming from," Matt said.

"Go on," I said, arms still crossed and foot tapping as my patience quickly dwindled.

"When Jase met you at the market, he was head over heels with someone he didn't even know. We all thought he was crazy when he spoke of this perfect girl he knew nothing about except that she drove a car with a New Jersey license plate. Then you came with Maggie to meet me at the bar and my brother couldn't believe it when you walked in. The girl who got away. The girl he'd talked about for two months nonstop. Jase told me he wasn't going to let you get away this time," he said.

Matt took a deep breath and continued. "I thought my brother had lost his mind. Jase had never been so enamored with a girl before—not even Luann, and he married her. The girls usually chased after *him*, not the other way around. After everything happened with my mom and he realized you'd left, he was pissed. He told me he felt you both had a connection, but after you left I saw my brother change. It was as if you took a piece of him with you," he said, sighing.

Matt shifted on his feet and watched me carefully to see how I was taking his words.

I looked down at the floor before looking back up at him. "He said I ruined him," I told Matt, feeling a little guilty.

He nodded in agreement. "I think you did," he said. "Before you showed up with Masen for Maggie's party, he had been doing much better. He was pretty much the old Jase. He was hanging out again and even registered for the last of his classes to finish his degree. Then he saw you with Masen and things went downhill. I saw how pissed and devastated he was because of you, and I reacted," Matt confessed.

His words struck home and a knot of guilt formed in my stomach. "It wasn't my intention to hurt Jase. I didn't want to lead him on or give him hope when I knew we couldn't work out," I told him.

As much as Matt needed me to understand his side, I very much needed him to understand mine.

"I get that now, but back then I was really pissed because I thought you were messing with my brother," he said.

I could see how he could have justified his actions. Matt didn't want Jase to get hurt and I could appreciate that. I knew I would do the same for Alayna or Maggie.

"I should have stayed out of it like I promised Maggie. When I found out she quit her job and moved back home, I thought I lost her forever. I tried to call and text her but she never once responded. After a few months I finally gave up," Matt said, shaking his head, clearly reflecting on what had happened. "That's all in the past. I'm grateful to have a second chance with her. I'm hoping you and I can do the same," he stated as he handed me the flowers again.

I uncrossed my arms and took them from him.

I looked down at the bouquet of white daises and thought of my best friend in the other room eavesdropping.

Maybe he does deserve a second chance. I know Maggie would do it for me without thinking twice.

I needed to be supportive of their take-two relationship and respect who she wanted to be with. "I accept your apology. But if you ever pull that shit again…"

Matt cut me off and put his hands up as if he were surrendering. "I know, I know. You'll dick-kick me. Maggie warned me," he said, laughing a little.

"Without hesitation," I said, shooting him a serious glare.

Matt nodded and I think he got the hint by my lack of a smile.

I let him off the hook and put a tight smile on my face as I walked toward the kitchen. "Thank you for the flowers. I guess Maggie told you I love daisies, huh?" I said over my shoulder.

It seemed to take a minute before Matt answered me. "No… umm, Jase did," he said, which took me by surprise.

Shit. Jase remembered my favorite flower. I couldn't help but look back at Matt, and I noticed his smile quickly disappear. Not having realized that my pace had slowed almost to a stop, I recovered and continued to the kitchen. I'd had my fill of niceties for one night so I yelled, "Maggs, your date is here!"

I walked into the kitchen and leaned on the sink, trying to get a grip. I could overhear Maggie and Matt talking in the living room. He was telling her how great she looked and how they needed to hurry to make their reservation. It was a relief that they were leaving. I needed some alone time to think. My mind was spinning. *What is it about Jase that makes me lose my shit?*

I reached under the sink for a vase to put the daisies in. While it was filling I looked out the kitchen window at the cold, dark, moonless night. My thoughts drifted back to my first date with Jase, when he'd surprised me with the picnic in the back of his truck. That's when I had told Jase that I loved daisies. A flurry of emotions and memories of that night filled my mind, and my whole body felt flushed. I remembered how his rough hands felt on my skin, how I got lost in those pale green eyes, and of course that panty-dropping smile. Those eyes and that smile were going to be the death of me.

At some point I needed to get used to the idea that Jase Hainsworth was back in my life. But how?

I looked down at the vase that was now overflowing.

Shit.

I turned off the faucet and dumped out half the water before putting the flowers in it. Just then Maggie came into the kitchen and gave me a big hug.

"Thank you," she said before letting go of me. "We're going, don't wait up." She was practically bouncing with excitement.

"Have a good time," I said back to her.

Maggie walked out of the kitchen and into the living room where Matt was waiting. I heard them shout goodbyes to me and then close the door. I stood looking at the white daisies, wondering how everything was going to play out.

Chapter 14 | Operation Lunch Date

It had been a couple of weeks since my meeting with the Rivers account. After getting over the initial shock of Jase being back in my life, I tried to find some normalcy again. Work was the biggest challenge. After I ended things with Ryan, he refused to speak to me. If I saw him in the hallway or elevator, he completely ignored me. I wasn't sure if I should try to talk to him or give him space to work through it. Either way, things were awkward and I hoped in time he and I would be okay.

On the upside, since Maggie and Matt's take-two date, things had been going really well for them. She even introduced him to her parents, and they loved him. They, of course, knew of Matt already because the two had dated before. She never did tell her parents or Masen the real reason why she had moved back to Jersey. She'd told them that it had to do with her job and they never asked any questions. I think they were so happy to have her back, they didn't care what the reason was. They were, however, concerned how the distance would affect Maggie and Matt's relationship. I wasn't quite sure how their relationship would fare, either—with her living and working in Jersey, him living and working in upstate New York, and only seeing each other on the weekends. But somehow they made it work.

Matt had asked her if she would consider moving back to upstate New York, and she told him not anytime soon. She was happy to be close to her family and friends again, plus her career seemed about to take off. There was even talk of her taking over the veterinary clinic when her boss retired in two years. Knowing this, Matt vowed to make things work between them. It seemed Maggie and Matt had their lives figured out, while I was still trying to figure out how to deal with Jase.

The week before, I had gotten a call from Jase's assistant, Maude. She was looking to set up a meeting at their office in Manhattan and needed to know my availability. After I hung up with her, I nearly had a panic attack. I kept thinking of our last encounter and what it had done to me. After Jase's email I had known that a face-to-face encounter was bound to happen sooner rather than later. I had been corresponding with him through email, but only regarding the account—which was fine with me, because I didn't have to deal with him directly. But now I had to see him in person, just him and me.

Ben offered to go with me, knowing the situation, but I told him no. I needed to put my big girl panties on and handle the situation. It felt like my life was one big "situation" lately. I was beginning to hate the word *situation*.

That day I had an eleven o'clock meeting with Jase at his office in Manhattan, and I was a tad bit nervous. I decided to work from home for an hour or two before taking the train into the city. It made more sense, since the train was only a couple blocks from my house.

I had just finished getting ready. I kept my makeup light, blew out my hair, and curled it. I decided to put it up in a bun until I got into the city, since it was so windy outside. I hated how cold it was in December. Since I was taking the train and walking in the winter weather, I decided to wear my most comfortable pantsuit, which consisted of a fitted black blazer and black pants. I chose my sleeveless, black-and-white polka dot blouse to wear with it. I paired it with my black patent leather belt and my five-inch patent leather heels.

I thought I looked hot in a corporate kind of way—not that I was trying to impress Jase, but I did want to look my best. It was a confidence boost for me, and given the day's audience I needed to be on my game. I checked the time. I had twenty minutes until my train arrived, so I needed to hurry. I grabbed my clutch and threw it in my messenger bag, put on my peacoat and scarf, and headed out the door.

I quickly walked to the train station. It was bitter cold, windy, and the sky was cloudy. Between the wind and the cold, my face was stinging. I'd heard on the news that they were calling for snow. I hoped it would hold off until I got back home. When I reached the platform, I bought a round-trip ticket and took a seat in the enclosed area. It wasn't as warm as I had hoped, but it was a break from the blustery wind. I had a couple of minutes before the train came, so I put my earbuds in and listened to my iPod.

I started to go over my plan of action for the day. My main objective was to stay focused on the account and not on Jase, his eyes, or his smile. I would focus on Jase and our past after the meeting.

The night before, I'd had a hard time sleeping. I was trying to figure out how I could have Jase in my life without another "situation" happening. I came up with a brilliant plan I'd decided to call Operation Lunch Date. Corny, I know, but that's what I got for watching *The Bourne Supremacy* before bed.

I had it all worked out. I figured that my meeting with him would take about an hour to an hour and a half. That would put us right at lunchtime or a little after. I planned on asking Jase to lunch, as friends, after our meeting. I thought it would be best to wait and ask him after the meeting, since there was actual work to do. Plus, it would seem more spontaneous rather than a premeditated plan. Then we could talk, lay everything on the table, and hopefully by the end of lunch we would have established a friendship.

I couldn't help but smile at myself for coming up with this plan. I only hoped he didn't have lunch plans already because, I didn't have a backup plan.

The train to New York pulled up to the platform. I stood and hurried onto the train to get out of the bitter cold, taking the first seat I found. While waiting for the conductor to punch my ticket, I tried to relax. It seemed impossible, and I knew my nerves would be on edge with my meeting with Jase and the plan on my mind.

Once I arrived at Penn Station, I walked through the terminal until I reached 8th Avenue. I found a taxi pretty quickly and gave the driver the address to Rivers Enterprises. Before I knew it, we were weaving in and out of mid-morning traffic. It was a short drive, so I quickly checked my makeup and reapplied some lip gloss. I unpinned my bun and shook my hair out. The curls where now replaced by waves as it hung loosely down my back.

The taxi arrived at the building in seven minutes. It was the quickest I had ever gotten there. I paid my fare, stepped out of the taxi, and walked up to the building, pausing right before going in. I took a deep breath, composed myself, and headed through the revolving door.

I rode the elevator to the eleventh floor, which was home to Rivers Enterprises. When I stepped out of the elevator, I noticed there was no one else in the reception area. I walked up to the receptionist and told her my name and who I was meeting with. She let me know it would be a couple of minutes and asked me to take a seat. I took off my coat and scarf and sat down.

Ten minutes passed and I was still waiting. I was trying not to fidget but my nerves were starting to get the best of me. Then the glass double doors pushed open and an older woman walked toward me. She was about five feet tall, plain, and dressed like she was stuck in the fifties.

She stopped in front of me and said, "Miss Shaw, I'm Maude, Mr. Hainsworth's assistant. We spoke on the phone." She stuck out her hand and I shook it.

"Nice to meet you Maude," I said.

"Mr. Hainsworth is ready for you now. Follow me, please," she continued.

I stood, grabbed my things, and followed her through the glass double doors. Maude seemed nice, and for a second I was glad his assistant was not young and attractive. I knew I shouldn't have cared, but a little piece of me was relieved.

I trailed behind Maude, past the conference rooms that we usually met in.

"Would you like coffee, tea, or water, Miss Shaw?" Maude asked.

"No, thank you," I replied.

We kept on walking, and I was curious as to where she was bringing me. We walked along a hallway, past a row of offices. About halfway down she stopped at what seemed like a random office, opened the door, and gestured for me to walk in. I stepped inside the office and saw Jase on the phone, sitting behind a desk with a window view of 8th Avenue.

I couldn't believe it. This motherfucker had an office with a window? All those years I'd been busting my ass to move up and prove myself, and all I had to show for it was a cubicle with a view of the copier. This asshole jumped right into the work grind and got an office with a window. We hadn't even started the meeting and I was annoyed.

I heard Maude close the door behind me. Jase was wrapping up his call, so I stood there and looked around his office. It was a little bare. There were some magazines, and a plant that may have been fake. There were also two frames: a picture of his parents in one and a picture of him with his three brothers in the other. I also noticed his college degree was nicely framed and proudly hung on his wall. I knew it meant a lot to him to finish school. He had told me he wanted more in life than just the family farm, and from where I was standing, he was off to a good start.

I heard Jase end his call, so I turned my attention back to him, only to see that he was checking out my ass. He looked up at me from his chair and saw that I had caught him. He smiled his sly smile and stood up, never taking his eyes from mine.

"Kenzie Shaw, welcome to Rivers Enterprises," he said.

I wanted to punch him in the face.

He walked to the front of his desk, where I was standing, and reached out his hand. I reluctantly shook it. The instant our hands touched, the anger I felt was replaced with electricity. My body began to hum with want.

I glanced down at our joined hands and quickly pulled mine back. I looked up through my lashes at Jase, taking in the country-boy-turned-corporate-man that stood before me. His head was slightly tilted. Expressionless, he looked at his empty hand before looking back at me. He dropped it to his side and walked back around to his chair. I couldn't help but watch his ass and notice how good he looked in his tan suit with a white button-up shirt and striped tie. I had thoughts of tying him up with his tie—or vice versa. Shit!

Jase sat back down and I did the same, placing my things in the empty chair next to me.

"Can I get you anything?" Jase asked.

A quick fuck would be nice.

Shit! I'm doing it again. Bad mind, bad! I mentally scolded myself.

"No, I'm fine. Thank you," I told him.

"Okay then. Let's get started," said Jase.

I grabbed my papers from my messenger bag and we began discussing the account and the status of the changes for 2015.

All in all, it was a good meeting. Jase and I worked well together, and for the most part I was able to hold my dirty mind at bay. Before I knew it, it was a quarter after twelve when Jase's assistant buzzed his phone.

Jase pressed the button and said, "Yes Maude?"

"Miss Roberts is here," she told him.

"Thank you. Please let her know that I'll be done shortly. We're just wrapping up," Jase said, ending their conversation. "I guess we're done here," he said, but the way he looked at me it seemed like he wanted to say more.

It was my chance to put my plan into action.

"Kenzie, are we okay? I mean, I think we worked well together today," he said, seemingly genuine.

"Yes, we did," I replied with a small smile.

Do I ask him now, I wondered?

"Let me walk you out," Jase offered.

Perfect. Now's my chance.

I gathered my things and draped my peacoat and scarf over my arm. He opened the door for me and I walked out of his office. It made me a little sad as it reminded me how much of a gentleman he had been during our brief time together.

We walked side by side, back to the reception area, and Jase began to make small talk.

"So, how are you?" he asked.

"I'm good. I see you're doing well for yourself," I told him.

He laughed a little. "Yeah, I'm doing okay," he said, shrugging off his new job like it wasn't a big deal.

His modesty annoyed me slightly. "Wow, really? You're doing okay? There are people out there that bust their asses for years to get where you are, and you make it seem like it's not a big deal?" I spat at him as we kept walking.

"Well, well. There's the Kenzie Shaw I know," he said.

I could feel him staring at me but I refused to give him the satisfaction by returning the look. We reached the glass doors to the reception area and I was beginning to question whether my plan for peace and friendship was a good idea. He held the door open and allowed me to walk through first. Once again, there was that sad feeling. Did I miss him? *Shut up, Kenzie and stop asking questions we may not want the answers to*, I chastised myself.

I was about to put my peacoat on when I realized that if I was going to put my plan into action, I had to do it right then.

I turned to face Jase and saw he was watching me. My heart nearly stopped when I looked up into those eyes that had graced so many of my dreams. My body began to get warm and I realized I had grabbed his hand without intending to. It still felt rough to the touch, and I remembered how they felt on my skin. My breathing hitched, and Jase noticed and zeroed in on my lips.

"Kenzie…" Jase said my name so softly I nearly came right there in the reception area.

I was struggling to keep it together. I was about to ask him to lunch or quite possibly a hotel when I heard, "Jase, honey, are you ready?"

What. The. Fuck.

I looked around Jase to see a beautiful tall blonde with big blue eyes and big boobs. She was dressed in workout clothes and was walking toward us. I let go of his hand and suddenly things felt wrong. When I looked back at Jase, his face was blank and his eyes were shut, no longer watching me. I couldn't read his expression. He turned and looked at the woman who walked up to us. She wrapped her arm around his and my blood began to boil.

I was this close to pulling down my pants and peeing on him to mark my territory. Only problem was, he wasn't mine and he never had been.

"Hey. Yeah, I'm ready. I was just walking Miss Shaw out. Leah Roberts, this is Kenzie Shaw. Kenzie works at one of the top advertising agencies in the country. Also, her best friend is dating Matt," Jase said, introducing us. Not that I gave a flying fuck who this bitch was.

Trying to be the bigger person, I reached out my hand to her and she shook it. "It's nice to meet you Leah," I lied to her face.

"Nice to meet you too," she responded dryly. "Is Kenzie short for something?" Leah the bitch asked.

Yes, she was officially known as *Leah the bitch* to me at that point.

I bit my lip and took a long, deep breath before answering her. "Yes it is. My full name is Mckenzie."

Leah the bitch only blinked at me and smiled before turning her attention to Jase.

Holy shit, this was not happening to me.

"Babe, if we're going to get lunch, we have to go now. I have to be back in an hour for my next class," Leah the Cunt said.

Yup, she went from bitch to cunt in under five minutes.

I wasn't quite sure what happened to me, but I turned into a raging, jealous bitch on the inside while I prayed that the outside seemed completely unfazed.

"Leah works at a gym a few blocks over. That's how we met," Jase explained to me. Like I gave two shits. He paused and looked at me, searching my face before looking back at Leah the Cunt. "We should probably get going then. Let me get my coat," Jase said.

I needed to get away from them.

"I better get going. Jase, it was good to see you again. Leah, it was nice to meet you," I lied again as I waved goodbye, turning and quickly walking toward the elevator.

"Kenzie!" Jase shouted, and I heard footsteps behind me.

Thankfully the elevator dinged and opened as I walked up to it. A person got off the elevator and I quickly got on, frantically pushing the door close button before hitting the button for the first floor. The doors closed just as I heard Jase's footsteps approach. I felt the elevator descend. I turned around and leaned against the wall, realizing I was alone.

"Fuck my life. Fuck Jase and fuck that cunt," I shouted at doors.

I was fuming for no reason, which made me even more pissed. He wasn't mine. He never was mine and I shouldn't have even cared, but I did.

The elevator doors opened on the first-floor lobby. I threw my peacoat and scarf on, and then I walked as fast as I could without people thinking I was running from a crime I had just committed. I shoved my way through the revolving doors, allowing the cold, bitter air to hit my face. Next thing I knew, I was on my ass and white shit was falling on my face.

What the fuck. I was now staring up at the cloudy sky, looking at the snow falling down as people walked past me. I saw a guy salting the sidewalk. A lot of good that did me.

"Jesus. When it rains it fucking pours!" I shouted to no one in particular as I attempted to get up.

"No—actually, young lady, it's snowing, not raining," I heard a man say in a gravelly voice.

I felt a hand reach around my arm and help me up. I turned to see an old homeless man with a dirty gray beard and more wrinkles then I could count, standing there in tattered clothes. He was holding onto a small cart with cans and some bags in it. He looked like he hadn't showered in months or maybe even years.

I rubbed my ass. I was almost positive that I would have a nice bruise in a couple of hours. "Thank you. I can see it's snowing. It's a saying, you know—when it rains it pours. I didn't mean it literally," I explained to the man, but wasn't sure why.

Then I remembered that Jase and his cunt might be walking out of the building at any moment. I reached into my messenger bag for my clutch. I pulled out a twenty-dollar bill and handed it to the man, which he gladly accepted.

I started to walk away from him when he said something that stopped me. "Thank you, young lady. Be careful, because it might have been the universe knocking you on your ass," the man said, smiling a toothless smile as he put away the twenty dollars.

"Excuse me?" I said in disbelief. "Why would the universe do that? What did I ever do to the universe, huh?" I said, mocking his crazy theory.

"How am I supposed to know? Probably knocked you on your ass to stop you from running from someone or something—or both," he told me.

Why was I even standing there in the cold, while it was snowing, having this conversation? I needed to get out of there.

"You can't screw with the universe. Believe me, I tried," he said, walking away from me.

Maybe I should have given him Maggie's number and they could talk about that universe shit together. So what if I was running from someone or something or both. What does a crazy old homeless guy know?

I stood on 8th Avenue and hailed a cab. Thankfully I didn't have to wait long. A cab saw me and pulled over to the curb. I opened the door and gingerly climbed in, attempting not to hurt my ass any more then I already had. I knew the forty-five minute ride home on the train was going to suck royally. I told the driver to take me to Penn Station. He pulled away from the curb and I felt relieved that I didn't see Jase again.

I looked out the back window to take one last look at the old homeless man who had helped me, only to see Jase and Leah the Cunt walking out of the building. He had his arm around her shoulders, pulling her close to keep her warm. The gesture seemed sweet and romantic, which was just like Jase. But it didn't seem right, because she wasn't right for him.

I tore my eyes away and looked straight ahead at nothing in particular. I felt envy stirring inside me and I didn't like it one bit. I thought about what the old homeless man had said about the universe. If he was right, then I was fucked.

Chapter 15 | Avoidance

Since my plan didn't work out the way I had hoped, I came up with another way to deal with Jase.

I decided I would ignore him.

Yup, that was my plan.

Was it healthy? Probably not, but it was working well for me at the moment.

Jase did call me the day after our meeting, but I didn't answer. Thanks to my business card, he also called my cell phone—but I didn't answer that either. Oddly enough, he didn't leave a message. I would have been lying if I'd said I wasn't curious as to what he wanted. Maybe it was to apologize for his girlfriend being such a cunt. Then again, those were my feelings and probably not his. I tried not to think about why he had called. They say curiosity killed the cat, and I didn't need any more fucked-up shit happening to me. Avoidance is bliss, and it felt so good.

Over the next few weeks, Jase called me several times. I never once picked up and he never once left a voice mail. It was strange, and no matter how hard I tried to ignore it, I found myself in knots each time. I wasn't sure if I was mind-fucking myself or if Jase was mind-fucking me. Then on Christmas Day, he called my cell phone. Again, I didn't pick up and there was no voice mail. It was pretty clear I was on his mind, just as he was on mine.

My mind had so many questions that I had no answers to. I, of course, quietly told Alayna this while we were opening Christmas presents at my house with our family. That was a big mistake. She decided to loudly tell me, for all to hear, that I should have answered his call. Yet again, I wanted to smack the shit out of my cousin. I gave her a death glare and she sat there smiling proudly that she had started a topic of conversation on my behalf.

Of course my family overheard her, and that led to twenty questions: Who was calling? Why didn't I answer the call? Was this guy my boyfriend? Why was a guy calling on Christmas if he wasn't my boyfriend? Is he a friend with benefits?

I then had to explain what a "friend with benefits" was to my Nan. She only shook her head at me and walked away, probably thinking I was a hussy. My mom wanted to know if he was cute and why I wasn't taking his calls. My aunt went on to tell everyone that he must be ugly if I wasn't calling him back. Then I overheard my mom whisper to my aunt that she would never have grandkids at this rate.

Ugh. I wanted to kill my cousin. I promised myself that one day I was going to tell my family about Alayna's threesome and see how that topic flowed over dinner. I did my best to avoid any questions while trying to convince my Nan that I wasn't a hussy. The questions and stress led to me stuffing my face with turkey, drinking lots of wine, and passing out on the couch.

Weeks had gone by since my meeting with Jase, and avoidance was how I continued to deal with him. I made sure I was on top of things when it came to the Rivers account. If Jase had a question or I had an update to give to him, I would send an email, always copying Ben and never with any phone contact. Ben noticed and asked me about it but I just brushed it off, telling him that I was covering my ass. He saw through me because he knew how I worked and knew this wasn't my style. So it shouldn't have surprised me when Ben called me into his office after lunch and asked, "Do you want off the Rivers account?"

I was shocked and speechless as I dropped into the empty chair. It took me a couple seconds before I could respond. "What? Why? Has something been said? Did I do something wrong?" I asked, worried.

"No, nothing has been said and you didn't do anything wrong," Ben assured me, leaning back in his chair. "We are making some changes, moving some people around. I've been keeping an eye on you and the Rivers account since you told me of your history with Jase

Hainsworth. I can see you're dancing around Jase, trying to avoid him. Don't get me wrong, you're still doing the work and it's good work, but whatever it is you think you're doing, you can't keep it up. I don't want you to get in over your head because of a past relationship you can't get over."

What did he just say? I can't get over Jase!

"First of all, *Ben*, with all due respect, I'm fine. Second of all, I am completely over Jase Hainsworth—not that it's any of your business. And third, well, I don't have a third yet, but give me a minute and I'm sure I will think of one," I said, annoyed, crossing my arms.

Ben laughed. He knew me too well, which meant he knew my first and second statements were lies.

Maybe I shouldn't think up a third. I'll only dig a deeper hole for myself.

"Kenzie, just think about it," Ben said, leaning forward in his chair, putting his elbows on the desk, and steepling his fingers. "You have been on the Rivers account for a while now. It might be good to change things up a bit. From what I hear, Jase is Mr. Manna's golden boy, and I don't see him going anywhere anytime soon. I'm proposing that you switch to another account so you can work to your full potential. Just think about it. That's all I'm asking," he said.

I knew Ben was looking out for me, but I was pissed. "So I'm being punished for past relations with Jase that you wouldn't have even known about if *I* hadn't told you? I don't think that's fair," I said sharply.

"This isn't a punishment or anything, Kenzie. I'm trying to look out for you. Let's put aside that I'm your manager. As a friend, I see you struggling. It's like you're off kilter. You're avoiding the client but handling the account. It's been a month that you and Jase have been working together and there's still no balance. You need that balance or things will start to fall apart," Ben said concerned.

"Well, if you didn't just put me in my place," I said, sulking in the chair. "I guess you're right," I told him, throwing in the towel.

"Of course I am," Ben said, smiling. "Listen, Kenz, I'm just trying to help you as a friend and as a boss," Ben told me.

"I know you are, but it doesn't make it any easier. This account was my first account and I worked my ass off over the years managing it. Since meeting Jase, all he's done is turn my life upside down, and now it's affecting my job," I confessed.

"Maybe it's not him doing it to you. Maybe you're doing it to yourself," Ben said, but I had no response. "You still have feelings for him, don't you?" he asked. I didn't know how to answer that either.

I looked down at my hands as I began to fidget. "I'm not sure," I told Ben. It was weird talking about my feelings for Jase. I tried very hard to avoid any feelings associated with him, but it was hard at times.

"You're not sure?" he questioned, then continued. "You do or you don't, Kenz? It's that simple."

I sighed and rolled my eyes. "Nothing in my life is that simple Ben," I told him. "Remember when I had a meeting with him at his office? I had a plan. I was going to talk to him about us, get it all out in the open. I thought working with him would be easier that way," I explained.

"What happened?" Ben asked, clearly curious.

I looked down at my hands again, fidgeting with the tie of my dress. "Jase walked me out to the reception area after our meeting and I was about to ask him to lunch so we could talk…" I paused, remembering the day like it was yesterday.

"And then?" Ben said, urging me to continue.

"…And then a woman called out to him. When I looked, it was a pretty blonde walking toward us. Then she wrapped her arm around his," I told him.

"Oh shit, for real!" he exclaimed.

"Yeah, for real," I confirmed, looking back up at Ben.

My face must have had pain, disgust, and sadness written all over it by the way Ben was looking at me.

"I'm sorry, Kenz," he said, apologizing.

"I'm fine, really. I don't need your pity. What's one more bump in the road when it comes to Jase?"

Ben was silent, which was never good. It meant he was taking everything in and thinking about how to respond, so I continued.

"The part that bothers me the most is how I felt about it. I was so angry at the way she was staking her claim by wrapping her arm around his. Then to see him look at me at that moment as if he was sorry I had to see them together. Plus she isn't right for him," I told Ben, annoyed as I thought about her, the cunt.

"But you are?" he asked.

"Huh?" I said, puzzled at Ben's question.

"Who would be right for Jase?" Ben asked me, but I just shrugged my shoulders as I continued to sulk in the chair.

"You may not want to know what I think, but I'm going to tell you anyway," he said.

That should have been my cue to get the hell out of his office, but maybe I needed to hear what he had to say.

"Kenz, it's pretty obvious that you still care for Jase. I actually wonder if you've fallen in love with him."

My mouth dropped open, speechless at his words, but I continued to listen.

"The hardest thing to do is watch the one you want with someone else. The pain, anger, and jealousy you felt when you saw Jase with that other woman was because you wished it was you. At some point you need to figure this shit out. Life's too short and there's no room for regrets," said Ben.

"Wow, that shit was deep. I feel like I should be paying you for a therapy session," I said, weakly laughing. "Take me off the Rivers account and put me somewhere else. I have to start figuring this shit out and I can't have it affecting my work," I told Ben.

I was saddened by this. I felt like I had just thrown in the towel. I had been on the Rivers account since I started, but maybe it was time for a change.

"I think it's the right decision. Once we figure out the details I'll let you know who will be handling what. Then I'll send out an email to our team and to the affected accounts," he said. "Remember, change is good," Ben added.

"Yeah, that's what they say," I said as I stood up to leave.

Just before I opened the door to walk out, I turned and faced Ben. "Thank you. As much as this sucks, I do appreciate you looking out for me and being a voice of reason when I needed it most. You're a good friend, Ben," I told him, flashing him a genuine smile of gratitude.

"Anytime. Now, why don't you head out of here? We're letting everyone go at two today. You can start ringing in the New Year a little early," he said.

"Okay, thanks. Happy New Year, Ben," I told him.

"Happy New Year, Kenzie," he said back to me.

I left Ben's office in a different mood from when I had entered. I was still upset, but had a strange sense of relief. Like a weight I hadn't even known was there was finally lifted. The more I thought about the change, the better it seemed. There were two accounts that came to mind that I thought I would like to handle. Before packing up my stuff for the day I quickly emailed Ben, letting him know my thoughts on those accounts. They were smaller than Rivers, but I knew I could do so much more with them. I sent my email, shut down my laptop, gathered my things, and headed out of the door.

Once I was in my car, I plugged in my iPod and played whatever song happened to be next on my playlist. I turned up the volume as "Bleeding Out" by Imagine Dragons blasted throughout my car. There was no traffic this early in the afternoon, so I sped down the highway. The sun was high in the winter sky, with only a few clouds. The scenery around me felt empty and my drive home felt lonely.

The song ended and "Someone Like You" by Adele began. I started to focus on the words of the song. My heart began to feel heavy. I didn't know who the lyrics were written for, but they touched a piece of my soul. I felt tears prick my eyes and then spill over onto my face. I quickly wiped them away, pissed that I was crying. What was I doing? I'd been trying to figure how to handle my life when it came to Jase, and apparently I sucked at it. It seemed like he was at the center of all of this shit. Goddamn him.

Then it hit me. Was Jase the center of *my* universe? Was it as simple as that? Were Maggie and the old homeless man right? All the time I fought tooth and nail to keep away from him, was it possible that we were supposed to be together?

I blindly crossed over two lanes to the side of the highway, my car screeching to a stop on the shoulder. I slammed my car into park, ripped my iPod from the plug, and threw it on the floor. I screamed obscenities while pounding on the steering wheel. I must have looked crazy but I didn't care. Thoughts of Jase and the way he'd touched me flooded my mind. It made me remember how I felt when I was around him.

I had never felt that way with anyone else. It was possibly the first sign of something more between us, and I'd pushed it aside. I was so sure things couldn't work out between us, but in all honesty I never even thought of trying. I was always so wrapped up in my job, myself, and what was good in the moment that I never thought about my needs or my heart. When I remembered the moments with him, every feeling, every touch we shared, good or bad, I realized what I wanted and needed. It was Jase.

I must have been parked on the side of the highway mulling over this newfound revelation for at least twenty minutes. I felt as if a fog had been lifted and I could see things a little clearer. A small smile began to creep up on my face but quickly disappeared when I realized it might be too late.

But I was never one to give up. If Jase and I were meant to be, then I would let things happen as they would. I would no longer put up a fight. I would no longer avoid him. I would no longer shut him out.

I immediately felt better after coming to these decisions. I guess I was an asshole for not doing it sooner. I was sure Ben would be proud of me, as would Alayna, Maggie, and the old homeless man. But this was going to be my little secret. For now.

I reached over to the floor, grabbed my iPod, and plugged it back in. I scrolled through my playlist and settled on "Heroes" by Alesso. I turned the volume up and got back on the highway. I decided to take the advice of the old homeless man and no longer fuck with the universe.

Chapter 16 | New Year's Resolution

"Wake up!" I heard someone shriek. "Wake up, wake up, wake up!"

I forced my eyes open to see Maggie staring down at me. Before I could react, she leaned over and began shaking my shoulder.

"Leave me alone. I need sleep and Advil. Can you go get me Advil, please? Oh, and a glass of water," I asked her, barely awake. I pulled the covers over my head. I was having a rough morning. Alayna and I had gone out for New Year's Eve with some friends. I drank way too much and now I was paying the price. If I didn't have a pounding headache, I'd probably be doing much better.

I felt my bed shift. Maggie must have parked her ass next to me. I had a feeling that she wasn't going to leave me alone.

"Mckenzie Shaw, wake the fuck up!" Maggie shouted, ripping the covers away from my face.

"For all that is holy in this fucking world! What the fuck do you want, Maggs?" I shouted back.

"Both of you shut the fuck up!" I heard Alayna yell from downstairs. I remembered my cousin had stayed the night and was probably in the same shape as me: very hungover.

"Shut the fuck up!" Maggie and I shouted in unison.

"Beer," Maggie said as she punched me in the shoulder.

"Ugh… please don't speak of any kind of alcohol," I said, holding my head, attempting to wake up. The thought of alcohol made my stomach queasy.

I tried to wake up but it felt like a chore just to blink my eyes.

"Wake up and open your eyes!" she pleaded.

"I'm up," I said, stretching and opening my eyes as they tried to adjust to the light. I didn't even know what time it was. It could have been four o'clock in the evening for all I knew.

The first thing I saw was Maggie's left hand about three inches from my face. It was so close my eyes were crossed looking at it. The second thing I noticed was the ring that sparkled on her finger. It was a beautiful round cut diamond. Two rows of smaller round accent diamonds framed it, which gave the setting an appearance of a square. It was stunning.

Holy shit, Maggie was engaged? Stunned, I stared at her in disbelief. She had a look beyond ecstatic. Maggie was ecstatic times ten.

"Holy shit, are you engaged?" I asked, still trying to register everything.

"*Yes!*" Maggie screamed, elated by her news.

I sat up in bed and hugged Maggie, and we both started bouncing. Bouncing was bad for my head, but given the situation, I didn't think I had a choice.

"Congratulations, Maggs! Who's the lucky guy?" I asked, busting her chops.

"Ha ha, very funny," she said as she let go of me. Maggie was transfixed by the ring that looked so perfect on her hand.

"So I take it Matt asked you last night?" I questioned.

"Why are you bitches so loud?" Alayna said, interrupting us as she dragged her ass into my room.

We looked at my cousin, who looked like a zombie minus the rotting skin.

"Wow, you look like shit," I told my cousin.

Alayna walked to the opposite side of my bed and crawled under the covers. "Thanks. I feel like shit. Remind me never to drink again," she grumbled. "What's going on? Why are you two always so fucking loud?" Alayna asked, burying her head in my other pillow.

Maggie shoved her left hand in my cousin's face, showing her the ring.

Alayna grabbed her hand. "You got engaged?" she asked, just as shocked as I was.

"Yes!" Maggie screeched.

"Holy shit! Congratulations," Alayna said, giving her a hug. "Now can you take the screeching down a notch or two? You're really hurting my head," Alayna told her, rubbing her temples.

"Sorry. I'm just so excited. I never expected this," Maggie told us.

Knowing what I knew, I honestly didn't think Matt would have ever proposed.

"How did he do it?" I asked.

Maggie was just about to tell us when I stopped her.

"Actually, hold that thought. I need to do something about this headache first," I told her. I quickly went downstairs to the bathroom and grabbed the Advil. I shook out three capsules and washed them down. I splashed some cold water on my face to help wake me up, but it didn't help. Not only was I exhausted, but I was still in shock from Maggie's news. I couldn't believe Matt had actually asked her to marry him.

I was making my way back upstairs, remembering when Jase had told me how Matt swore he would never get married. I guess he changed his mind. Maggie and I had talked a lot about their relationship since they'd gotten back together. He was determined to make things work, and their relationship was better than ever.

Even though I was a little skeptical, I was happy because Maggie only deserved the best. At the end of the day, all that mattered was her happiness. I did think his proposal was a little soon—they had only been back together for a few months—but what did I know? When it came to relationships, I still had a lot to learn. My longest had been with Masen. That was in high school, and I wasn't sure if that really counted.

I reached the top of the stairs and turned in to my room.

"It's about time. The bride-to-be is itching to tell us how he popped the question," Alayna said.

"I'm sorry. Next time you have earth-shattering news, please make sure I'm not hungover," I joked as I crawled back under the covers. I nodded at Maggie, prompting her to start her story.

She had a constant smile on her glowing face as she told us about their night in the city. I was a little worried she might end up like Jack Nicholson's Joker from *Batman*.

Maggie went on tell us how Matt had always wanted to see the ball drop in person at Times Square. I, personally, was not a big fan of freezing my ass off while being surrounded by a million people—but who am I to judge?

They made plans to spend the day sightseeing in Manhattan. Lucky for them, they got a room to stay overnight, even though it cost an arm and a leg. Maggie said they had a great day walking around, and then came back the hotel to shower and get ready for a casual dinner. She said the whole time Matt was calm and she would never have thought that he had something like a proposal planned.

Maggie told us their night was great, and when it was almost midnight they got as close as they could to Times Square, squeezing through the crowd. They held hands, counting down with everyone around them. When the ball dropped, they kissed. Shortly after, they decided to head back to the hotel.

Maggie said that when they got into the room, she noticed there was champagne on ice in a silver bucket, two toasting flutes, and some chocolate-covered strawberries on a silver tray. There was also a card.

She walked over to the tray and picked up the card. It was blank on the outside, but when she opened it up it said "Happy New Year" at the top and "I love you" beneath it. She turned to tell Matt how thoughtful and sweet it was of him, but he wasn't there.

She told us she heard water running and followed the sound into the bathroom to find Matt starting a bubble bath. He told her to get undressed and relax in the bath. She was exhausted from all the walking, so a bath sounded like a good idea. She dropped her clothes and slid into the tub. It was huge and had a dozen jets. Matt joined her a few minutes later, with the silver tray and everything on it.

Once in the tub, Matt popped open the champagne and poured some in both of their flutes. They talked about the day and then Matt asked what her New Year's resolution was for 2015.

Maggie told us she didn't really have an answer. She never made resolutions because she never kept them. So she said the first thing that came to mind, which was to eat less pasta since she had eaten so much at dinner that night. They both laughed.

She said she asked Matt what his resolution was. Matt told her it was to marry her and to make her the happiest woman alive.

"Oh my god, what did you say after he said that?" I asked Maggie, who was still smiling and starting to creep me out.

She seemed to somehow smile even wider and continued with her story. She explained how his resolution didn't really register right away. She made Matt repeat himself, and even though his lips were moving she didn't hear a word. He was clearly relishing the situation and took his sweet time to reach behind the strawberries and grab a black velvet box.

Somehow, once again, Maggie's smile grew even wider as she explained how Matt then sat up and took a knee, naked in the bubble bath. Then he stared into her eyes for what had felt like an eternity to her before asking, "Maggie Rowe, will you do me the honor and marry me?"

"Wow. That's great, Maggs. I bet you're not going to tell your parents that version," Alayna said, being funny.

"Actually, we called both of our parents this morning and told them. We gave them the PG version, of course, leaving out the bubble bath and nakedness," Maggie said laughing.

"I'm really happy for you," I told her, and I truly meant it.

"Are you sure? I know you're not crazy about Matt, but I love him and I really want you to be happy for me—no, for *us*." Maggie said.

"I am happy for you, Maggs. I can see Matt has tried very hard to make things right. If you're happy, then I'm happy for you," I told her with all sincerity.

Maggie's eyes began to tear up and she reached over, giving me a big hug. "Thank you, Kenzie. That means the world to me," she said in my ear. Then let go of me, wiping her eyes. "Matt and I talked this morning and we want to get married in the spring," she said.

"That's good, a little over a year to plan," I told her.

"Umm no, *this* spring," Maggie said.

"What?" Alayna and I said together, shocked.

"I know, I know. But we don't want to wait. We told his parents and they want to throw an engagement party for us in a couple of weeks," Maggie said.

"Shit, that doesn't leave much time for planning. What about the church, reception, flowers, DJ, and like fifty other things?" I spouted off to her.

Maggie's beaming smile suddenly turned suspicious.

"Wait, what aren't you telling us?" I asked her, arching an eyebrow.

Her eyes fell to the ground before saying, "Well, Matt mentioned that his parents built a new barn in the fall because their old barn was falling apart. He said we could ask his parents if we could have the wedding there," Maggie said, excited.

I glanced at Alayna and she had the same pained look of confusion on her face that I probably did. A fucking barn wedding? Where would people go to the bathroom, the pasture? The more I thought about it, the crazier it sounded.

I didn't want to rain on her parade, but a wedding in a barn was hardly my style. Alayna and I both smiled reassuringly, but our silence was a dead giveaway.

"I know it doesn't sound grand, but Matt swore to me that the barn would totally work. It's new and can fit over a hundred people. It only has a few pieces of farm equipment in there currently, so they could clear it out and we can decorate it however we want," Maggie said, trying to sell us on the idea.

We both looked at each other and then looked back at Maggie.

"To be honest, a barn wedding sounds fucking insane, but if that is what you want then I will help you make it the best fucking barn wedding ever," I told Maggie.

"Pinterest, here we come," said Alayna.

"Thanks, guys. That leads me to my next question: Kenzie, will you be my maid of honor?" Maggie asked me.

"Holy Shit! Of course, Maggs," I told her.

"And Alayna, will you be one of my bridesmaids?"

"Yes, I totally will. Whoa, wait. You said *one* of your bridesmaids. Who's the other?" Alayna asked.

"Matt wants his cousin Amy in the wedding," Maggie told us.

"Oh okay, I'll allow that," said Alayna, being funny but serious at the same time.

Maggie rolled her eyes. "Amy is really sweet. You'll like her. Right, Kenzie?" Maggie asked.

"Yes, she's very nice. Who are the groomsmen?" I asked, afraid of the answer.

Maggie looked at me, hesitating to speak, but then said, "Matt asked Jase to be his best man. Reid, Cole, Casey, and Masen will be the groomsmen."

Great. Now I'm going to be in a wedding with Jase.

This had to be a good thing, right? Then I remembered that Jase was seeing the Cunt. I kicked myself in the ass again for not doing something with Jase while I had the chance. Gotta love my life.

"Kenzie, you okay?" Maggie asked, looking concerned.

"Yeah, sure. I'm fine. I'm just a little hungover. The Advil hasn't kicked in yet," I said, lying through my teeth.

"Oh, okay. I wasn't sure how you would feel being paired up with Jase with everything that's happened. I know you said working with him has been okay," Maggie said.

"Nope, it's fine. But I won't have to worry about him and work because they're moving me off the Rivers Account," I told them.

"What?" they both said, shocked.

"What aren't you telling us? Isn't the Rivers account your baby?" Alayna said, eyeing me suspiciously.

"Yeah, what's going on?" Maggie asked, losing her smile.

Crap. They were onto me.

"Nothing. They're just shuffling around some people at work between different accounts. Fresh eyes, fresh ideas. That's all," I told them.

"You're lying," Alayna said, jabbing her index finger into my shoulder.

Shit. If there was anything I was terrible at, it was lying. Honesty was my thing. I was usually too honest.

"Okay, okay. You got me. I surrender," I told them, throwing my hands up.

I knew I didn't have a choice but to tell them. The question was, how much to tell. I took a deep breath, wondering how they were going to take what I was about to say.

"Ben asked me if I wanted off the account. When I found out Jase was working for Rivers, I told Ben about my past with him. Apparently he had been keeping an eye on me and noticed that I was having a hard time balancing Jase and the account," I confessed, and continued. "He suggested moving me to a different account. At first I was pissed, but the more I talked to Ben about it, the more it made sense," I explained.

"Damn. Is this why you haven't been answering his calls?" Alayna said, jabbing me again for answers.

"Wait, Jase has been calling you? Why didn't you tell me?" Maggie asked.

Fuck. I have such nosy people in my life.

"Because I didn't want to deal with the questions. Plus he never leaves a voicemail, so it must not be that important," I said, thinking of all the times he'd called. "Or, he could be calling to tell me something I don't want to hear," I said, realizing the flurry of questions it was going to bring.

"Wait a minute. What do you mean by that?" Alayna asked.

"How long have you been ignoring his calls, and what don't you want to hear?" Maggie demanded.

"Since their meeting at his office," Alayna told Maggie before I had a chance to answer.

I was now glaring at my cousin as she smiled back at me.

"I thought the meeting went well," Maggie said, confused.

"It did go well," I said.

"I'm getting the sense that something happened. Why would he be calling you and why wouldn't you pick up?" Maggie questioned.

"Yeah, what's going on, Kenz? Oh shit, did you fuck him in his office?" Alayna asked.

"I'll tell you what happened and what I've realized, but I need both of you to promise not to push or pry after this," I stated.

"Promise," they both said in unison.

"To answer your question, no, I didn't fuck him in his office," I told Alayna.

"But you wanted to," Alayna interrupted.

"Not that it matters, but yes, I did. Now shut up and let me talk," I said.

Alayna made a zipping motion across her lips, but I knew it wasn't that easy to keep her quiet.

"The meeting with Jase at his office went great. I planned to ask him to lunch to clear the air. I thought it would make work and personal life a little easier. A sort of fresh start, you know. Jase had walked me out to the reception area and just as I was about to ask him to lunch, someone called his name. It was some tall blonde with big boobs wearing workout clothes. She walked over to us and wrapped her arm around his. The receptionist had buzzed Jase during our meeting, letting him know someone was waiting for him. I never thought it would be someone he was dating," I told them.

"Why not? He's single and totally hot," Alayna said.

I knew it wasn't that easy to keep her quiet. If looks could kill, Alayna would be dead and Maggie and I would be digging a hole in the backyard.

Alayna gasped and covered her mouth when she realized she had spoken. "Sorry," she apologized.

"Getting back to my story," I said, eyeing my cousin, "Jase introduced Leah the Cunt to me and shared how they met at the gym where she works."

I started to fidget with my blanket as I thought about how much more to share with them. I figured it was best to tell them everything and see what they said.

"There's something else. I was really pissed off seeing them together. In the past it was Jase chasing me, and me walking away or turning him down. Now the roles are reversed and I don't like it," I confessed to them.

"I knew it!" Alayna said so loud that Maggie and I both jumped.

"I swear to god, Alayna, I will get duct tape and tape your mouth shut," Maggie told my cousin, but Alayna responded by sticking her tongue out.

"Anyway, after the introduction I got out of there as quickly as I could," I said.

"Can I speak now?" Alayna asked sarcastically, raising her hand like she was in class.

I nodded yes at her.

"Besides the obvious, why is she a cunt?" she questioned.

"Well, since I didn't like her touching Jase, I decided she was a bitch. But then she spoke and it was obvious she was a cunt. Pretty simple," I stated matter-of-factly.

"Okay, I accept that. Cunt she is," Alayna agreed.

"I've met her and I don't care for her. No one does, actually. His mother can't stand her," Maggie told us.

"Wait, she met his parents? Are they serious?" I questioned.

"I'm not sure. All I know is she doesn't seem right for him. She's clingy and needy. I didn't think it would last this long," Maggie explained.

Shit.

"Kenz, there is one thing that I don't understand. You say you have feelings for him but you've been ignoring him. You don't take his calls. You don't call him back. And now you're pissed he has a girlfriend. What am I missing?" Maggie asked, always so perceptive.

"Just before the cunt interrupted Jase and me, we were having a moment. It felt like he was going to say something significant, but then she announced her presence and wrapped her arm around his, staking her claim. After that he barely looked at me and I surely didn't want to see them together. That's when I left. He called after me but I didn't turn around," I told them.

I took a deep breath to prepare to come clean.

"I haven't been taking his calls or calling him back because I'm afraid of what he might say. I'm afraid Jase might say he's happy with her. Maybe that's what he was about to tell me when she interrupted us. I want him but I think I realized it too late," I said, looking at both of them.

Alayna and Maggie were silent and looked dumbfounded.

Of course it was Alayna who broke the silence. "Whoa. So you want him because you're jealous or you want him because you want to be with him?" she questioned.

"Because I want to be with him," I said meekly, barely more than a whisper.

"He told you he wanted you at that meeting you had when you found out he was working for Rivers," Maggie chimed in.

"He did say that, but he's with that cunt now so maybe his feelings have changed," I told them.

"I guess we'll have to find out," Maggie said.

"No! If something is going to happen with Jase, I want it to happen naturally—not because people got involved and forced it," I said.

Alayna and Maggie looked at each other and smiled.

"I mean it, you two," I warned them.

"We promise. Right, Alayna?" Maggie said.

"Yup, I promise," Alayna said, winking at my best friend.

Shit. I was in trouble. Maybe telling them had been a bad idea.

I had a feeling that it might be an interesting year for me. If I had to make one New Year's resolution, it would be to remember the lessons from past mistakes so I could find love in spite of my fear.

Chapter 17 | Memories

"Let's go, Alayna!" Masen impatiently shouted from the driver's seat.

"I'm coming. Stop being such an asshole," she said, annoyed, as she locked my front door.

I watched my cousin rush about. I wasn't sure how she wasn't ready. All she had to do was pack enough shit for the weekend and get over to my house. It was Friday and we had left work early to beat the rush hour traffic. Yet here we were running late as usual.

Things never go the way you plan them to.

"We were supposed to leave an hour ago. Now we're going to hit traffic," Masen said, equally annoyed.

"What's the rush to get there? It's the fucking boonies!" Alayna said in a snarky tone, tossing her duffel bag on the seat and climbing in behind me.

Alayna and I were practically twins in our sweat outfits. Thankfully she was in gray and I was in black.

"Because I left before my parents to pick you guys up, and now they'll probably get there before us. Then it's gonna be twenty questions about why we're late and how I'm never on time," Masen snapped.

"Both of you, cut the shit!" I yelled at them. We hadn't left the driveway and I already had thoughts of murder.

It was the end of January and we were driving to upstate New York for Maggie and Matt's engagement party. Matt's mom, Nancy, insisted she throw the party at her house. Can you say control freak? Usually it's supposed to be the bride's parents' responsibility to throw the party, but she had insisted. Luckily, Mr. and Mrs. Rowe didn't put up too much of a fight.

Maggie had a very small family, and the only people she'd invited to the engagement party on her side were her parents, Masen, Alayna, and me. I, of course, was not thrilled about seeing Jase's mom again. I hoped she wouldn't recognize me, but a small part of me hoped that she would. Maggie had warned me that Jase was bringing Leah the Cunt. Yup, fun times would be had in the boonies that weekend. I was sure of it.

The only thing that made me feel better was knowing that no one else liked Jase's girlfriend. Alayna told me she was going to accidentally spill a drink on her. At first I thought it was a brilliant idea and told her to make sure it was red wine. Then I thought, *what if the Cunt says some shit to my cousin after the unfortunate accident?* No way would I let that happen. I'd end up punching the Cunt, and I couldn't ruin Maggie's engagement party, no matter how much satisfaction I would get from it. Plus Nancy would really think I was trash then. Not that I really cared.

I had asked Maggie about the sleeping arrangements. I was worried about the whole Jase and Leah the Cunt situation. I wasn't sure if I would have to get a hotel room. I wondered if they even had hotels in the boonies. Maggie assured me that they did have hotels in the boonies and not to worry. We were all staying at Matt's house while Matt stayed with Jase, per Nancy's request. Maggie said Matt was completely annoyed by this. He'd told his mom that he was an adult and could sleep with Maggie if he pleased. Apparently this didn't sit well with his mom and she'd spouted off about it not being proper, especially with Maggie's parents being in the same house. It seemed that Nancy only cared about keeping up appearances. I knew Mr. and Mrs. Rowe wouldn't care. Maggie told Matt it wasn't worth it so he decided to give up the fight. I wished Maggie luck with her future mother-in-law before she left with Matt to head upstate.

"Can you turn the radio down a little?" Alayna asked.

I took a quick peek behind me only to see my cousin resting her head against the door.

"No," Masen said.

I turned and shot him a look, shaking my head.

"What crawled up your ass?" Alayna asked Masen. The tension was clearly building and I was sick of it.

"Jesus, I can't listen to this shit the whole ride. Masen, stop being a dick. Just ignore each other and shut the fuck up!" I shouted.

That was the last thing I said to either of them for the rest of the ride to Matt's house. Masen listened to the radio while Alayna fell asleep. I also tried to sleep, but wasn't so lucky. So for three and a half hours, I passed the time by thinking about the weekend, but mainly Jase.

The previous week my boss, Ben, had made an announcement on the reorganization in our department and who was working on what account. Following the announcement, individual emails were sent to the affected accounts and their contacts. It notified them of the changes and who their new contacts would be. I expected an email or call from Jase, but I got neither.

For once I hoped and prayed that he would reach out to me. Days passed without a peep. Maybe he figured that since I had ignored his past attempts, why reach out to me now? Why would he be concerned about me or the changes that affected my job when I never even took his calls? I was pissed at myself for that. Actually, I was very pissed at myself. It was a painful reminder of all the times he'd made an effort but I'd avoided him, and now he was with someone else. Fuck my life.

The navigation said we were only a couple of miles away. My nerves hit me and my stomach started to churn. This wasn't good. Maybe things would be better once we got there and settled in. Wishful thinking, right?

My phone started to vibrate. It was Maggie. She must have texted me ten times in the past hour, asking where we were.

I swiped my phone to answer it. "Hey Maggs," I said to her.

"Where are you guys? My parents are worried," she said in a hushed tone.

"No need to worry. We're right down the road. We left a little late. We'll be there in five minutes," I told her.

"Okay. See you in a few. Bye," Maggie said and hung up.

Masen gave me a look. I guessed he'd overheard my conversation with Maggie. "What? Don't start your shit, Rowe," I said, pointing at him. "The last thing I need is to be the referee between you and Alayna this weekend," I told him.

"Did I say anything?" he asked.

"Not yet," I said, eyeing him so he knew I meant business. I knew him too well.

"You need to relax, Kenz. You're always so serious," Masen said, laughing to himself.

"Says the guy who flipped out because we were running late," I told him sarcastically.

Masen grinned and winked at me as he drove. "Keep an eye on the road, Rowe. All kinds of shit will jump out. It's like the animals have a death wish or something up here. Maybe it's the altitude or the country air," I said, trying to lighten the mood and take my mind off the weekend.

I looked out the window. Damn, it was dark out there. Everything was a blanket of white from a recent snowfall.

"Don't worry, Kenz, I'll protect you. I got your back," Masen said.

I could only smile. His words were so sincere, and I had no doubt he meant every one of them. Masen was a great guy and a great friend. I felt a little better about the weekend knowing he was there with me. I did wonder what he would say if he knew the story between Jase and me.

The navigation said our destination was ahead on the right. Masen slowed and made a right turn onto the snow-covered gravel driveway, hidden by trees that lined the road.

"Wake up, sleepyhead. We're here," I said to Alayna.

There were several cars parked in the driveway and on the grass. My heart stopped beating for a couple of seconds when I recognized a certain black Chevy Silverado pickup truck. It was Jase's truck.

I felt stuck in my seat, unsure of what to do next. I repeated, *you can do this, you can do this*, as I internally psyched myself up. I had known I would have to see Jase the following night. I guess I shouldn't have assumed that everyone wouldn't get together tonight as well. Fuuuuuuuck!

Masen spotted his parents' car and parked behind it. I opened the door, and as I stepped out I felt the snow crunch under my feet. Then the winter cold hit me like a freight train.

"Damn, it's fucking cold up here!" I said out loud, to no one in particular. I was trying to reel my emotions in when I looked up. I couldn't help but take notice of the stars.

Alayna stepped out and stood beside me as we stared at them together. They were ridiculously bright in the night sky. It was almost as if they were welcoming us—or maybe warning us. Either way, they were beautiful.

"The country at night makes me miss streetlights and sidewalks," Alayna said out of nowhere, still staring at the stars.

"I couldn't agree with you more," I said before lowering my voice to a whisper. "Let's get our bags before Masen freaks out again. Plus I'm freezing."

We both laughed. The three of us grabbed our bags and headed for the house.

Masen rang the doorbell as we impatiently waited while freezing our asses off. We heard lots of voices and laughing inside. I started to get more nervous. Alayna must have noticed because she put her free arm around my shoulders and gave me a tight squeeze.

"Just relax. Everything will be fine," she whispered.

Then the door opened. It was Reid, face-to-face with Masen. Was Reid the official doorman? It seemed every time I went someplace and a Hainsworth was there, he was always answering the door.

"Masen," Reid said.

"Reid," Masen replied.

I swear their chests looked puffed out, and I couldn't help but roll my eyes. I guess both guys remembered their last interaction with each other.

"What are you two, cavemen? It's friggin cold out here," Alayna said.

I couldn't help but shake my head and laugh. Reid looked shocked and taken aback.

"Look, I'm not sure how *y'all* do it in the country, but making us stand out in the cold is rude. I've been in the car for three and a half hours and I have to pee. Now, if you'll excuse me," Alayna said, pushing past Masen and Reid, walking through the door, and dropping her bag by Reid's feet.

I overheard Alayna ask someone inside where the bathroom was while Reid stood in the doorway, probably wondering what had just hit him. The dumbfounded look on his face was priceless and I couldn't help but laugh a little.

Wondering if Reid had forgotten that Masen and I were still standing there, I cleared my throat. "Earth to Reid," I said, waving my free hand up at him.

"Oh right, sorry. Come on in," he said, not even offering to take our coats or help with our bags. I heard Masen mutter "asshole" under his breath, so I lightly punched him in the shoulder as Reid closed the door behind us.

"Who was that?" Reid asked, still looking in the direction of the hallway where Alayna had disappeared.

"That would be my cousin, Alayna. She is also Maggie's bridesmaid," I told him.

"I heard my name," Alayna said, rounding the corner and walking toward us. "Are you talking about me?" she asked.

"Reid asked who you were," I said.

"Alayna this is Reid, Matt and Jase's younger brother. He also has a twin brother, Cole."

"Hi," Alayna said, picking up her bag, which was still on the floor at Reid's feet.

"Hhhhi," Reid stuttered. "Let me get that for you," he said, quickly helping my cousin with her bag.

"Thanks!" she replied.

Masen and I looked at each other and rolled our eyes.

"You're finally here!" Maggie shouted, coming over and hugging all of us. "Come on, I'll show you guys to your rooms," she said.

We followed her upstairs, and I couldn't help but feel like I'd been there before. It was an odd sensation.

I noticed Reid walking behind Alayna, still carrying her bag.

"Masen, you can stay in the office. There's a pull-out couch I made up for you," Maggie told him as we walked to the next room.

"Kenz and Alayna, you guys are staying in this spare room. It's a queen-sized bed. Hope you guys don't mind sharing," Maggie said.

"Nice. You guys are sleeping together," Reid said smiling, doubtlessly imagining some girl-on-girl action.

"They're cousins, Reid. Get your mind out of the gutter," Maggie said, shaking her head.

"Hey, a guy can dream, can't he?" Reid asked and winked at Alayna.

With that being said, Masen turned to go into his room, dropped his bag and coat on the floor, and headed downstairs. I think Masen could only take Reid in small doses. It was going to be an interesting weekend for sure.

"Why are you even up here, Reid?" Maggie questioned.

"I'm helping Alayna with her bag," he replied, shaking the bag for emphasis.

Maggie eyed him suspiciously. "Sure you are. I think we got it from here," she told Reid, grabbing Alayna's bag from him. "Why don't you see if Matt needs help with anything?" she suggested.

Reid realized that was his cue to leave. "It was nice meeting you Alayna," Reid said before walking back down the stairs.

"He's kind of cute," Alayna whispered as we watched him disappear down the stairs.

I didn't know what to think about her comment. I couldn't imagine the three of us hooking up with Hainsworth men. The holidays would surely be interesting.

Alayna and I were taking our coats off when Maggie closed the bedroom door and locked the three of us in the room. She grabbed both of our arms and walked us to the bed, making us sit down. She started to pace and I was immediately nervous, thinking it might have to do with Jase. I couldn't even bring myself to ask what was wrong.

Alayna looked at me, and then back at Maggie. "Ummm, Maggs, is everything okay?" she asked.

"There are a couple things I need to talk to you guys about," Maggie said, still pacing. "My future mother-in-law is freaking me out.

I can see this wedding getting out of control real quick if it's left up to her. I'm not sure how to handle the situation," Maggie told us.

I took a deep breath, relieved that the news wasn't about Jase. "No worries, Maggs. We'll help out with whatever you need because it's your day. Oh, and Matt's too. By any chance, did you talk to him about this?" I asked her.

"Yeah, and I think he's just as freaked out as I am," Maggie said, obviously worried.

"Seriously, it will be okay. Let's just get through the weekend," I said.

"You're right," she said, nodding her head in agreement. Maggie took a deep breath and shook out her arms and hands. She looked like a freak, but it was her way of dealing with stress.

Sensing the worst was over, Alayna and I stood to leave.

"Okay, so there's one other thing. Jase is looking for you," Maggie quickly blurted out.

Fuck.

I immediately sat back down. My head started to spin and I needed to get a grip. Maybe he wanted to talk to me about work and the account changes. I just needed to keep calm and all would be okay.

"Is she with him?" I asked, looking up at Maggie.

"Yup, the Cunt is here," she stated.

"This is your chance, Kenz. Don't fuck it up," Alayna said, poking my shoulder.

"Thanks for the vote of confidence. You should pray I don't smother you in your sleep tonight," I said, looking up at my cousin.

"Hey, I'm rooting for you. You're the one who finally realized that Jase is the guy that you want to be with. It only took you how long?" Alayna asked sarcastically.

"Shut up, Alayna," I told her as she laughed at me.

She bent down and looked me in the eyes. "Kenz, stop being a pussy and just talk to him. See where the conversation goes. Don't freak out until you have something to freak out about," Alayna said, trying her best to calm me down.

"We should probably head downstairs before somebody comes looking for us," Maggie said, grabbing my arm and pulling me up.

Maggie unlocked the door, and as I walked out of the spare room my stomach dropped, knowing that the next couple of days were going to be spent with or around Jase. Alayna was right—I had to stop being a pussy.

I followed Maggie and Alayna down the stairs into the kitchen and it was like déjà vu. That's when it hit me: Matt's house was set up just like Jase's. The foyer was different and so was the décor, but as I looked around, I saw that the floor plan was the same.

The memories of that night spent with Jase came rushing back to me. I remembered how my body had felt when he'd slammed me up against the wall and begun to kiss me. I remembered how he'd looked at me with want, and I wondered if he would ever look at me that way again. I tried to shake away the memories but they were right on the surface, and I wasn't sure if that was good or bad.

We rounded the corner and I saw everyone standing around talking. The downstairs had an open floor plan, and everyone was mingling between the kitchen and living room area. Maggie stopped us just inside the kitchen and introduced Alayna and me to everyone. I tried to make a mental note of names along with faces. We waved and said a general hello to the room.

I saw Maggie's mom talking with Jase's mom, Nancy. She must have felt my gaze and looked over to me. Her brow furrowed and her head tilted to one side, as if she were trying to match my face with a memory. I was sure if I'd had fewer clothes on and a just-fucked hairstyle, she could've picked me out of a lineup. I quickly turned my back before she could remember.

Maggie walked up with drinks for Alayna and me. I took mine happily, not knowing or caring what was in the cup. I took a long sip that made my throat—followed by my chest, then my stomach—instantly on fire.

"Holy shit, Maggs! What the fuck is this shit?" I asked in a raspy voice, trying not to choke on whatever it was that I had just ingested.

"Yum. I kind of like it," Alayna said.

I looked at my cousin like she was fucking crazy.

"I'm not sure. Reid and Cole are making them. I just told them to make us something strong," Maggie said.

I sipped my drink, which tasted like death, hoping it would take the edge off and not kill me in the process.

Alayna and I naturally gravitated toward Maggie's family, joining in their conversation. I kept an eye out for Jase, but he was nowhere to be seen and I didn't want to ask. I began to feel very warm and fuzzy from the drink, which was now empty. Reid the doorman/bartender filled up our cups and made small talk with Alayna. Reid seemed to be smitten with my cousin, and she was clearly enjoying the attention. They looked like they were hitting it off and I wasn't sure how I felt about that.

I was leaning against the couch, keeping an eye on Alayna and Reid just in case my cousin needed me.

Masen noticed me watching them and walked over. "Don't worry about her. She can handle him," he said.

I nodded in agreement. "I know she can, but I think I'm more worried that she actually likes him," I told Masen in a low voice.

He just shook his head. "Does she ever date anyone who isn't an asshole?" he asked me just as quietly.

I could only shrug my shoulders and roll my eyes.

"I'm going to get another drink. You want me to fill you up?" Masen asked, gesturing toward my cup.

"No. I'm good, thanks. I'm already feeling tipsy from whatever I've been drinking," I told him.

"Okay," Masen said as he turned and headed for the kitchen.

The hairs on my neck stood up and a chill ran through my body as I had a sudden feeling that I was being watched. What if this house was haunted? Shit. I scanned the room to see if anything weird was moving or floating. That's when I saw someone standing in the hallway, leaning against the wall, arms crossed. It took my eyes a few seconds to focus on the face, and even less time for my stomach to drop. It was Jase.

I wondered how long he had been standing there. He didn't walk toward me. He just stood there staring. My heartbeat began to race and I felt the need to be closer to him. I wouldn't fight the draw anymore. I began to walk toward Jase as he continued to stare. I was two feet away when I stopped, thinking it was a safe distance for us to talk.

"Hey. Maggie said you were looking for me?" I asked him, looking up through my long eyelashes.

When my eyes met his, I could have passed out from the intensity of his stare. I couldn't read him, and what I had hoped to see wasn't there.

My heart sank, and to make things worse, he didn't say anything. I was so confused and thought maybe talking to him had been a mistake. I started to back away, but couldn't help but hold his stare as I searched for a glimmer of hope.

Jase noticed me retreating and quickly grabbed my arm. "We need to talk," was all he said as he pulled me down the hall.

Jase opened a door and turned on the light. There were stairs that led down to what I assumed was the basement. He gestured for me to go first, which I did without question, and he followed me, closing the door.

Once at the bottom of the stairs, I looked around to see Matt's man cave—complete with a bar along the back wall, theater seating, and a huge TV opposite from the bar.

"Damn. Nice room," I said under my breath. I could feel Jase standing behind me, watching me.

He walked past me to the bar. For the first time, I actually took notice that he was dressed in work clothes. He had on charcoal gray dress pants with a navy blue shirt that had the sleeves rolled up to his elbows.

I watched as he grabbed a glass, some ice, and a half-empty bottle of whiskey and poured himself a drink. Then I watched as he drank it, never once asking me if I wanted one—or anything, for that matter. That kind of annoyed me. I was still wondering what he wanted to talk to me about. His silence and apparent shitty attitude left me quite confused.

"No thanks, I didn't want anything," I said sarcastically, crossing my arms.

This must have hit a nerve because he polished off what was left in the glass and slammed it down on the bar. I jumped, not expecting that from him. My body was trembling and I wasn't sure if it was due to the excitement or the uneasiness of the past ten minutes. His pale green eyes stared at me and I could see anger. Jase may have been pissed, but I'd had enough of his bullshit for one night.

Maybe his cunt of a girlfriend tolerated the silent treatment while he slammed shit around, but I surely didn't. Come to think of it, I hadn't seen the Cunt, and Maggie did say she was here. Trouble in paradise? Maybe. One can only hope.

"I don't need this," I said, throwing my hands up in surrender. "I think I'll go back upstairs where there's less bullshit."

I turned and started to walk away.

"Why did you switch accounts? Was it because of me?" Jase asked, stopping me in my tracks.

I wasn't ready for that question and didn't know how to answer. I took a deep breath to gather my thoughts before turning around to face him. "There was an opportunity for a change, so I took it. Did I do it because of you? Yes, I did. My boss noticed the difference in my work, and I can't afford to fuck up my career because of a one-night stand," I told him honestly.

That really pissed Jase off. He rounded the bar and walked right up to me. "Are you still trying to convince yourself that that's all it was? Just a fuck? Because if it was, you wouldn't have changed accounts," Jase said through gritted teeth. "I fucking called you but you never answered. Why?" he hissed, determined for answers.

I looked at him, ready to come clean. "I was afraid," I told him as calmly as I could.

"What does that mean? What the fuck were you afraid of?" he said a little too loudly.

I was starting to worry that someone upstairs might hear him.

My patience was running thin and I wished I'd taken Masen's offer of another drink. I sure could have used one right then, especially since this asshole didn't offer me one.

"I was afraid of what you might say," I spouted back at him, no longer calm. "I was afraid of hearing your voice and the way you said my name. I was afraid of the feelings I had for you," I hissed back at him.

Jase tore his eyes away from me and ran both his hands through his clean-cut hair. He walked over to the bar, reached for the same bottle, and poured himself another drink. He downed it in one gulp, still never offering me one. Fucking asshole. This shit was now officially old.

I'd given him the answers he wanted but now I was left more fucked up and confused. I decided I'd had enough. I walked up to him and grabbed the bottle of whatever the fuck he was drinking. "Are we fucking done here?" I asked him.

He didn't even move.

I took that as a yes and stormed up the stairs with the bottle in my hand, leaving him in the basement with his shitty attitude.

I could hear everyone still talking and laughing, but I was in no mood to join them. I walked down the hall and toward the stairs. I quickly hurried up to the spare bedroom I was sharing with Alayna and shut the door behind me. I needed to be alone. I sat on the bed crying and couldn't stop. I'd fucked it all up. I felt hopeless. The more I cried, the more I drank. Before I knew it I was passed out on the bed.

At one point I remember having a dream that felt so real. It was Jase, caressing my face, telling me how beautiful I was and how he wished he had a second chance. I wanted to tell him how sorry I was and how I felt about him, but I couldn't find the right words. It seemed my dreams were just as cruel as my reality. All I had left were my memories, and I wasn't sure I wanted them anymore.

Chapter 18 | Little Taste of Home

My stomach was on fire. I felt it churning and making god-awful sounds. Wherever I was, it was bright, even though my eyelids were closed. I was so tired and my eyes felt swollen from crying. Something didn't feel right. Suddenly I began to gag. I sat up immediately, covering my mouth with my hand.

"What the fuck is going on?" I heard Alayna ask.

I jumped off the bed, not knowing where I was. I saw a garbage pail next to the dresser and dashed toward it. I fell to my knees and began to heave.

"Holy shit, Kenz! Are you okay? Maggie!" Alayna shouted.

Masen opened the door, nearly hitting me. "What's going on? Jesus, what's wrong with her?" Masen asked, sounding barely awake.

"I don't know. She just woke up and started puking," Alayna replied with panic in her voice.

"Oh my god, get her in the bathroom." Maggie said, rushing into the spare bedroom.

Masen scooped me off of the floor between gags and carried me to the bathroom.

"Where's Mom?" Masen asked Maggie. "Mom and Dad got up early to have breakfast with Matt's parents," she said, frantic.

I realized where I was. I was at Matt's house. It was all coming back to me now. The mysterious drinks the twins had made. My conversation or lack thereof with Jase. The crying and finishing of the whiskey.

Ugh, the whiskey.

My stomach rolled at the thought and I began to gag again.

"Call Mom. Tell her to get back here right now. Tell her something is wrong with Kenzie," Masen ordered his sister.

"No. Don't call anyone. I'm not a fucking child. I'm fine," I told them all.

"You're far from fine, Kenzie," Masen told me.

I began to throw up again. "Leave me alone," I said between heaves as I hugged the toilet bowl. "I don't need a fucking audience. Please leave me alone," I told them.

I heard Alayna and Maggie talking in the hallway, and then my cousin walked back into the bathroom.

"What the fuck is this?" Alayna asked, holding up the empty bottle of whiskey. "Please tell me you didn't drink this whole fucking bottle, Kenzie. Because if you did, I'm taking you to the fucking hospital and I hope they pump your stomach dry," my cousin shouted.

"Ugh! Get that bottle away from me," I pleaded.

The thought of alcohol at the moment was far from appealing. I wanted—no, I *needed* the burning in my stomach to stop.

"Mckenzie Shaw, did you or did you not drink this whole fucking bottle?" Alayna insisted.

Was she my mother, using my whole name like that? My cousin was making me feel like I was five years old again.

"It wasn't full, so stop yelling at me," I pleaded with her again.

I heard Maggie on the phone with someone. I really hoped she wasn't calling her parents. Meanwhile Masen sat next to me, not saying a word. Knowing him, he was probably freaking out. He rubbed my back and held my hair while I continued to violently remove anything and everything in my stomach, which was mainly alcohol.

"Did you eat anything last night?" Maggie asked, petting me like a dog.

"No," was all I could get out before I began to throw up again.

"That's why she's so sick. She drank on an empty stomach. She's lucky she doesn't have alcohol poisoning," Maggie told them like I wasn't in the room, but I didn't care. I just wished they would let me puke in peace.

"Maybe she does have alcohol poisoning," Alayna said.

Someone started swirling my hair into a bun and I felt a clip hold in it in place. I knew it wasn't Masen. It had to be Alayna or Maggie. I had no energy to lift my head to check, and honestly, it was one more thing I didn't care about. I felt a cool, wet compress being draped on the back of my neck and it felt like heaven.

This went on for about an hour before I was done. Toward the end I was mainly dry heaving but I clung to the toilet bowl, refusing to move. I felt better just resting there. The porcelain was nice and cool and I was exhausted. Eventually Alayna and Maggie made me get up. I was still in my clothes from the day before, so they stripped me down to my bra and thong and got me in the shower. Unfortunately I had no energy to stand, so Masen had to get in the shower with me. He held me up while Alayna washed my hair.

I heard voices coming up the stairs.

"Is she okay?" I heard a man's voice ask.

I couldn't even ask who it was because Alayna was trying to brush my teeth and she was making me gag. The last thing I wanted was to start puking again. I could hear Maggie explaining, to whomever it was, that I'd started puking and that they had found an empty bottle of whiskey in the room. She wondered how much I had drunk and if the bottle had been full.

"It wasn't full," I heard another man's voice say.

"How do you know that?" I heard Maggie ask, and by her tone I was sure her hands were on her hips.

"Because I do," was all he said. I knew then that it was Jase.

Alayna must have thought I was clean and smelling much better, because she shut off the water and pulled back the shower curtain. I looked up and saw Maggie, Matt, and Jase standing in the bathroom doorway. They were staring as I stood there soaking wet and half-naked while Masen held me up. The look on Matt and Jase's faces were priceless. I wasn't sure if it was because I looked like death or because I was in a hot pink bra and thong. I couldn't help but laugh a little.

"You still look like death," Maggie said.

I didn't feel like talking so I gave her the finger. Maggie rolled her eyes and shook her head.

I looked at Jase and saw worry and anger written all over his face. His eyes were looking over my body but then his focus snapped to Masen.

Oh crap, not again. Why do I get myself in these predicaments?

"Are you guys going to fucking stand there all day, or can someone get her a fucking towel?" Alayna yelled.

Everyone started moving, but it was Jase who took charge. He grabbed a towel from the towel rack, walked up to the shower, and wrapped it around me while Masen still held me up. With one swift motion he scooped me up and carried me out of the bathroom. I laid my head on his shoulder and watched as everyone stood there, speechless as we walked past them.

Being so close to Jase, I recognized his smell, and it made me smile inside. I was exhausted and still felt like shit, but in Jase's arms, with the way he held me so close, it felt like home.

He carried me into the spare bedroom, gently laid me on the bed, and sat next to me. Everyone else followed us.

"Okay, everyone out. I want to get her dressed," Alayna ordered, and everyone did as she said—everyone except Jase, who didn't budge. He sat there rubbing my arm and looking over my face.

"That means you too," Alayna said to him.

He looked me in the eyes and ever so lightly brushed the side of my face with the back of his fingers. It sent chills down my spine. If I had been feeling better, I was sure my already wet panties would have been dripping.

"I'll be downstairs if you need anything," Jase said, looking at me.

Too tired to even answer, I gave him a weak nod.

Alayna walked next to the bed. "She needs rest. If you want to be helpful, why don't you make her some toast and get her some Aspirin or something," she said, keeping up with the orders. She was going to make a great mother someday. I could see her kids saluting me at family functions while they stood single file.

"Are you always this pushy?" Jase asked. His back was to me and I couldn't tell if he was being funny or serious.

Alayna, on the other hand, was very serious as she shifted her hips and crossed her arms. "Always. It's a family thing. We're also loud and opinionated. Is that a problem?" my cousin questioned.

"No. No problem here," Jase said, putting his hands up in surrender.

"Good," Alayna said while getting in Jase's face, arms still crossed. "Because I have a feeling that this mess has something to do with you. Just know this: you break her heart, I will fuck you up. Are we clear?" Alayna spat without one ounce of humor.

Jase didn't say a word. He walked out of the room and closed the door without looking back.

Alayna took a deep breath before she turned to me. "Sorry, but it had to be said," she told me.

"Don't apologize. I should be the one apologizing. I'm so sorry, Alayna. I feel so bad," I said, apologizing in a low voice.

"Don't worry about that right now. Let's get you changed," she said.

Alayna grabbed my pajamas out of my bag and helped me get dressed. Afterwards she tucked me back under the covers.

"You're lucky you had cute matching underwear on. I could only imagine what Jase thought when he saw you half-naked, looking like death with Masen in the shower," Alayna chuckled, trying to lighten the mood.

"Don't remind me," I said quietly, my throat sore from my puke marathon.

"There's never a dull moment when it comes to you and him, is there?" she asked, and I could only shake my head no.

About twenty minutes after I got dressed, Maggie brought up a tray with tea, water, two kinds of crackers, toast, half a corn muffin, apple slices without the skin, and most importantly, some aspirin. I guessed Jase had passed along Alayna's demands and they had given me everything they could think of that might make me feel better. I felt a little more human, so I ate enough to take some aspirin. I closed my eyes and eventually fell asleep.

Every so often I would hear someone checking on me, but I never opened my eyes. I just lay there because I was so tired, and honestly, I didn't want to talk to anyone. I knew Jase was one of the people who checked on me, because he was the only one that would caress my face or touch my lips with his rough fingers. It was like he was trying to remember what I felt like. I didn't mind. When he would leave, I would pray he would check on me again. I seriously had issues. After a while, everyone seemed to leave me alone when they realized I wasn't going to die.

Hours later I woke up to Alayna sitting on the bed reading a book, looking freshly showered, hair and makeup already done.

"Why hello, McPuky. How are you feeling?" she asked.

I slowly sat up and my stomach felt like I had done a thousand crunches. "I've had better days," I said weakly. I reached for a glass of water only to see it had been replaced by a can of ginger ale with a bottle of aspirin sitting next to it. I grabbed the can, opened it, and took a sip. The soda felt raw going down my throat. I grabbed the aspirin and shook out two pills.

"What time is it?" I asked Alayna.

"It's four o'clock in the afternoon. We were wondering when you'd wake up," she said.

"Where is everyone?" I asked. The house seemed quiet.

"Maggie and her parents just left to go to the Hainsworths' house to help set up. Maggie told everyone you weren't feeling well and that you wouldn't be coming to the party tonight," she said, filling me in.

"What? I'm going! I wouldn't miss her party," I told her.

"Good, because if you did I'd be pissed at you. Now let's get you ready. We can drive over with Masen, but first you need to eat something," she insisted.

Alayna helped me out of bed and down the stairs. The more I moved around, the better I felt.

Masen came downstairs looking freshly showered while I ate a peanut butter and jelly sandwich Alayna had made for me.

"The dead rises," Masen said, bumping me in the shoulder as he walked past me.

"Ha ha, very funny," I said, showing him the chewed-up food in my mouth.

"You're gross. Don't you think I saw enough of that shit for one day?" he said, clearly grossed out.

I wanted to laugh but my stomach muscles wouldn't allow it.

"Are you going tonight?" Masen asked. "Yes. I wouldn't miss it," I told him.

"You need to hurry up," Alayna jabbed.

I felt better but I wasn't sure I could pick up the pace like she wanted me to. I felt like this was a theme for me when I visited upstate: drink too much, end up hungover, and then rush to go somewhere or do something. You'd think I would have learned my lesson by now. There was no way I could eat any more of my sandwich, so I threw the rest away and headed upstairs.

"Don't leave without us, Masen," Alayna shouted to him.

"Yeah, yeah. Just hurry up," he shouted back.

I tried to hurry per my cousin's instructions. I took a quick shower then started to get ready. I blew out my hair and curled it to give it some life. Alayna did my makeup since she was done getting ready. She made me look like I had a healthy glow rather than looking so pale.

"Before we go, you want to talk about last night or this morning?" Alayna asked while blending my eye shadow.

"Nope," was all I said.

"Interesting. Did you talk to Jase last night?" Alayna pushed on with the questions like I knew she would.

"Yes," I replied. I also knew how she hated one-word answers.

"O-kay, and how did it go?" she asked.

"Okay," I said as I counted down in my head.

Three, two, one...

"Kenzie!" Alayna shouted at me. "Stop being an ass and spill," she said, losing patience. "

"There's nothing to say. Jase asked about work and I told him. He asked why I never answered his calls, and again, I told him. He clearly wasn't happy with what I had to say. Actually, he seemed mad even before we talked. Maybe he was just mad that I was there. Either way, we said some things. I left pissed off with his bottle of whiskey and woke up puking. End of story," I explained.

Alayna took a step back, looking over my face, making sure everything looked good. At least I hoped that was what she was doing. "I think I know why he was mad before you talked to him," Alayna said smiling, grabbing the mascara.

"Really? Did you hear something?" I asked, hopeful that I wasn't the whole reason he was so angry last night.

"Yes. I overheard his mother complaining to Matt that Jase had to bring his girlfriend back to his house because the country air was giving her a headache or some shit," Alayna said.

"Shut up! Seriously?" I questioned. Who gets a headache from fresh air?

Alayna sighed. "Yes, and Jase was pissed. That's why he was gone so long, because she was acting like a baby and didn't want to be by herself."

"Wow, I can't believe he would want to be with someone like that," I said, shocked, while Alayna applied mascara to my eyelashes.

"I know. I said the same thing to Reid. His family can't stand her, but she will be at the engagement party tonight," she said, a devilish grin spreading across her face, "soooo, I decided to drink red wine tonight. If at any point you feel the need for me to be clumsy, just say the word."

That really did sound tempting. Actually, it was fun just thinking that we might do it—even though I knew we wouldn't. We couldn't... could we? I heard an evil laugh echo in my head.

"You're all done," Alayna said, motioning for me to check myself in the mirror.

"We should have a code word," I said, playing along while looking over my face. Wow, I looked good. You wouldn't have known I had been puking my guts out twelve hours before.

"How about balls-deep?" Alayna said laughing.

"Are you kidding me? How the fuck would I work that into a conversation? I think you've been talking with Reid a little too much," I said, shaking my head.

"You have twenty minutes before we have to leave," Masen shouted from somewhere in the house.

"Okay," Alayna shouted back. "Look, you don't have to say the code word out loud. Just whisper it to me in passing," she said to me. Alayna was taking this very seriously—maybe a little *too* seriously.

"Fine, balls-deep it is," I said, caving to her request.

The two of us just laughed.

I was rummaging through my bag, pulling out my clothes. I had packed seven outfits—which I admit is a bit much, but I needed options.

I stared at the mess in front of me, then looked at my cousin. She looked so comfy wearing a gray wrap-style sweater dress with black riding boots. I wished I had more time. I laid my outfits on the bed and realized most of them were wrinkled.

"Fuck. I don't have time to iron something," I said, starting to freak out.

"Relax. We're going to an engagement party at a house in the boonies. You could wear a bag with a belt and you'd look hot. Just pick an outfit that doesn't require ironing," she told me. She did her best to calm me down, but honestly, I was exhausted and my anxiety was kicking in. I wasn't even sure how I was functioning, but I was determined to be there for Maggie.

I looked over my clothes and found the one outfit that didn't need to be ironed. I grabbed a watercolor floral V-neck camisole, black stretch-knit pants, and my collarless electric blue blazer. I quickly got dressed and slipped on my five-inch black seude platform heels. It was my least favorite outfit, but hot damn, I looked really good.

"Wow, I guess you really can polish a turd," Alayna said, cracking herself up.

"Thanks, asshole," I shot back.

"You're welcome. Now let's hurry before Masen freaks out on us," Alayna said, grabbing our clutches.

We walked down the stairs to see Masen waiting for us.

"Wow, you guys look amazing," he said, giving us the once-over.

"Thanks," I said back, looking into his beautiful blue eyes.

"I started the truck so it's not cold. Matt said his parents' house is less than ten minutes down the road and that we can't miss it," Masen told us as we put our coats on.

Bundled up, we filed out of the house. Masen stopped me, looked over my face, and said, "You truly are beautiful, Kenzie. Not just tonight, but always."

I was a little taken aback. I hadn't been expecting that, and wasn't too sure what to say. I smiled up at him and said, "Thank you."

He nodded in acknowledgement, returned my smile, and then closed the door behind us. The three of us got into his truck and off to the party we went.

I had a flurry of emotions swirling around my mind. I was excited to celebrate Maggie and Matt's engagement. Thankfully they had kept a lid on my whiskey-drinking adventure the night before. Everyone thought I had a stomach bug and that's why I couldn't come. Now that I felt almost human again, I was determined to make the party, with the added bonus of surprising my best friend.

Then there was the dread that I felt knowing I'd have to see Jase and his cunt of a girlfriend together. I didn't want to see him touching her, knowing that hours earlier he was holding me like I belonged to him and only him. His gentle touches were so familiar and comforting. My body cringed at the thought of never having that feeling again. I could only hope that he would open his eyes to the possibility of what could be.

Chapter 19 | Balls-Deep

Matt was right—there was no way anyone could miss his family's home. It was a few miles down the road from Matt's house and it was enormous. It had a big, ornate, lit-up sign that said "The Hainsworth Farm." Unlike Matt or Jase's homes that had a driveway hidden or lined with trees, this house was open for everyone to see.

The house was set a ways back from the road. There was up-lighting on the bare, dormant trees that dotted the front yard. The driveway was lined with lights that were slightly buried by the snow.

The house itself was enormous. It had huge windows that would be a Peeping Tom's dream. Maggie had told us that years before, Matt's parents had had two big additions added on to either side of the old farmhouse. She'd said the one addition was for a master bedroom, larger kitchen, and family room. The other one was a great room, and that's where tonight's party would be held. You could still see the original structure and it had the old farmhouse charm, even with the recent additions being so big. Somehow, it made the house more beautiful.

Masen parked the truck at the first open spot he saw. There must have been twenty to twenty-five cars and trucks parked on the side of the house. Out of all the vehicles, Jase's truck immediately stood out. I was instantly on edge and I could feel my nerves tingling throughout my body. I got out of the truck without saying a word. Masen and Alayna were talking amongst themselves, but I was too preoccupied with thoughts of Jase and the previous night's encounter to join in their conversation.

We walked up to the huge house and rang the doorbell. The door opened and I half-expected Reid to answer it, but instead it was Matt's mom, Nancy.

"Hello, come in from the cold," she said. "Here, let me take your coats."

We obliged, slipping them off and handing them over.

I couldn't help but look around at how grand the entrance was. "You have a beautiful home, Mrs. Hainsworth," I said.

"Thank you, but please, call me Nancy," she said, watching my face, seeming a little puzzled.

Shit. I should have kept my mouth shut.

"Forgive me, but ever since last night I feel like we've met before, and I never forget a face," Nancy said, still staring, wondering who I was.

Crap, now what do I say?

I heard footsteps behind me. I turned slightly to see Maggie.

"Oh my god, you came!" Maggie shrieked as she ran over and hugged me. "You were so sick I didn't think you'd make it," she said, ecstatic.

"I wouldn't miss this even on my death bed," I told her, hugging her back. Quietly I whispered, "I think your future mother-in-law is starting to recognize me."

Maggie released me and turned to Masen and Alayna. She quickly acknowledged them and ushered us into the great room before Nancy returned from putting our coats away. I heard my inner umpire scream "SAFE" in my head. It would be great if I could get through the rest of the weekend without Nancy figuring out where she remembered me from.

Maggie walked us into the great room, pushing open the double doors. The room looked like a page out of a magazine. No words could truly describe how picturesque it was.

The room was huge with a cathedral ceiling that had big wooden beams going across it, spanning the room. The far wall had an enormous cobblestone fireplace that looked like it had been plucked from a castle. Above the fireplace was a ten-point buck, mounted proudly. I looked up and saw a huge chandelier that was made of deer antlers, which added to the outdoorsy feel of the room. To our left was a bar that spanned the length of the entire wall and would put some taverns to shame. Despite all the conversations being had, I could hear a piano being played. Given the size of the room, I wouldn't have doubted that there was a baby grand somewhere nearby.

As I looked around, I noticed there were probably more than fifty people mingling, eating, and drinking.

"Wow," Alayna and I said in unison.

"It's beautiful, isn't it?" Maggie said, looking around.

"And why would you want to get married in a barn when I'm sure you could have your wedding here?" Alayna asked, clearly puzzled as she stood next to me.

Maggie linked my arm with hers. "Because Matt and I want simple and the barn is just that. We can make it whatever we want," she told Alayna. "Plus, being that it's a barn and not his parents' house, we'll have more control over it all," Maggie whispered to us, leaning in like a conspirator. "Come on. Let's join the party. Oh and Kenz, lay off the whiskey tonight, okay?" she said with a smile and a wink.

"Ugh, please don't remind me," I said, cringing at the thought.

The four of us started to walk into the crowd of people when I heard someone calling Maggie's name.

"Maggie dear," I heard again, stopping Maggie and me in our tracks while Masen and Alayna continued ahead of us.

Maggie and I turned to our right and saw Nancy descending a set of curved stairs. I looked up and saw that they led to the second floor of the original house, which looked over into the great room.

Holy shit, this is a nice place.

"Maggie, if you see Jase can you tell him I'm looking for him?" Nancy asked before her eyes landed on me with a smile and a slight tilt of her head.

Oh shit, she knows.

I didn't know what to do. I wanted to say "yes, I am the trash that slept with your son," but instead I gave a weak smile.

"Sure, will do Nancy," Maggie said politely as she quickly turned us in the opposite direction of her future mother-in-law. "Did you see that?" Maggie asked.

"I sure did. I think it's safe to say that she remembers who I am," I told her.

"It's never a dull moment, is it?" she asked.

"It never is," I said, agreeing with my best friend.

With our arms still linked like we were each other's lifeline, Maggie walked us through the crowd. There were a few servers passing out hors d'oeuvres and I grabbed some food as they passed. We stopped at the bar, where everyone our age was congregating. After the night before, the last place I wanted to be was anywhere near a bar. My eyes swept over all of the faces and one in particular looked at me and rolled her eyes. It was Jase's ex-wife, Luann.

Great, just what I need tonight. Not only do I have to be around Jase and his cunt of a girlfriend, plus his mother who I think figured out why she remembers me, but now I have to put up with his ex-wife who is currently giving me the evil eye.

I wondered if anyone else got themselves in fun situations like this.

I leaned against the bar, half-listening to the conversations, while my other half wondered where Jase was. I thought he would be there with everyone else but he wasn't.

"Can I get you anything?" I heard someone say. Then there was a light tap on my shoulder.

I turned and saw it was the bartender.

Again he asked, "Can I get you anything?"

"Water with lemon, please," I told him.

"Sure thing, ma'am," the bartender said with a smile.

I turned back around to see Jase walking toward us with Leah the Cunt hanging on his arm. She stood there like she was bored to death.

My world felt like it was going to come crashing down. I wanted to look away but I couldn't, and the sight of them together crushed me. Jase looked so handsome and carefree, wearing a white button-down with the sleeves rolled up and khaki pants. The Cunt's outfit totally contradicted Jase. I couldn't help but look her over, because I'm a female and that's what we do. I was appalled by what she was wearing to an engagement party. She wore a really short, coral-colored, strapless cocktail dress that was more appropriate for a Harrah's pool party than an engagement party… in the boonies… in the dead of winter.

I turned to the bartender, who had just put my drink on the bar. "I changed my mind. Can I get a shot of vodka and a Captain and Sprite?" I asked, knowing that it probably was a bad idea, but my inner jealous bitch said *fuck it*.

He nodded at me and began to make my drink.

"Can you get me a glass of red wine please?" I heard Alayna order behind me.

"Sure thing," he told her.

Alayna stepped up to the bar and put her arm around my shoulder. "Remember those two little words. Balls-deep," she whispered in my ear.

I couldn't help but smile. "How could one forget such important little words?" I told her, giving her arm a gentle squeeze.

The bartender had placed our drinks on the bar. I took the shot of vodka and threw it back, feeling it burn as it went down my raw throat. I grabbed our drinks and passed Alayna hers. We clinked our glasses, silently toasting to our premeditated shenanigans. The smiles on our faces were devilish.

"Is that such a good idea? Especially after this morning," a man's voice questioned.

I recognized it all too well without looking. Jase.

I took a sip of my drink and looked over at him, with no Cunt in sight. He watched me carefully. My heart skipped several beats while I stared into his pale green eyes. They looked different from how they had the night before. There was no anger or rage, only concern and question in them.

"As long as you don't give her any more whiskey, I think we'll all be fine," Alayna told him in a chastising tone.

He looked at Alayna and you could see how her words struck a chord with him. But he let it go, his eyes falling back on me.

"I heard you weren't coming to the party. I'm glad you're feeling better," he said sincerely. He gave me a quick once-over and smiled his sly smile. God, how I loved that smile.

My heart began to pound and I started to get tingly all over.

"You look beautiful, Kenzie," he said, not taking his eyes off of me. Of course the way he said my name totally put me over the edge. I had an instant puddle in my panties, because that's what this hot piece of ass did to me.

I should literally carry extra panties with me when I know I will be around him.

"Thank you. You're not so bad yourself. Although I'm not a fan of the clean-shaven look. I miss the day-old scruff you used to have," I confessed, reaching up to his face without even thinking.

When I realized what I was doing I pulled my hand back, but Jase grabbed it and put my hand to his cheek. His hand still felt rough, like I remembered. Ever so lightly, he rubbed his thumb over the back of my hand. It sent chills down my spine. With my hand on his cheek I felt the hours-old light stubble. My body was on fire, melting inside and out. Realizing where we were and who was around, I quickly pulled my hand from his.

Alayna was still standing beside me, frozen, watching the intimate exchange between Jase and me. Her eyes darted from me to Jase and back again.

"Well, that was somewhat awkward," I heard my cousin say under her breath, but I just ignored her.

Our eyes locked and Jase was about to say something when the fucking Cunt walked over interrupting him, yet again. This bitch had the worst timing ever. Can you say cock block?

"Jase, did you get my drink? Oh and your brothers are being mean to me again," Leah the Cunt said, pouting. Maybe she should have taken a fucking hint and realized that no one liked her.

Leah noticed that Jase was talking to someone and looked over at Alayna and me. She must have recognized me from Jase's office.

Note to self, change up appearance when I get home so I'm not so recognizable.

"Kelsie, right? We met at Jase's work," she asked, pointing at me.

Doesn't she know it's not nice to point? I think I learned that when I was two years old.

I could feel my anger building. I prayed I could keep it in check. I felt my ankle being kicked and I knew it was Alayna, just waiting for her cue.

I looked at the Cunt's finger, still pointing at me, before looking up at its owner. "It's Kenzie, and yes, we met before," I said, trying my hardest to be nice. I glanced over at Jase to see him looking distant. He didn't say a word. The look in his eyes pained me. They looked unreadable and he seemed so conflicted.

"Oh right. It was short for something," she said. Then she completely lost interest in our exchange and looked at Jase, who was still standing in front of me. "Did you get my drink or do I have to order one for myself?" she whined, sounding as spoiled as ever.

I couldn't believe what I was seeing. This bitch was acting like a fucking baby. I loathed this chick and I barely knew her.

I felt Alayna kick me again, a little harder this time. I looked at her and flashed a tight smile. She winked at me.

"What did you want to drink? I'll tell the bartender," Alayna asked Leah the Cunt. What was she doing? Why would she do anything for this bitch?

"Really? Well aren't you sweet. I'll take a glass of merlot," the Cunt said, smiling as if Alayna had made her year.

I held my drink in both my hands, afraid that if I had a free hand I might choke the Cunt.

"The sweetest," Alayna said, agreeing with her. "One merlot coming up," she said with an exaggerated smile.

My cousin ordered Leah the Cunt's drink, and when she looked at me I mouthed *balls-deep*.

The bartender poured it and handed Alayna the glass. From that point on, everything that happened felt like slow motion. Alayna took a step toward her, reaching across me to make her move. Leah, with a big smile, was reaching out to take the glass when I grabbed it from Alayna. She looked surprised.

"Here, let me get it for you," I said, hoping devil horns weren't popping out of my skull. Just then Reid walked up behind Alayna, startling her, causing her to bump me.

What happened next was flawless. I exaggerated the handoff, purposely tipping the glass of wine on the Cunt's outstretched hand. Her smile turned into a pained "oh" face and my smile was something that probably mirrored the Joker. The wine spilled all over her arm and the front of her coral-colored dress.

Bravo, I shouted in my head. *Brav-fucking-o*. I wanted to clap, but instead my hand flew to my face, covering my smile. This was pure enjoyment. I was going to mark this day on my calendar. Today is officially Balls-Deep Day. "Oh my god, you fucking asshole!" Leah the Cunt shouted at me as she stood there, not sure what to do next. She stared at me like I was pure evil, and I was loving it.

Jase was shocked, and I wasn't sure if it was due to the supposed accident or the fact that she had loudly announced that I was a fucking asshole in his parents' house, in front of all their guests. The once-loud room seemed to get quiet as I was truly trying to hold back a laugh.

"Don't just stand there, get me something," Leah the Cunt demanded, still staring at me.

Jase was still frozen, as was everyone else. This was actually fun to watch. I saw Maggie and Matt walking through the crowd, heading toward us with Nancy in tow. Oh, great.

"Hello, earth to Kelly," Leah said, waving her hands in front of me and calling me by the wrong name yet again.

It was so entertaining to watch that I couldn't even get mad at her for fucking up my name a second time in the matter of five minutes.

"Are you going to get me a towel or just stand there?" she said, shouting at me again.

I glanced over at Alayna, who looked like she was ready to whoop ass at any given moment. "Neither," I said to Leah. "I'm a fucking asshole, remember? Get your own fucking towel," I said quietly and calmly, so not too many people could hear, and then walked away.

As I walked away, I heard a mix of shouting and hushed voices. Leah the Cunt was complaining to Jase while he tried to tell her it was an accident and that she was wrong for yelling at me. I also heard Reid telling them it was his fault because he'd bumped into Alayna, who bumped into me. I thought it was sweet of Reid, trying to take the blame, but I was good with owning this one. Someone grabbed my hand as I pushed through the now-growing crowd of people. I looked back and saw it was Alayna. She had a wicked smile on her face and I couldn't help but smile back at her. Maggie, Matt, and Nancy stopped us in the crowd. Nancy didn't seem pleased.

"What's going on? Who was shouting?" Nancy demanded, visibly pissed off.

Alayna stepped in front of me and said, "Leah is shouting. She got wine spilled on her."

"What? How did that happen?" Nancy asked.

I was sure heads where going to roll for this one.

Maggie eyed me suspiciously, like she knew I'd had a part in it. "I was handing Leah her glass of wine when Reid bumped into Alayna, who bumped into me, and I accidently spilled the glass all over her," I confessed to them.

"It's a good thing you have hardwood floors and not carpet," Alayna added.

I saw a small smile creep across Matt's face, and Maggie covered her mouth but I knew she was smiling.

"Then she freaked out on Kenzie, calling her a fucking asshole in front of everyone, and demanded that she get her a towel like she was her personal servant," she said.

"Then what happened?" Nancy asked, very stone-faced.

"I told her to get her own fucking towel and walked away," I said nonchalantly, shrugging my shoulders.

Maggie and Matt started to laugh.

Nancy began to smile. "Good. I hate that dress she's wearing. Who wears such things?" Nancy questioned. "I better go check on her and then see what needs to be cleaned up," Nancy said as she walked away.

"I'll help," Matt said, following Nancy.

I couldn't believe my ears. Everyone really hated her, and it seemed like I had just scored points. Bonus!

"Balls-deep, huh?" Maggie said in a low voice.

I looked at my cousin, who had clearly spilled the beans. "What? Maggie and I were talking about Jase's girlfriend last night while you were passed out, and I told her about the plan and that's when I came up with the code word," Alayna said, smiling proudly.

Maggie shook her head. "I didn't think you two would actually do it! But since you have, I wish I could have seen her face," Maggie said.

"It was priceless," I said, recalling the last few minutes in my mind. I smiled, just as proudly as Alayna.

"I should probably go check on things as well. We'll talk later," Maggie told us before walking away.

We spotted two leather barrel chairs on a bearskin rug, which happened to be next to a baby grand piano. There was a man playing, so Alayna and I sat in the chairs listening, steering clear of the chaos we had created.

"We're going to hell, aren't we?" Alayna asked, looking at me.

"Probably, but it was worth it just to see that look on her face," I said happily.

"You're so bad, Kelsie—or is it Kelly?" she joked.

We both laughed until our eyes teared up. We blotted them, and after several minutes got our laugher under control.

The mood and conversations in the room started to continue where they had left off. Things seemed to return to normal, and you wouldn't have known there had been drama ten minutes prior.

"There you two are. Remind me never to have you hand me a drink," Masen said.

"Hey, accidents happen," Alayna said, pointing at Masen and then looking at me. We broke into hysterics all over again.

Masen looked quite puzzled, as if he'd missed the joke.

Reid, Cole, and their cousins Amy and Casey came over and joined us.

"I feel bad that I caused this whole thing and that you got the brunt of it from Leah, but it couldn't have happened to a better person," Reid said to me, smiling.

"Where is she?" Alayna asked. I was glad that she did, because I was wondering myself. And I knew that wherever she was, Jase was probably with her.

"Jase was taking her back to his house to get cleaned up. My mom wasn't too happy about her outburst and she let them both know it," Reid said, laughing.

"I'm sure it will be a while before Jase hears the end of it from Mom," Cole said.

"Yeah, just like when she found Kenzie naked in Jase's kitchen," Reid blurted out. "Mom was so pissed and wouldn't talk to him for weeks," he added.

Things suddenly got really quiet and awkward. I wanted to crawl under the bearskin rug and hide.

Out of nowhere, a hand came up and smacked Reid in the back of the head.

"Ouch, Amy! What the fuck?" Reid said, annoyed.

"You don't blurt things out like that, Reid. What's wrong with you?" Amy yelled at him.

I had always liked Amy, and I did even more so now.

"You slept with Jase?" Masen asked, shocked by the revelation.

Fuck. My. Life.

"See, this is why you keep your mouth shut," Amy said to Reid.

"Dun-dun-*duuun!* And the plot thickens," Reid said to Masen. He was clearly trying to get under Masen's skin, and by the look on Masen's face, it was working.

"If you only knew..." Reid began to say before I cut him off.

"Enough, Reid!" I said through gritted teeth. "For the record, I wasn't naked. I had a shirt on," I told them, defending myself. I stood and grabbed Masen's arm. "Can I talk to you, please?" I asked, pulling him away from Reid's big mouth, but not before shooting Reid a nasty look.

There were a few couples slow dancing. I pulled Masen next to them and made him take the lead. As we swayed back and forth I gave him the quickest rundown of my history with Jase. Masen seemed a little taken aback, and I hoped he didn't think any less of me.

I explained how I had viewed what happened between Jase and me as a mistake, but now I'd realized that it wasn't.

"I would be lying if I said I wasn't a little pissed, Kenz," Masen said, frowning. "I think somewhere deep down I thought you and I would get back together. Like you were my last resort," he said with a weak smile.

"Wow, Rowe, that's probably the shittiest thing you've ever said to me," I told him, annoyed as I tried to pull away from his arms.

"Kidding, Kenz, kidding. Well, maybe just a little," he confessed. "It's just we get along so well. We have history and we never really get seriously involved with anyone. I figured if we didn't meet someone in the next five to ten years, maybe we could give us a second chance. Plus, I don't mind when you snore. I think it sounds cute," he said with a smile.

This was the most perplexing thing I had ever heard. I looked at his face and could tell he was serious.

"It must be nice to live in La-la-land," I told him, annoyed. "I wouldn't give us another chance just because it would be convenient or a last resort. I love you, Masen, but not in that way—not anymore. I hope you understand," I said, pulling away from him.

I had begun to walk away when I heard Masen calling after me. I didn't turn around. I just kept on walking. I needed a couple of minutes to myself. I went to the nearest bathroom, but someone was in there. Then it hit me: I had to pee. I left the party in search of a bathroom. I asked one of the servers who was walking into the party. She pointed me in the direction of one, so I hurried down the hall and made a right like she had instructed. I found the door and grabbed the handle but it was locked. I knocked, only to be told by the person inside that it might be a while. Fucking great! The more I thought about finding a bathroom in this huge house, the more I felt like I had to pee.

I backtracked my steps and almost walked right into Matt's mom. "Excuse me, Nancy, can you tell me where a bathroom is? The two down here are occupied," I said.

"There's one in the kitchen but it's not flushing right. You can use the one at the top of the stairs," she told me.

"Great, thanks," I said to her, trying not to act like a four-year-old doing the pee-pee dance.

"Oh, and Kenzie...," Nancy said, her words holding me in my place. "I knew I remembered you from somewhere. It took me a little while to figure it out, but every time I've seen you recently you've had clothes on. Or should I say more clothes than the first time we crossed paths," she said, not amused. "For what it's worth, I'm sorry for how I treated you that morning. It was my son's house and I had no right to talk to you that way. For that I'm sorry," she told me.

I was shocked and wasn't expecting that from her. Maybe I did score points when I'd spilled wine on the Cunt. "Apology accepted," I said to her.

Nancy only smiled and nodded, then walked away. I had to pee so badly, I ran up the steps taking two at a time in my five-inch heels. I reached the top and prayed that the first open door was a bathroom.

Hallelujah! I quickly shut the door and took care of business.

After I washed my hands, I leaned against the counter, thinking of how I could win back Jase. That was if he wanted me. I wasn't even sure I would see him again tonight after what happened. Maybe I should have considered that before spilling wine on his girlfriend.

I was wrapping up my thoughts when I heard a knock at the door. "I'll be right out," I yelled.

I checked my face in the mirror and applied some lips gloss. I opened the door to see Jase leaning against the wall, looking over at me. "It's funny how we keep meeting like this. You know—you, me, and bathrooms," he said, smiling that sly smile of his. He seemed different from before, more at ease. I wondered where Leah was and hoped that was the reason for the change.

"Except this morning I looked like death," I pointed out.

"This is true," he agreed.

Jase pushed off the wall and I noticed he had my coat in his hands. "I need you to take a ride with me," he said, handing it to me.

I must have looked confused, but he gave me nothing.

"Where are we going?" I asked.

"It's a surprise," he said, helping me into my coat.

"A surprise?" I questioned. The last time he had surprised me with a picnic in the back of his truck. I clung to the memories of that night.

"Just trust me," he said, reaching out his hand for me to take it, so I did.

Chapter 20 | Taking a Chance

Jase and I slipped out of his parents' house through the garage. I prayed no one would look for me. I had so many questions for him, but wasn't sure I wanted the answers to them just yet.

We walked over to his truck. He opened the door and took my hand, helping me get in. His brief touch along with sneaking away had my heart pounding in my chest. We paused at the déjà vu moment to look at one another, both with questions in both our eyes. I wanted him to reach out and touch me like he had in the past, but he didn't. Jase was the first to break our gaze before shutting the door.

I wasn't sure what was going on or where we were going, but it seemed we were both on edge. Being so close to him made my body hum. I would be lying if I said I wasn't excited about the surprise. All kinds of thoughts, dirty and clean, ran through my mind. Mainly dirty, though.

Jase pulled out of the driveway onto the road. I felt my phone vibrate in my clutch. I pulled it out and saw a text message from Masen. I swiped it open and read,

> I hope you know what you're doing. Remember he has a girl-friend.

I think it was safe to say that Masen had seen me leave with Jase. After reading his text, I wondered what I was doing but I knew it was a chance I had to take.

Yes, I knew he had a girlfriend—hell, I'd just spilled wine on the bitch not too long ago—but I also knew I needed time alone with Jase. I didn't know what would happen and I wasn't even sure what I wanted to happen. Totally lying about the second part. The fact of the matter was that he was with the Cunt. I didn't want to be that girl who tried to steal someone else's man, but I needed to see if there was still something there between us—something worth fighting for.

Rather than text Masen back, I put my phone away, ignoring him. I wasn't trying to be mean, but I surely didn't need a reminder of the obvious. Plus, I thought it was best given the one-sided pact he'd made about us.

We weren't more than five minutes from his parents' home when Jase turned off the road into a field. If there was a road there, I couldn't see it. I could only see the snow being lit by the headlights of his truck as we drove slowly. I looked over at him. He was focused on the path ahead.

"Jase, where are we going?" I asked him.

"Maggie asked me to take you to the barn. She said you needed a visual for decorating it for the wedding," he told me.

I hoped he was going to tell me he was whisking me away from everyone to have me all to himself, but I was sadly disappointed. I couldn't help but frown a little. He was doing this for Maggie, not for me. On the bright side, it was still just us, and if this was the only chance I had then I needed to make the most out of it. I made a mental note to thank Maggie later.

The truck began to slow and I saw a building coming into view, lit up by the truck's headlights. Jase parked about twenty feet from the big barn, turning the truck off but leaving the lights on, illuminating a snowy path. With it being so dark, it was hard to see anything but what was right in front of us.

"Wait in the truck while I go open it up," Jase said as he exited his truck. I did what I was told and watched him traipse through the snow-covered ground.

Then it dawned on me: how the fuck was I going to walk to the barn? No way was I ruining my heels. As I pondered my dilemma, Jase unlocked the barn, turned on a light inside, and then walked back toward the truck. He walked over to my side and opened the door.

"Come on, I'll help you down," he said, extending his hand.

"Ummm, I'm not really wearing the best footwear for this," I told him, showing him my heels.

178

He looked down at my shoes and shook his head. "Okay, I'll have to carry you then," he told me.

My heart skipped a beat and my inner whore screamed with excitement. I was more than thrilled to be back in his arms. Jase scooped me up from the seat and pushed the door closed with his back.

It was just him and me in the dark winter night. It could have been twenty below outside and I don't think I would have noticed. My body was on fire, my heart was pounding, and I wondered if he could hear it. Our faces were so close. It wasn't hard to see him looking at me, taking notice of my slightly parted lips. I couldn't help but watch him back. Being in his arms felt so right as he held me.

"Shall we?" Jase said, breaking the moment we'd shared.

I nodded my head as he walked toward the barn.

The winter night was so quiet you could only hear the crunching of snow underfoot. Once we reached the newly built barn, he set me down inside. I looked around at how big and empty it was, except for a dirt-covered green tractor. Maggie and Matt could easily have at least a hundred people inside.

I walked around, thinking of all the possibilities. I was sure Pinterest would be my best friend over the next couple of months.

"My parents plan on moving everything from the old barn to here this spring, then tearing down the old one. That's why it's so empty," he told me.

"Do you think your parents would let us do whatever we want to the barn? Decorating-wise, I mean," I asked him.

"I don't see why not. At the end of the day it's going to end up housing the farming equipment," Jase explained.

I could totally see a wedding in there, and it would look great.

I started to make a mental checklist of lights, tulle, white fabric, research port-a-potties, and table and chair rentals. Oh, and I couldn't forget the dance floor and bar.

"Can I take a couple pictures?" I asked Jase.

"Sure, go ahead," he told me, leaning against the big tire of the tractor. I pulled out my phone and saw I had a text message from Maggie. I swiped it open and read it,

You're welcome ☺

That little shit had set me up. God, I loved her.

"What are you smiling at?" Jase asked.

"Oh, nothing," I quickly retorted.

I backed out of the message on my phone and pressed the camera icon. I took a couple pictures of the barn to reference later on.

"You think you can make this presentable for a wedding?" Jase questioned.

"Yup. This is my niche," I told him. "I love to decorate. I'll need help, of course," I added.

I walked over to Jase, who was still leaning against the tire.

"I'll help with whatever you need," he said, looking at me with a small smile. Oh, if he only knew what I needed from him. The list could go on for days.

Focus, Kenz. Reel yourself in.

I put my phone away and thought maybe I should make some small talk. "Hey, I'm sorry about spilling the wine on Leah," I said, lying through my teeth while fidgeting with my clutch. I was a terrible liar.

"Are you?" he asked, pushing off the tire to stand right in front of me.

My heart began to pound and I felt like I was being put on the spot. "Of course I am," I said, still lying terribly.

I couldn't look at him any longer, so I focused on the strap of my clutch. Jase's hand came up and gently lifted my chin so our eyes met. I peered at him through my long lashes.

"Are you?" he questioned again, but this time he had a sly smile on his face.

"No," I said, barely audible.

"You don't like her?" Jase asked, still holding my chin.

"Not particularly, but that seems to be the theme with her, from what I hear," I said honestly.

The smile left his face and as his hand left my chin.

Shit. Can you say "foot in mouth"?

"We should get back to the party," Jase said. He began to walk toward the barn doors.

I chased after, reaching him just as he turned the light off.

It felt like the stage was set. The barn was partially lit by the headlights, casting a soft spotlight on us through the doors.

"Why are you with her?" I questioned.

Jase stopped walking, his back to me, and looked up at the ceiling. "Why do you care?" he asked, sounding frustrated by the question.

It seemed safe to say I wasn't the first person to ask him that question.

"Because I need to know, Jase," I said, stepping to the side of him so I could see his face.

"Why, Kenzie? Why do you need to know? You don't give a shit. Remember, you *had* feelings for me. Isn't that what you said the other night?" he said, annoyed, but kept his tone even.

Did I tell him that? I tried replaying our conversation in my head.

"I don't have time for your bullshit games. This weekend is about my brother and your best friend. Let's leave it at that," he said as he began to walk out, but I grabbed his arm.

"No, wait. Please listen to me. If that's what I said, that's not what I meant. We were both pissed off when we talked. Maybe it came out wrong," I said, trying to salvage the situation.

Jase shook off my arm and ran both his hands through his hair.

"I never stopped having feelings—" I told him before he cut me off.

"You want to know why I'm with Leah? Because I can fucking count on her," he said, getting very close to my face, which made me take a step back. "I didn't want some country girl again. I wanted different. I wanted more. I wanted you, but you didn't want me, remember?" he said.

I took another step back from his ranting. The glow on his face from the headlights made him look so angry. And it made me so sad.

"She may be whiny, demanding, and spoiled, but she's there, and she wants to be there, with me. That's more than I can say about you," Jase shouted at me. His words were honest and true as they stung my sinking heart. I had lost. I'd fucked up royally. *Where do I go from here? Do I just exist without him?* It would be torturous, but what choice did I have?

I must have snapped, or something in my brain must have shut off. One minute I was standing there shocked, dying inside from his words. Then without conscious thought I slammed my body into his, rocking him back against the doorjamb. I took his face in my hands and kissed him as fiercely as I could. I put all I had from my dying soul into that kiss. Maybe it was a kiss goodbye or maybe it was my white flag, surrendering myself to him, in a last-ditch effort.

At first he was tense and unsure, but then he relaxed and I felt his arms come up to embrace me, holding me to him. His mouth parted as our tongues danced together once again. The electricity from our touch was real, and I swear our hearts were pounding in sync. In that moment we were so right for each other, but I knew it was the end.

I pulled away from our embrace, not bothering to look at him. I couldn't look at him even if I had wanted to. I walked out of the barn through the snow, not caring about my shoes or feet. I opened the door to the truck, climbed in, and pulled it shut.

I stared out the passenger window thinking about how the universe continually fucked me over. That old homeless man didn't know shit. It took a couple of minutes before Jase appeared from the barn and after he locked it up. A part of me wondered why he had taken so long, but then the other part of me remembered my loss and that I shouldn't care. Our drive back to the house was quiet. Neither of us spoke. In my mind I drew a line in the sand, leaving my past with Jase behind me in that barn.

We pulled into the driveway at Jase's parents' house. As soon as Jase put the truck in park, my door was open and I quickly got out. I didn't run to the house, but I didn't take my time. I needed to put distance between us and I needed Maggie and Alayna.

With wet feet and probably fucked-up heels, I headed into the house through the garage. I took off my coat and threw it on a chair in the hallway as I made my way to the party. The closer I got to the party I noticed that the piano, which was being played before we left, had been replaced with guitars and maybe a banjo. As I moved through the crowd, I noticed that the atmosphere had changed. It was clearly louder, people were clapping, and some were line dancing. It was like I'd walked into a fucking hoedown.

I moved through the crowd in search of my lifelines. Maggie spotted me first and waved me over with a big smile on her face, and I knew why. I was sure she thought that giving me the opportunity to be alone with Jase would work in my favor. Not so much.

Alayna was right beside her, with Reid's arm draped around her shoulders. I couldn't help but feel a teensy bit jealous. Fuck it, I was a lot jealous, okay? Why was it so easy for everyone else? Where was my happy ending?

When I reached them, Maggie knew something was up. "What happened? Did it go well?" Maggie asked, excited about her sneaky setup.

I thought of Jase's words and forced a smile on my face. "Everything is fine. Tonight is about you and Matt, not about Jase and me. We'll talk about it another time, okay?" I said.

"Oh, okay. Are you sure?" Maggie asked, puzzled by my lack of details. Her eyebrows were scrunched together and I was sure she knew something was up.

"Yes, I'm sure," I said, reassuring her. "And thank you for having Jase show me the barn. We'll have our work cut out for us, but we're going to make that place look amazing," I told her, trying to change the subject.

She smiled at me with excitement. "Thanks, Kenzie," Maggie said, pulling me in for a hug.

I glanced over at Alayna, who gave me a sad smile. She must have known I was with Jase, and I was sure she could tell it hadn't gone well. She did the only thing she could do and handed me her drink. I gave her a weak smile as Maggie and I pulled away from each other. I secretly toasted myself to the end of this cruel joke called my love life and threw back the drink in one gulp.

The rest of the night went off without a hitch. It was great to see Maggie and Matt so happy, celebrating their engagement with family and friends. Jase kept his distance and I tried not to look for him. Key word being *tried*. The Cunt never reappeared, which was a blessing. I surely didn't need to see the girl who was "there" for him.

Before I knew it the party was over and we were back in Masen's truck, heading back to Matt's house. Maggie, Masen, and Alayna were drunk, and since I barely drank I was declared the designated driver. Thank god we were only five minutes from Matt's house, because the three of them were so annoying. Maggie stole a platter of cookies as we were leaving—yes, stole from her soon-to-be in-laws. They were eating the cookies while I was driving. It was like three Cookie Monsters, and crumbs were flying all over the place. No doubt Masen would have a shit fit the next day. I didn't say a word because I had other things on my mind—plus you can't argue with drunk people.

Once we got to Matt's house, the drunken trio staggered up the stairs and everyone got ready for bed. Maggie decided to crash with Alayna and me. Three people in a queen-sized bed was not ideal, but we made it work. Alayna and Maggie quickly fell asleep while I lay there with thoughts of Jase in my head. As much as I tried, I couldn't fall asleep. I tried to think of other things, but my thoughts always came back to him. Before I knew it the sun was shining through the windows.

Once everyone got up, we packed, said our goodbyes, and headed home. Since I hadn't slept, I decided to ride in the back and let Alayna sit in the front. There was also the fact that I didn't want to talk to Masen, just in case he asked me about sneaking out with Jase. Honestly, I just wanted to be by myself and hopefully get some sleep. I didn't want to talk about his harsh but truthful words, and I was grateful no one asked.

Once Masen pulled out onto the road, I lay across the back seat—but not before brushing off the cookie crumbs. I closed my eyes and hoped for a dreamless slumber. I couldn't help but think about what I had learned over the weekend. Something that I never knew was possible: a person's heart could be broken into a million pieces. I knew this because that's how mine was right then. My question was, could it ever be put back together?

Chapter 21 | Acceptance

After we came home from our weekend upstate, I locked myself in my room for two days. I had every intention of going to work, but once my alarm went off I ignored it. I couldn't bring myself to physically get out of bed. Then I would text Ben to tell him I was sick and couldn't make it in. Was I sick? No. Well, maybe lovesick, which sounded pretty pathetic. Either way, I didn't want to face the world or work.

That was until Maggie and Alayna pried my bedroom door open with a butter knife. Yes, pried. Those bitches were lucky they didn't break the door. If bothering me wasn't enough, they proceeded to dump a pot of ice-cold water over me in my own bed. I was furious and soaked. There was a lot of yelling back and forth. They wanted to know what was wrong, but I refused to tell them. I didn't want to relive that night in the barn. I wanted to forget about it, but that seemed to be an impossible task. The memory was always there, his words echoing in the back of my mind. I swore to Maggie and Alayna that I was fine, but again, lying isn't exactly my strongest attribute.

I forced my cold, wet self out of bed and stormed downstairs to the bathroom to take a hot shower. Once I was done, I went back to my room and saw Maggie and Alayna dusting, changing my sheets, and picking up my dirty laundry from the floor. Deep down inside I appreciated what they were doing for me, but it was too much and I needed my space. I ignored them both as I got dressed, and thankfully they didn't ask me anything else.

I left the house but didn't go far. I took a ride to the nearest park and just sat in my car and stared out the windshield. I told myself from that point on I needed to make an effort for everyone else so they wouldn't worry.

So that's what I did.

Three months later, I was making progress. At least that's what I was telling myself. Although I think it was the denial talking. Maggie and Alayna didn't worry about me as much, so I guess they saw me making progress too. I couldn't lie—my heart still hurt. Every day, thoughts of Jase would pop into my mind and I would have to hold myself until the pain in my chest subsided. I guess it was true what they say: in time things do get better, and I did feel like my heart was slowly piecing itself back together. It was a painfully slow progress, and I figured by the time I was forty-seven years old it would be whole again.

Dramatic much, you ask? *Yup!*

I kept myself busy by helping Maggie and Matt plan their wedding. It wasn't easy. Being broken-hearted over a guy you lost to some cunt sucked enough, but then planning a wedding for his brother who was marrying your best friend sucked even more. Don't forget, Jase was the best man and I was the maid of honor, so that meant we had to walk arm in arm and dance together. How did I end up in these situations?

Thankfully, I worked with Matt a lot on the planning for the barn and it seemed to help the strained relationship we'd once had. I could now say I really liked Matt, and was really glad he was marrying my best friend. Maggie must have told him something had happened, because he would always ask how I was but would never mention Jase's name, ever.

The new and improved relationship that we shared also helped when Maggie and Matt sat me down to ask about living arrangements. Maggie wasn't willing to move back upstate, which was something that Matt had known when they got back together. She was set to take over the veterinary clinic she had been working at in less than two years. This was her dream.

Knowing this, Matt worked it out with his parents to split his time between the farm and Maggie. He would spend three or four days at the farm and the rest in Jersey. Being that he was splitting his time between two states, he didn't want Maggie to move just because they were getting married. Naturally, their question to me was would I mind if Matt lived with us when he was in town.

I didn't hesitate to answer. I told them I didn't mind and even suggested that they take one of the other spare rooms and make an office for themselves. Strange how things come full circle with relationships. Matt was at my house most of the time when he was in Jersey and if he wasn't I assumed he was at Jase's, but like I said, we were on better terms so I didn't mind.

Life was looking up. I just needed to get past the wedding and then all would be good, I hoped.

Masen and I were better too. Not that we hadn't been talking, but things were little awkward after that weekend upstate. We had a long talk and we both agreed that we were better as friends. He actually met some girl and had been seeing her quite often. That was pretty serious for Masen, and I was happy for him. But it was just one more person in my life that was moving forward while I felt stuck.

Even Alayna and Reid were still talking. Apparently he came down to stay with Jase a couple of times and they met up for dinner. The first time he came down, he'd asked Alayna if she wanted to go on a double date with Jase and the Cunt. Alayna told him she would rather stick a hot needle in her eye than spend an evening with them. She also told him if he ever wanted to see her again, he would refrain from asking such a question in the future. When my cousin told me, I laughed so hard. He never asked about double dating again.

I was very lucky to have such caring people in my life—although it seemed like they thought I was going to snap at any moment. It felt like they were tiptoeing around me at times, but I wasn't sure why. Then one day I found out the reason.

I came home from work early one night and saw that Matt and Maggie's cars were in front of the house. I was happy because I needed to go over some last-minute details since their wedding was in three weeks.

When I walked through the door I was welcomed by Susi. She was always the first to greet me when I got home. She rubbed against my leg, purring like she usually did. I gave her a quick scratch on the head before putting my stuff down in the living room. I stopped in my tracks when I heard loud voices that were borderline-shouting coming from Maggie and Matt's bedroom.

I didn't want to be nosy, but their voices carried so it wasn't hard to hear. I had walked closer to their room when I thought I heard my name.

"You have to tell her, Maggie," Matt said, annoyed.

"I know I do, Matt, but I don't think now is the right time," she said.

"When would be the right time? At our wedding? Or were you hoping she would find out some other way? It's been a little over a month, and Kenzie deserves to know." Matt's voice got a little louder. "I wanted tell her but you said to leave it to you," he added.

My heart started to pound in my chest, and my body started to tremble. I had no idea what it could be. What would they keep from me and why? I was beyond annoyed and worried.

I pushed open their bedroom door with such force that it crashed against the wall. "What is it that I deserve to know?" I asked, crossing my arms.

They both jumped. Maggie looked like she might be on the verge of tears and Matt looked furious.

"I swear to god, if you two have decided not to get married or have changed your minds about getting married in the barn, I will beat you both," I told them in all seriousness.

I had spent so much time preparing for their wedding. I had a detailed floor plan on how they were to set things up. I had even Skyped with Nancy and Amy to make sure we were all on the same page. Matt put them in charge of coordinating the family to help decorate.

"Kenzie," Maggie said, my name laced with pity.

"Yes, that is my name. Now, what the fuck is going on?" I demanded.

"Maybe you should sit down," she said, patting the spot next to her on the bed.

"I don't want to sit down, Maggie. Tell me what the fuck is going on!" I shouted.

"Kenz, Maggie wanted to tell you sooner but—" Matt told me, but I cut him off.

I was tired of the song and dance with these two. I wanted answers and I wanted them now. "Yeah, I heard that much. What is it that I should have known about but you didn't think it was the right time?" I said, staring right at Maggie.

"It's about Jase," she began to say.

Story of my fucking life. When wasn't it about him?

"And…?" I said, waiting to hear the rest of the story.

"He's… he's engaged. It happened about a month ago. I wanted to tell you…" Maggie quickly confessed.

I put my hand up, stopping her from saying any more.

I didn't want to hear it. My body was instantly numb from the news. Tears started to well up in my eyes, but I refused to let them spill in front of Maggie and Matt. I looked up at the ceiling, hoping to dam them in.

"I'm sorry, Kenzie," Maggie said, and I could tell she truly was. She started to walk toward me but I backed away.

I didn't want anyone's pity and I surely didn't want someone comforting me.

"Kenzie, if it's any consolation, no one is happy about this," Matt said, trying to comfort me the only way he could.

"I'm guessing everyone knows, including Alayna?" I asked Maggie. I knew she talked to Reid quite often, and I was sure his big mouth would have told her.

Maggie confirmed my suspicions and slowly nodded her head yes.

"Alayna and I wanted to tell you together, but we weren't sure how or when the right time was," Maggie said, feeling bad.

"You keep saying that!" I said, annoyed, and stomped my foot. "You both fucked up. You guys should have told me when you found out. Not three weeks before your wedding," I shrieked. "Whatever! It is what it is, right?" I said, looking at them both and shaking my head.

I knew they didn't want me to hurt any more, and that's why they didn't know how or when to tell me. I couldn't fault them for that. At the end of the day, Maggie and Matt were still getting married in three weeks and there was still a lot to be done. I had already lost Jase months ago. What difference did it make if he was engaged now? I took a deep breath and let out a long sigh, trying to regain my composure.

"I have some wedding things to talk to you both about. Maybe we can talk over breakfast," I suggested.

Maggie and Matt looked at each other in disbelief. It's like they couldn't believe I was able to flip my sanity switch so quickly after the news they'd just dumped on me.

"Oookay," Maggie said, looking at Matt for confirmation.

Matt nodded his head yes.

"Good. I'll be in my room if you need me," I told them, but I hoped and prayed they wouldn't bother me. I really wanted to be alone, but I didn't want to say that because they would then worry. I was sick and tired of people worrying about me.

I walked away and headed upstairs.

"Kenzie," Maggie called out, stopping me on the landing of the stairs.

I slowly turned toward her, readying myself for whatever she was going to say.

"You're taking this better than I thought. Are you sure you're okay?" she asked, concerned. "I was so afraid you'd lose your shit over this, Kenz," she added.

I gave her a weak smile, choosing my words carefully before answering. "I can't lose my shit over someone that isn't mine, Maggs. Jase made that very clear that night in the barn. He chose her and I have to accept that," I said sadly, before turning and walking up the stairs.

Maggie didn't say another word. I expected a call or text from Alayna, but thankfully no one bothered me.

After that night in the barn, I must have been in denial. I liked denial; it made functioning daily easier. A big part of me hoped, even prayed, that Jase would change his mind sooner or later.

As time went on that hope had grown smaller and smaller. To-night's news had brought me out of denial and made me feel raw and vulnerable. My heart crumbled as I thought of Jase down on one knee, asking for that cunt's hand in marriage. My stomach was in knots and the pain in my chest was overwhelming. I sat on my bed, hugging myself, trying to do the impossible and hold it together.

I vowed to myself to lay my denial to rest and replace it with acceptance, because what choice did I have?

None.

Chapter 22 | Last Day as Maggie Rowe

It was wedding time.

Maggie and Matt were getting married the next day, so everyone was in preparation mode. I wondered where the time had gone. I remembered when Maggie had first told me about Matt, and how she wanted me to meet him. A lot had happened since then. I remembered when I wanted to dick-kick him for being such an asshole. Thankfully he had seen the error of his ways after losing my best friend, and was able to win her back. They'd had many ups and downs, but it had all worked out in the end.

It was going to be a busy weekend. After helping Maggie take care of some errands at home, Alayna and I made the trip to upstate New York with her. My best friend was beyond excited to be getting married, and I was excited for her. She told us that Matt's family had been busy transforming the barn for the wedding. Since I had a big part in the planning and design, I was excited to see my visions come to life.

I had OCD about checking the weather, and lucky for the soon-to-be bride and groom, it was supposed to be beautiful. That would definitely make setting up much easier and less messy. Rain on a farm equals mud, and the last thing we needed was a rainy and muddy wedding.

Once we got to Matt's house, we quickly dropped our stuff off and then headed over to the barn where they were setting up. About a mile from it, I noticed a sign on the side of the road. It happened to be one of the signs I had made for the wedding.

Maggie slowed down as we came up to it. "Look, Kenzie, it's the wedding sign," she pointed out, practically bouncing in the driver's seat. I was equally excited to see it.

The sign was made from wood reclaimed from the old barn that they had begun to tear down. I had asked Matt a month before if he could bring me some of it so I could make signs for their big day. This sign was a wooden plank cut to the shape of an arrow and nailed to a stake with the word "Wedding" painted neatly in white. It pointed toward the direction of the barn. I had made a few of these to be put along the road a mile from the barn in every direction.

When we drove up to the dirt road that led us to the barn, there was another rustic sign I had made. It was bigger and had three planks, one right under the other, nailed to a longer stake. The words were also painted neatly in white. The first plank read "Happily," the second was "Ever After," and the last was "Starts Here." There were three bales of hay stacked around it. In front of the hay, someone had put an old milk can and planted some flowers. It looked great, and I thought it was a perfect way for the guests to be greeted as they turned off the road.

We turned off the main road and drove slowly toward the barn. We could see it in the distance, along with lots of pickup trucks and people walking around.

Maggie pulled up and parked. I saw Nancy, Amy, and some people setting up outside. The three of us got out of the car and headed over. I noticed they had bales of hay stacked nicely outside for added seating. Some of the seats were just two tiers of hay in the form of a square with flowers at the center. Then I realized that someone had made two couches of hay, which I thought was an amazing idea.

The barn doors were open, and next to each door were stacked bales of hay. Nancy and Amy were accenting them with flowers potted in silver, galvanized buckets that I had ordered. The buckets were also going to hold the flower centerpieces on the tables.

"You girls made it," Nancy said. "We've been working all week on the inside. Wait until y'all see it!" she said proudly. "You have a knack for decorating, Kenzie. We were able to do everything you asked, and the guys even got the chandeliers hung last night," she told me. I was beyond elated.

It was weird how our relationship had started. First Nancy had thought I was some trashy whore and kicked me out of her son's house, but over the last two months, things had changed. We chatted through email about the wedding preparations. It seemed our mutual interest paid off and put us on good terms. If someone would have told me a year before that Nancy Hainsworth would actually like me, I would have told them they were batshit crazy. I also think I scored points with her when I spilled my wine on the Cunt.

She went on to tell us about all they had done and what was left to do, which wasn't much.

"Come on, let me show y'all the barn," Nancy told us.

As we walked toward it, there was another sign leaning against the door.

This one I was most proud of because it took the longest. I'd wanted to give up on making it several times, but in the end, it turned out amazing.

It was a four-foot chalkboard I had found at a garage sale. I'd had to repaint it with chalkboard paint, since it was a little worn. I'd trimmed it with the leftover barn wood, which gave it the rustic look I was going for. I had written the bridal party's names and the wedding date on it in white paint. Then I'd used stencils and pastel-colored paints to accent it. I couldn't help but stare at the names—especially the one directly across from mine, which was Jase's. I was the maid of honor and he was the best man, which meant we would be paired up.

It felt a little ironic and sad. I was neck-deep in the dread I was feeling, knowing I would be seeing him. Knowing we had to dance together and make eye contact made it even worse. I wondered if the connection was still there between us. Would he feel what I felt? I was scared to look into his pale green eyes and see what truths might lie there.

"Wow. Kenzie, that looks amazing," Alayna said. "I can't wait until I get married so you can do all the planning for me," she said, smiling, and I knew she was only half kidding.

Before I had a chance to respond, Nancy beat me to it. "I think you have time, dear," she said dryly to Alayna.

Everyone knew Reid and Alayna were talking, and it seemed Nancy was in no rush to marry off another son so soon—especially since Jase was now engaged. Not that anyone was happy about it, including me.

There was an awkward silence hanging in the air after Nancy's comment.

"How about we go see the barn," Maggie said, ushering everyone inside.

Even though the doors were open, inside the doorway there were long white linen curtains draped on either side. They were tied back with old rope. When we walked inside, the three of us gasped in amazement as we looked around. The barn had been transformed into something straight out of a magazine. All this time I had an idea in my head as to what it was supposed to look like, but to see it actually come to life was breathtaking.

It was lit by thousands of globe lights. There were rows upon rows of them draped through the rafters along the length of the barn. In between the globe lights were yards upon yards of ivory tulle with lights inside, making the fabric appear to glow. It draped through the rafters as well and ran down the sides of the barn walls.

"I thought you were crazy wanting all these lights hung, but as we hung them it gave the barn an enchanted feel to it, don't you think?" Nancy asked.

I nodded in agreement because I couldn't find the right words to describe the newly transformed space.

I was speechless, which was a rarity. I looked up to see the old wrought iron chandeliers that I'd found on eBay lit up and hanging from the main beam like Nancy had said. They were an amazing find, even though the pictures had shown them being quite dated and with plenty of rust. I preferred to think of them as having character, and thought that they looked perfectly at home high up, suspended from the main wood beam. To think this space was going to end up housing farm equipment in less than a week. Just the thought made me a little upset. I personally thought they should leave the barn the way it was and just build another one. I doubted they would agree.

The tables and chairs were set up, with only the centerpieces missing. There were people all over. Some were putting together the dance floor, while others were setting up the buffet table and stocking the bar.

"Is there anything we can do?" I asked Nancy. Not going to lie, I was itching to do something—anything.

"Nope. You girls go and relax. We have this covered," she said.

"Are you sure?" Maggie asked, sounding a little disappointed.

I was sure this was the controlling part of Nancy that Maggie had been afraid of.

"I'm positive. Everything is almost done here. I had Amy call and confirm with the band, florist, and caterers for tomorrow. Your day will be perfect, I promise you," Nancy said, smiling.

I think it was only the second time I had ever seen her smile. I realized then that Maggie's soon-to-be mother-in-law wasn't trying to be controlling. She just wanted the wedding to be perfect for her son and his soon-to-be wife. I thought it was very sweet.

Given the way the barn looked, there really wasn't anything for us to do. It was plain to see that everyone had put a lot of effort into transforming it for the wedding.

"Why don't you girls take Amy and go back to Matt's house and relax before the rehearsal tonight," Nancy said, gently grabbing Maggie's shoulders. "Enjoy your last day as Maggie Rowe, because tomorrow you will be Mrs. Matthew Hainsworth," she said, smiling proudly at Maggie.

Whoa. Smile number three. Hell might freeze over at this rate, but who's keeping track?

"Okay," Maggie replied, beaming. Just hearing her new name, Maggie went from looking sad and defeated to ecstatic in three seconds flat.

Nancy ushered us out of the barn. Once in the car, Amy told us that Nancy had Matt stock his house for us. It was definitely going to be a packed house. Besides Maggie and her bridal party, we had Maggie's parents, Masen and his new girlfriend, Ally, staying with us.

The four of them were driving together and would arrive around two o'clock.

I had yet to meet Masen's new girlfriend, and I hoped she was as nice as Maggie said she was. He deserved someone nice, because he was such a great guy. Maggie told me things seemed to be moving along nicely with them, and I was truly happy to hear it. Everyone had someone—except for me, of course. Yup, I was slightly bitter and I knew it. It was something I needed to change, so I'd set a goal for myself, but it would have to wait until after the wedding. The Monday after the wedding, to be exact.

After finding out about Jase's engagement, I'd decided to take a two-week vacation from life. That is exactly what I called it—"A Vacation from Life."

Alayna told me I was being a bit dramatic, which was rich coming from her. I think she was a little hurt and upset that I didn't invite her. She did try to invite herself, but I quickly shut that down and only felt a little bit guilty. Alayna and I were so close and we always did stuff together—especially vacations. But this was different. I needed the time to myself. Plus, I didn't want to hear her mention Reid or any news about the Hainsworth family. I just wanted to sit my ass on a beach and relax without a care in the world.

Maggie thought it was a great idea and even helped me pick my vacation spot in Maui. She was a little jealous, since she had to wait to go away but things on the farm were a little hectic, and unfortunately the honeymoon would have to wait a month. At least they had the house to themselves for two weeks while I was away.

Every day I would check the weather in Maui. I couldn't wait to enjoy the eighty-degree weather. I looked forward to lounging by the pool or snorkeling with the brightly colored fish and turtles in the clear waters surrounding the island. It sounded amazing right then, and it was only three days away.

That would be the start of a new chapter in my life—a life that didn't involve Jase but did involve me moving forward and hopefully finding love and happiness. But, first things first, I needed to get through the weekend. It was about love, friendship, and happily ever after for my friends, not my pity party. I took a deep breath, quietly sighing.

I refocused my attention on Maggie, who was going over our plans for the day.

"Hey Maggs, where's Matt?" I asked, because I hadn't seen him at the barn. Now thinking about it, I was so wrapped up in the barn and all the details, I hadn't seen any of the Hainsworth boys.

I know, shocker that I wasn't looking for Jase.

"I don't know. I'm sure Nancy has them doing something." Maggie said.

"They're celebrating," Amy said nonchalantly.

"You want to be more specific?" a curious Alayna asked. I'm sure she was wondering if the celebration consisted of strippers and making dollar bills rain from the sky.

Amy laughed at that question. "They went to the bar in town. They all did—Matt, Jase, Reid, Cole, my brother Casey, and some of their friends," Amy told us.

"Umm, its ten o'clock in the morning. What bar is open that early?" I asked.

"Matt's friend owns the bar, so he opened up early for them to hang out and celebrate," Amy said, answering my question.

"Fuck!" Maggie shouted. "I will kill Matt if he is hungover for our wedding day," she said, slightly annoyed.

"I'm sure he will be fine, or my aunt will kill him for you," Amy told her.

I was sitting next to Maggie in the car, and I could see her mind buzzing with different scenarios stemming from the guys' mid-morning celebration.

"I'm sure they will be fine, Maggs. Don't worry," I told her as she turned in to Matt's driveway.

She parked the car and gave me a look like she wasn't convinced. I couldn't help but chuckle.

"Let's get inside and unpack our stuff. We can go over the last-minute details to make sure nothing was missed. Then pamper ourselves and celebrate as well," I said, trying to ease Maggie's worries about her future husband being hungover for their nuptials.

"You're right. It'll be fine and the wedding will be perfect," she said, cracking a smile.

After settling in at Matt's house, the four of us sat on the floor around the coffee table. We chatted while opening a couple bottles of wine and snacking on cheese and crackers. Maggie broke out her wedding planner and began going over her last-minute checklist with us.

Thankfully she hadn't been a bridezilla, and had wanted everything to be easy and simple. She'd even let us pick out the bridesmaids' dresses. Maggie didn't even want to see them until the day of her wedding. Alayna and I thought she was off her fucking rocker, but Maggie insisted. She wanted to be surprised, and she knew we would look amazing in whatever we picked out. Her only requirement was the color had to be plum. Amy was just as easygoing as Maggie. She didn't care about what the dress looked like. She said she would wear whatever.

Alayna thought it would be funny to play a joke on Maggie and have us all wear burlap sacks. I quickly nixed that idea. The thought of playing a practical joke on the bride on the day of her wedding was probably bad karma. Considering my shitty love life, I wasn't about to take any chances on fucking it up any more with a practical joke.

As Maggie went over her list, she realized she didn't have anything else to do but show up for the rehearsal that night and her wedding the next day.

"I guess everything is pretty much taken care of," she said.

"Awesome!" Alayna said. "Let's do a celebratory shot. I'll get the tequila," she told us, and by her excitement I didn't think we had a choice.

"I'll help you," Amy told Alayna.

They both walked out of the living room and headed downstairs to the basement, where Matt's man cave and bar were.

"Thank you for everything you have done for me and for my wedding. I really appreciate it," Maggie said, grabbing my hand and giving it a gentle squeeze. "You're my very best friend and I can't imagine my life without you. I love you, Kenzie Shaw," she said with tears in her eyes.

I could see she was more than grateful and I was more than happy to be a part of it all. "You're very welcome, Maggs. Thank you for making me your maid of honor. Your next chapter of life as Mrs. Hainsworth will be amazing, I just know it," I told her.

Alayna and Amy came back into the room with mini red Solo cup shot glasses and a bottle of tequila. Of all the alcohol in Matt's bar, why did they have to choose tequila? And those shot glasses, really? I felt like we should have been listening to fucking redneck country music while drinking out of those.

Amy lined up the shot glasses as Alayna poured the tequila.

"I just want to point out that I found these shot glasses. Aren't they cute?" Maggie asked, proudly holding up the little red Solo cup shot glass. "I got them for Matt for Christmas as a stocking stuffer," she said, like they were the deal of the century.

I could only roll my eyes and shake my head.

"Yeah, they're great. Fabulous, even. Are you going to do the shot or bore us to death on your deal-of-the-day find?" Alayna spouted.

I couldn't help but crack up, as did Amy.

Maggie was not impressed, but couldn't keep a straight face for long. "You're an asshole, Alayna," Maggie said, pointing at my cousin.

"Oh shut up and let's do this," Alayna told Maggie, then stuck out her tongue.

I raised my glass and the others followed suit. I looked at my best friend and smiled before I spoke. "Through the good, the bad, and the ugly, our friendship is still here like a bad rash, annoying the shit out of each of us like no medicine can cure. You're my very best friend and I wish you a lifetime of happiness. Cheers to you, Maggie Shaw, and your big day tomorrow," I said, still smiling at her.

We all raised our red Solo cup shot glasses together.

"Fuck yeah. Well said," Alayna shouted.

"Hear, hear," Amy said, a little more calmly than my cousin. Then we all threw back our shots.

I felt the warm but welcoming burn as the liquid made its way from my mouth, down my throat, and into my belly.

"One more shot!" Alayna shouted.

This wasn't going to end well if we kept this up. No good could come when it involved Alayna and tequila.

"One more and that's it," Maggie scolded Alayna, who then started to pout.

She didn't argue. She poured us all another round and held up her own shot glass. "To us, looking fabulous tomorrow and not waking up with any pimples," Alayna said.

"Hear, hear," the bride and her bridesmaids all said, and then threw back our last shot of the night, hopefully.

Chapter 23 | Checklist

The four of us had had at least two to three glasses of wine plus the two shots of tequila. Needless to say, we were all feeling pretty good. We sat on the floor of the living room, exchanging stories and laughing our asses off. Amy seemed to break out of her shell and even used the word "fuck" a couple of times. It was great.

Maggie was expecting her parents to arrive in an hour with Masen and his new girlfriend.

"I don't think we should drink any more," Maggie said.

"But we can drink after the rehearsal, right?" Alayna questioned.

"What are you, a lush?" I asked jokingly.

"No. Maybe a little. I need clear and precise instructions. This way I don't get myself into trouble," she said, smiling.

"Ain't that the truth," I said.

"I'll drink to that," Maggie said, laughing.

"Wait, I thought no more drinking," Amy said.

"Loosen the fuck up, Amy. Shit!" Alayna said, laughing at her.

Amy seemed confused, so she picked up the bottle of wine. Then, carefully watching Alayna, she put the wine bottle to her mouth and took a long swig. We all looked at each other. We had totally corrupted this country chick. When Amy was done, she wiped her mouth with the back of her hand and burped loudly.

"You should definitely not drink any more," I told Amy.

She only smiled and burped again.

"Yes!" Alayna said to Amy as they smacked their right hands together, giving each other a high five.

The front door shut and the four of us jumped in unison. I hadn't even heard it open.

"Hello. Is anyone here?" I heard Mrs. Rowe call out.

"In here, Mom," Maggie said as she got up from the floor. They'd arrived earlier than we had expected. Mrs. Rowe walked in with who I assumed was Ally.

Ally was a tall Asian girl with a cute figure. She had shoulder-length, straight black hair that was parted in the middle. She stood there with a meek smile while looking at us, unsure of what her next move should be.

"Your father and brother are getting the rest of our bags," Maggie's mom said.

Maggie went over and gave her mom a hug and kiss, then gave Ally a hug. She turned toward us and introduced Masen's girlfriend, Ally. We all stood, said hello, and introduced ourselves. She seemed nice, just really quiet.

Once Mr. Rowe and Masen finished unloading the car, we decided to make a late lunch for everyone. This was a brilliant idea. We needed to soak up the alcohol we'd just consumed, and we wouldn't be eating dinner until late.

After our late lunch, Maggie's parents decided to take a little nap before the rehearsal, so Maggie set them up in the bedroom upstairs. When she came back downstairs, we all went into the living room.

Masen took notice of the empty wine bottles and tequila on the coffee table. "Celebrating a little early, are we?" he asked, and I couldn't help but cringe like we were about to get in trouble.

"That's all you noticed? I mean seriously, look how cute these are," Maggie said, holding up the little red Solo cup shot glasses.

"Enough with the fucking shot glasses! When did you turn into a redneck?" I said to Maggie.

She took a page from Alayna's book and stuck her tongue at me, so I flipped my middle finger at her. Ally's eyes got wide and darted back and forth. It was pretty clear she wasn't sure what to make of us.

Masen put his arm around her and rubbed her arm reassuringly. "It's okay, babe. They're like this all the time. Don't worry, they won't bite," he told Ally. "Worst case scenario, that one over there might spill wine on you by accident," he said, nodding in my direction. "Or at least she'll make you think it's by accident, but it'll really intentional," he added, clearly thinking it was appropriate to bring that up.

Yup, he went there.

Masen laughed as he looked around at us. He stopped laughing when he saw the unhappy expressions on our faces. I swear I heard crickets chirping, it was so damn quiet.

"What? Should I not have said anything?" Masen asked. "It was funny when it happened. Remember, you guys were laughing," Masen said, trying to backpedal.

Maggie shook her head at her brother and Alayna crossed her arms in annoyance. Amy placed her hands on her hips and shocked all of us by saying, "That was fucked up, Masen."

I couldn't help but smile at her for breaking the awkward silence.

"No more alcohol for you," I told her.

Ally went from looking confused to scared, and I wondered if she would take off running any minute.

Masen looked at me and I could see he felt bad. He was trying to be funny, but given my fucked-up situation with Jase and how it had last ended, it just wasn't funny. The Cunt had won, end of story.

"It's fine, Masen, really. I'm okay guys, so relax. And Amy, you should drink some water. Lots of water. Ally, you should drink lots of wine or tequila if you want to get on board with this shit show," I told her, hoping to ease her discomfort.

I sat down on the floor in front of the coffee table and everyone seemed to follow suit. Masen and Ally sat on the couch across from me. Masen poured himself and Ally a shot, and I prayed he would keep his stories to a minimum for the rest of the weekend.

Alayna watched me carefully through the corner of her eye. I could see the wheels were turning, and I was sure she was wondering if I was truly okay. I hadn't talked about Jase's engagement since I'd found out three weeks before. I thought she and Maggie were hoping I would, but I wanted to push forward and leave well enough alone.

There was nothing to talk about, nothing to say or do. That topic was dead in the water, so push forward was what I did.

"Soooo," Alayna said, really dragging out the *O* sound. "Since Masen brought up your 'situation and unleashed the elephant in the room, are you okay? Are you going to be okay? Do you want to talk about it or anything?" Alayna asked in her usual machine gun style.

I needed to start talking before she started asking more questions. "I'm fine, really," I told them. I lied. "I have a plan to get me through the weekend," I said, smiling as I thought of my flawless plan. I prayed it would get me through the emotional turmoil I was sure to endure over the next couple days.

"What's your plan?" Maggie asked suspiciously.

I couldn't blame her after Balls-Deep was so successful.

"I made a mental checklist of things I should and shouldn't do. Every day I go over it in my head to make sure I don't leave anything out," I told Maggie.

"Do tell us of this checklist that lives in your head," Maggie asked again, and by the look she was giving me I wondered if she was questioning my sanity.

"Okay, sure. I'll tell you," I said. I glanced at everyone and I noticed I had five sets of eyes on me.

Pressured much? Shit.

"Since I found out that Jase got engaged..."I said before getting cut off.

"Hold up, Jase is engaged!" Masen said, shocked. "Why am I always the last to know these things? See, I told you Kenzie..." he began to say before Maggie and Alayna yelled, "Shut up!"

There was a brief pause before he practically whispered, "Sorry, Kenz. Continue."

I was definitely sure Ally thought we were a bunch of crazy bitches.

"So, like I was saying, I found out Jase got engaged and I knew the wedding was only three weeks away, so I needed to mentally prepare. I started to think of all the things I should do or try to avoid, so I came up with a plan. I made a mental checklist and I recite it to myself every day," I said proudly.

Alayna was the first to speak. "You're fucked up! Do you know that? When did my cousin hitch a ride on the crazy train?"

"Shut it, Alayna. What am I supposed to do, cry myself to sleep every night? I'm handling it the best I know how," I said, annoyed.

Maggie was pretty quiet while she listened to Alayna and me squabble back and forth.

"Can you tell me your checklist?" Maggie asked curiously.

I was a little hesitant, considering my cousin thought I'd lost my mind. Little did she know I'd probably lost it a while ago.

"Sure, I'll tell you. Just don't judge me," I said.

"Got it, no judging. Now spill," Maggie said.

"Okay, so my list of things I should and shouldn't do are: One, keep my shit together. Two, no crying unless they're tears of happiness. Three, don't choke, trip, kick, or punch the Cunt. Four, keep a safe distance from Jase and his cunt. Five, drink whenever possible. That's the list I recite to myself every day," I told them as they sat there, quiet.

Ally looked so lost, and concerned for her well-being.

"I think it's a good list, Kenzie," Amy said, putting her arm around me and giving me a squeeze.

"Yes, it's a very good list. I know this is terribly difficult for you. I really appreciate you putting aside your heartache to make my day special," Maggie said, leaning over to give me a hug.

If they only knew I wasn't putting aside my heartache. I didn't even know if that was possible, but I could try to pretend—and if they were convinced, then I must have been doing a good job.

I heard a little voice say, "Excuse me."

I looked and saw it was Ally.

"I know it's none of my business, but I'm a little confused. Can someone tell me what's going on?" she asked politely.

Before anyone had a chance to explain, Alayna jumped in. "What's going on is my cousin is batshit crazy, but you probably figured that out by now," she said before continuing. "The problem is she's in love with Jase, who's also Maggie's soon-to-be brother-in-law. Kenzie and Jase had a one-night stand a couple years ago and it was love at first site, or love at first fuck. Who knows, really? But the last couple years they have been popping up in each other's lives, him wanting her but her not wanting him. Now the crazy bitch realizes she's loved him all this time, but now he's engaged. End of story," Alayna ranted, then poured herself a shot and threw it back, slamming the plastic red Solo cup down on the coffee table.

Honest and true, Alayna rang it loud and clear. It left the room quiet once again, and I swear I could hear a fucking cricket chirping.

"Wow, Alayna, harsh much?" Masen said with a tone.

"She's right. She pretty much summed it up," I said, shrugging my shoulders. It was my story and I was sticking to it whether I liked it or not. "So this is why I need to stick to my mental checklist and get through this weekend," I said with a weak smile.

"That's crazy. I hope everything works out for you," Ally said with a sincere tone.

Her words were genuine and I appreciated them. I smiled back at her.

"Everything will work out for her. I just know it in my heart," Alayna said, rather confident-sounding. She then grabbed the tequila and poured us all a round of shots in the little red Solo cups. Did someone say no more drinking? Nah.

Alayna made a toast to everything working out. We all clanked our red Solo cup shot glasses together and threw back the tequila. I welcomed the warmth of the liquid as it made me feel a little bit more numb. I smiled at myself and mentally checked off number five on my checklist: drink whenever possible. Done and done.

Chapter 24 | Wedding Rehearsal

Maggie's mom rounded all of us up to head to the church for the rehearsal. Given our current blood alcohol levels, Mr. and Mrs. Rowe took Maggie's car and Masen drove the rest of us in his truck.

Once we reached the church we all climbed out, giggling over nothing as a result of the fabulous buzz we all had. Maggie gave us the get-it-together speech before we walked into "God's house"—her words, not mine. I wasn't sure when she had become religious, but we got our shit together and would be respectful in "God's house." We all stood around waiting for everyone to arrive. I made Amy sit in the pew because she had started to sway.

It was a good thing we were in church, because I prayed for Amy to make it through the rehearsal and that she would not puke or pass out while we were in church. After my silent prayer, I made the sign of the cross. Alayna noticed.

"What are you doing?" she whispered.

"Praying, what the fuck does it look like?" I whispered back.

"You just cursed in god's house. He's going to strike you down," she said, laughing quietly.

I gave her a smug look. "If god is going to strike me down for saying 'fuck' in his house, then surely you would have burst into flames the moment you crossed his threshold," I told her.

We both looked at each other and started to giggle a little too loudly.

"Touché, Kenzie. Tou-fucking-ché," Alayna whispered.

Maggie cleared her throat and gave us the death stare, so Alayna and I quickly shut up. We couldn't help but grin. I looked around at all the people there. My stomach dropped as I saw those pale green eyes curiously watching me. It was Jase.

I felt tears prick my eyes and I quickly turned, but not before I noticed the gaudy accessory latched onto his arm: the Cunt. She rubbed her head on his shoulder like a cat wanting attention from its owner. Pathetic.

My stomach was in knots and I began to break out into a cold sweat. *You can do this*, I mentally chanted. I took a couple of deep breaths and got myself under control. Alayna looked at me like I was crazy, and it probably sounded like I was practicing some form of Lamaze. She looked past me only to see what I saw. She grabbed my hand and held it tightly. I tried not to focus on anything but her death grip. I thought of number one on my checklist: keep my shit together. I had to get through this. It was only a matter of moments before I would be standing across from Jase, walking down the aisle with him as we rehearsed our roles for the big day.

The voices in the church quieted as the priest, who spoke softly, introduced himself to everyone. He was a tall but scrawny man with a warm smile. His white hair made him look older, but his lack of wrinkles made me second-guess his age. The priest gave a brief history of his relationship with the Hainsworth family. They had known each other for many years. After the introduction, he explained the ceremony to us all from start to finish.

All that was left was to go through the motions. The priest made Matt and his groomsmen take their spots as he ushered Maggie, her parents, and all of her bridesmaids out into the hallway and closed the double doors.

We waited for our cue, which would be everyone inside the church humming the wedding march. After a few minutes we heard it begin. Alayna and I each grabbed a handle of the double doors and opened them. Amy took her position in the doorway with minimal swaying. She began to walk slowly up the aisle. When she was about halfway, Alayna took her place in front of the doorway, and then started to walk up the aisle, mirroring Amy's steps.

Maggie looked at me and smiled. She mouthed *You can do this* to me and I wished that was enough to unknot my stomach. *It'll be all over soon,* I thought to myself, taking a deep breath.

Alayna was at the halfway point, so I stood in front of the doorway. I took one last look back at my best friend and started the slow walk up the aisle as everyone continued to hum. I made sure not to look in Jase's direction.

As I took each step, I thought of the pictures of the hotel I had booked in Maui. I tried to focus on the white sandy beaches, the beautiful, bright flowers, and the snorkeling pictures from the hotel website. It helped and made me feel a little less nervous. When I reached the first pew near the alter, I took my place next to Alayna. She smiled and gave me a reassuring wink. I turned to see Maggie walking up the aisle with her parents on either side of her. She had her arm linked with her father's while her mother held her hand.

The priest told Mr. and Mrs. Rowe to take their places after they pretended to give Maggie away. He went over the next steps, told Maggie and Matt to kiss, and then announced them as the soon-to-be Mr. and Mrs. Hainsworth. We all cheered as they turned and walked back down the aisle. This only meant one thing. It was my turn to walk down the aisle with the best man, Jase.

I looked across from where I was standing and saw him stepping into the aisle as the priest had instructed. I stood there frozen as he approached me. Alayna must have noticed my hesitation, and she slapped my ass so hard it made me jump forward, right into Jase. I whipped my head around, ready to slap the bitch who was now smiling at me. But then I felt rough fingertips gently grab my wrist.

I slowly turned to see Jase looking at me with an unsure smile. He wrapped my arm around his, holding it in place as he led me down the aisle. My heart was pounding so hard I could barely hear. I kept my eyes focused on Maggie, who was standing at the end of the aisle with Matt, waiting. I stole a quick glance at Jase, who seemed puzzled by the expression on my face.

When we reached Maggie and Matt, I pulled my arm from Jase's and stood next to Maggie. Even after I pulled away, I could still feel his touch on my skin. This was the last thing I needed. Number four on my mental checklist was already shot. And number one wasn't looking too good either.

I watched Reid and Cole escort Alayna, and then Casey and Masen escorted Amy. Mr. and Mrs. Rowe walked behind them, followed by Matt's parents. Done, finally. The knot in my stomach felt a little better, knowing I was halfway through tonight.

An arm draped over my shoulders and I knew its owner before I even looked. Alayna.

"Are you mad at me?" she asked.

I decided the silent treatment was better than answering her.

"You know you can't be mad at me for long. I'm too annoying." She was spot on with that comment. "You looked totally freaked out, so I figured a good slap on the ass would help you out," she said, hugging my shoulders like she had done me a favor. I wouldn't admit it, but it had worked.

"I'm annoyed," I finally told her.

"What else is new?" she said.

I wanted to slap her. "You're a bitch, Alayna. Go bother someone else," I mumbled under my breath.

"Nope. I'm going to stick to you like glue. Especially since he keeps checking you out," Alayna whispered to me.

"Who?" I asked, whipping around to look at her.

I regretted the question as soon as I asked it. She rolled her eyes at me and mouthed his name: *Jase.* My heart skipped a beat. Fuck my life.

The priest came over to Maggie and Matt to go over some last-minute details, and then sent us on our way. Everyone began to file out of the church and head to the restaurant for the rehearsal dinner. Alayna was true to her words, wrapping her arm around mine as we walked toward the truck. I, of course, couldn't understand why he would be checking me out. He'd gotten what he wanted, and what he wanted wasn't me.

Chapter 25 | TMI

Masen drove, following the cars in front of him. We were just on the outskirts of town when everyone turned in to the restaurant parking lot. It dawned on me in that instant that I'd been there before. My stomach dropped when I realized it was the same place that Jase had taken me to. I closed my eyes tightly and tried to breathe. Of course it would be the place. It was the only big restaurant in town, and I remembered Jase talking with the hostess about his family. Of course she knew them. Everyone knew everyone up here.

We got out of the truck and followed everyone inside the restaurant, where the hostess sat all of us immediately. Several tables were pushed together to make one long table. Alayna and I hung back to see where everyone was sitting. Once we saw where Jase and his cunt were, we sat toward the opposite end but on the same side.

I wanted to make sure I couldn't see them, and I surely didn't want him looking at me. I took a seat between Alayna and Matt. I looked around at the restaurant and noticed it was still as quaint and cozy as I remembered it had been. The memory only made it that much more difficult. I tried to focus on the conversations swirling around the table. But I started to think about Jase and our first date. How I thought he might kill me and chop me up, but instead ended up surprising me with a picnic. It was a good memory and one I had thought of a trillion times.

"Earth to space cadet," Alayna said, waving her hand in front of my face.

"Huh, what?" I said, breaking my daydreaming.

"What's going on in that head of yours that's making you smile so much?" Alayna asked me curiously.

"Maui. I'm thinking of Maui," I told her. I lied, of course.

My cousin eyed me suspiciously and handed me a glass of wine. I willingly took it from her, thinking of number five on my mental checklist.

Alayna grabbed her glass of wine then clinked my glass with hers. "Here's to you being a terrible liar, Kenz," she said with a sly smile.

I said nothing and only smiled back before taking a sip.

The waitresses began bringing out the appetizers, so I decided to run to the bathroom. I pushed my chair away from the table and stood up.

"Where are you going?" Alayna asked.

"I need to pee. Is that okay, or did you want to come with me to make sure I wipe front to back?" I asked in a snarky tone.

Alayna made a face at me and stuck her tongue out. I rolled my eyes and walked toward the sign that said "Restrooms." I pushed open the ladies' room door. Both bathroom stalls were unoccupied, so I chose the first one on the left, closest to the sink.

I was answering nature's call when I heard the door open and close. Then I heard heels on the tile floor stop in front of the sink. After I pulled up my pants the toilet automatically flushed, which surprised me for a restaurant in the boonies. I opened the door of the bathroom stall and saw Leah the Cunt at the sink, primping herself. I thought it might be best to quickly wash my hands and get the fuck out of there.

Unfortunately I couldn't help but watch her out of the corner of my eye. She was checking herself out in the mirror, making duck faces. God, I hated her.

She noticed me looking. "Oh hey, I remember you. Kerry right?" she asked.

"Yeah, Kerry," I said, wanting to choke the stupid bitch for fucking up my name once again.

I remembered number three on my checklist, and choking was one of the things I couldn't do. I needed to hurry up and get the fuck out of the bathroom. I shut off the water and grabbed some paper towels. I was about to leave when the Cunt grabbed my arm, stopping me in my tracks. I stared at her hand on my arm before looking at her. She was crossing a fine line and she didn't even know it.

"Kerry, I wanted to apologize for yelling at you for spilling the wine on me. It was an accident and I get that now," she said, in a somewhat sincere tone.

Like I gave a fuck that *she* finally got it. I didn't need her apology. Little did she know, my actions had been intentional.

"Yeah, sure," I replied, because I needed to speed this along. Last thing I wanted was to converse with her.

I started to leave when she started to talk again. "Just think, next week it will be me!" she squeaked with excitement, then started humming the "Wedding March" as she applied lipstick.

That stopped me in my tracks again and I literally backed up two steps. "I'm sorry, what?" I asked as my heart began to pound in my chest. I clenched my fists, readying myself for the unknown words she was about to speak.

She stopped humming, looked at me in the mirror, and smiled. "Next week Jase and I are flying to Vegas and eloping," she squeaked again and clapped her hands in excitement. That's when I saw the light catch the diamond ring on her finger.

It was all too much. The room started to spin and I seriously felt faint. My heartbeat had begun pounding in my ears and I needed to get out of the bathroom.

The Cunt turned to look at me. "Oh, and please don't say anything. We didn't want our news to take away from Matt and Maggie's wedding," she pleaded. Little did she know every syllable that this bitch spoke was one more syllable closer to me kicking the shit out of her.

I tried to regain some composure and began to walk toward the door. I felt my ears burning and I was sure my face was a shade of red that wasn't in the crayon box.

She clasped her hands together and seemed lost in thought.

My eyes focused on the sparkly diamond on her hand.

"I can't wait until our wedding night. The things I'm going to do to that man. God, he is so hot, don't you think?" the Cunt said.

I couldn't believe she was seriously asking me this.

"And *my god,* he is *amazing* in bed," she added, as her eyes rolled back, really emphasizing the words she spoke.

Holy Fuck. No she didn't.

If you were inside my mind, you would have heard a snapping sound. That sound was me mentally losing my shit over her last comment. I'm sure my eyes were bugged out, and I think I started twitching. I felt like I was having an out-of-body experience, hovering above as it all transpired.

I began to think a teensy bit more clearly. I thought my checklist didn't apply to a situation of this magnitude. I was sure any other woman would agree with me. I got past the red I was seeing, and out of the corner of my eye I noticed the lock on the bathroom door. Usually in a situation like this I could count on my internal voice to calm me down, to make a better decision. I decided in that moment that my internal voice was female because all I heard in my head was chanting... *Fuck her up! Fuck her up! Fuck her up!* So I slowly reached over and locked the door.

The Cunt looked a little confused when she saw me lock the door. That confusion quickly changed to fear as I rushed her, grabbing her shoulders and slamming her against the bathroom wall, hard. Her head bounced a bit on the tile.

I could never be more thankful for wearing heels. She was taller than I was, but with my heels on they put me at her height.

I got an inch from her face before unleashing on her. "You disgusting pig! I don't give a fuck about your personal life or what you do behind closed doors. Don't you dare talk to me or even look at me or I swear to god, the next time I will punch you in the fucking throat! Do you fucking understand me?" I said through gritted teeth.

She frantically nodded yes, so I released her shoulders and turned on my heel to leave.

I unlocked the bathroom door, swinging it open wildly and with such force that it slammed into the wall. I walked out, leaving that stupid bitch to ponder my words and the very real threat I'd offered her. I walked back to the table pissed off on so many levels that I was trembling. I pictured her sliding down the wall scared and crying, regretting that she'd shared such intimate details with me.

Taking my seat next to Alayna, I grabbed my glass of wine and in one big swallow made the liquid disappear. Alayna's eyes grew wide as I took her wine glass from her hand and drank it as well.

"Did peeing make you thirsty or something?" she asked me with a look of confusion on her face.

"Just sticking to my checklist is all," I told her.

"Right, number five: drink whenever possible," Alayna quoted.

I nodded.

"But that doesn't mean you should drink mine as well," she protested.

I was still so angry and my head was pounding. My body started to unwind and I tried to will away the trembling. Just then I saw the Cunt return to her seat with a worried look on her face. She must have taken my threat seriously, because she didn't even look in my direction. Smart girl. Now if she could only get people's names right.

I overheard someone ask if everything was okay but I didn't hear her answer.

"Kenz, are you all right?" Alayna whispered.

I wanted to lie and tell her yes, but since I was a terrible liar I doubted she would believe me. I lifted my head to look at her. I paused before I spoke. "I truly don't know, Alayna," I told her honestly in a hushed tone. "This may sound crazy, but he's mine and I'm his. I know in my heart that's how it's supposed to be. He and I are supposed be together and it's not going to happen," I added.

Alayna looked at me with pity in her eyes.

She didn't have an answer for me, and nothing she could say would make me feel better. I had to look away before I started to cry, so I stared at the salt and pepper shakers that were on the table. I felt like a lost cause. My life was the same sad story. Just a different day, week, month, or year.

I wanted to tell Alayna about what had happened in the bathroom, but that would have to wait until after dinner. I didn't need her to flip her shit or ask a ton of questions. My cousin grabbed the bottle of wine off the table and poured some into our glasses. I was grateful for the third glass and every other one after, which seemed to help the pounding in my head as well as my trembling nerves.

I didn't say much the rest of the night. After we ate, both Matt and Maggie's fathers stood proudly and gave heartfelt speeches. Most of the women were crying or holding back tears. Not me. I was still too angry to shed a tear. I was done with everything and everyone. At that point, if something didn't change soon I would probably end up old and alone with thirty cats all named Pretty or Mr. Whiskers.

Chapter 26 | Truth

After dinner we said our goodbyes and headed back to the house. Once we arrived at Matt's, everyone headed for the kitchen or living room, but I headed upstairs. I wasn't feeling chatty, so I decided to get ready for bed. I grabbed my bag of toiletries from the bedroom, then went into the bathroom to brush my teeth and wash my face. It was the first time I had been alone since the incident at the restaurant. Thinking about it made me start to tremble again. I thought about tonight and how hard it had been, and I was sure the next day would be a thousand times worse. My stomach knotted just thinking about it, and I wouldn't have been surprised if I ended up with an ulcer.

I walked back into the bedroom, changed into my pajamas, and got under the covers. I lay there with only the bedside lamp on, lost in the shadows it cast on the ceiling. My mind was still buzzing from the unsolicited information I'd received earlier that night.

There was a light knock on the door. "Kenz, are you in here?" Alayna asked as she opened the door.

"Yes," I answered.

"Wow, you're in bed already? You're a party pooper. At least you made it to bed. Amy passed out on the couch. We tried to wake her, but she wouldn't get up so Maggie covered her with a blanket," Alayna reported. She staggered into the room and sat on the corner of the bed. "What's up with you? I know you're upset, but—" Alayna was saying, but I cut her off.

"Jase is eloping next week!" I blurted out like my life depended on it.

It wasn't my news to tell, but knowing it felt like my insides were being poisoned. I had to tell someone, and that someone could only be my cousin.

"Oh fuck," Alayna said slowly, blinking her eyes, processing the news I had just dropped on her. "Are you sure?" she said, questioning me.

"Yes I'm sure, and you can't say anything to anyone. I don't want pissed off people for the wedding," I told her.

"How do you know this?" she asked, skeptical.

I told Alayna what had happened in the bathroom at the restaurant, but only after swearing her to silence.

"You should've kicked her ass," she said angrily. "What are you going to do now?"

"Nothing," I told her.

"What do you mean nothing? You have to do something. You said it yourself at dinner tonight: he is yours and you are his. You said you know it in your heart that you both belong together. If you truly believe that, how can you walk away?" she asked.

"I just have to. I confessed my feelings for him months ago and he turned me down. What more can I do, Alayna?" I asked her.

"Talk to him," she suggested.

"I'm not going there again. I can't. I can barely make it through this wedding," I told her truthfully.

"Something's got to give. Maybe he'll realize what he's doing is a mistake and break off the engagement," she said, sounding hopeful.

The pain in my chest from my already broken heart would not allow me to be so hopeful. I had to begin again. A new chapter in my life was just a few days away. I shut the bedside lamp off before I rolled onto my side, tucking myself farther under the covers. It left the room dark except the hallway light that peeked through the door. Alayna took that as sign that the conversation was done, but she didn't leave. She kicked off her heels and crawled into the bed next to me.

"No matter what, Kenzie, you will always have me by your side. Your battles are my battles. Your heartache is my heartache. You're never alone. Don't ever forget that," Alayna said softly.

I silently cried as the tears streamed down my face onto my pillow. Her words were so touching and one hundred percent the truth. All I wanted was happiness. I didn't think that was too much to ask for. I would make it happen, because then, my happiness would be her happiness too.

Chapter 27 | Country Wedding

I was quite comfortable in bed when I was woken up by a scream. I thought I was hearing things, so I just lay in bed to see if I heard it again.

"What the hell was that for?" I heard Masen question.

Okay, I guess I wasn't hearing things, since he heard it too. But who was he talking to? I remembered Alayna sleeping with me, but when I looked over she wasn't there.

"Do you see the size of this fucking pimple on my face?" I heard Alayna say. Maybe it was her screaming... but over a pimple? Come to think about it, Alayna *would* scream over a pimple, especially on the day of the wedding.

I tossed the blankets off of me when Alayna threw open the bedroom door. "Do you see this? This is your fault," she told me, pointing at the blemish on her cheek.

I saw the red bump, but I had to squint just to see it. "What? How is it my fault?" I asked her.

"Because you let me go to bed last night without washing my face!" she said, continuing her rant while stamping her foot.

"You're a crazy bitch, and it's way too fucking early for this shit. Go put some toothpaste on it," I told my cousin while I got out of bed. "We have a wedding to get ready for and you're screaming and carrying on about a pimple," I mumbled, walking past her, trying to wake up.

I headed downstairs to get some coffee and breakfast. Alayna joined me shortly, after showering and applying toothpaste to her pimple. I tried not to stare at the white dot on her cheek, but I couldn't help it.

"It's rude to stare," she told me with an attitude. Clearly she was not as refreshed as I had hoped. I didn't say a word. I only smiled, giving her the middle finger as I shifted in my seat.

Everyone was up and doing stuff around the house. Maggie was buzzing around happily with nervous excitement. I couldn't help but smile at my best friend, but her energy was making me even more tired. I sat there slowly sipping my coffee, trying to feel a little more human and a little less hungover. It didn't help that the dread of today was making me move at a snail's pace.

Once I had two cups of coffee in me, I began to get my shit together. The caffeine I ingested was jump-starting my body. The day was going to be tough, and I needed to stay focused for the wedding and my best friend.

After I showered, a couple women from the salon in town came over to do our nails, hair, and makeup. Alayna and I opted out of the hair and makeup, since we preferred to do our own. While Maggie, her mom, and Amy where downstairs getting primped, Alayna and I were upstairs with Ally doing the same.

Ally barely wore any makeup. Her idea of makeup was some mascara and lipstick. When she told us that, Alayna looked at her like she was from another world. We took our time doing our makeup, which consisted of more than two products. Although we did keep it simple, with natural tones on our eyes and coral on our cheeks with a pale pink lip gloss to make our lips pop.

While we were doing our hair, Masen interrupted our beauty session and thoughtfully brought us some mimosas. I was eternally grateful to him, hoping it would help settle my nerves a little. After Masen left us to finish getting ready, Ally tied her hair back in a simple chignon bun. I was quite jealous at how easy she made it seem. I'd tried it several times before and failed miserably.

Alayna and I curled our long brown hair and let the loose curls hang down our backs and over our shoulders. After lots of hair spray to keep us from losing the curls, we were ready. Well, almost ready. We only needed to get dressed.

We headed downstairs to check on everyone and their progress. We were rounding the corner to the kitchen when we nearly walked into Maggie and Amy. Maggie's makeup looked so fresh yet stunning. Her caramel-brown hair was put into a ballerina bun on the top of her head with a braid that wrapped around it. The stylist had clipped the white silk gardenia flowers to the left side of her hair, close to the bun. Attached to the flowers was the netting of the birdcage veil that was pulled down over her face. Her smile shone through, showing that she was one step closer to the altar.

Amy had her long, golden-blond hair pulled into a side ponytail with loose waves. Some of her hair wrapped the ponytail to hold it in place. Amy didn't have much makeup on. Her face seemed light, yet bright with some blush and mascara. She looked like the all-around American girl. I wished I could look that good with some blush and mascara.

"You girls look amazing," I told them. "Maggie, you took like a million bucks! You're a beautiful bride," I said, smiling at my best friend.

"Thank you. I'm starting to get butterflies in my stomach," she said, fidgeting with her engagement ring. "The photographer should be here within the hour, so we should probably get dressed," Maggie said.

The four of us headed upstairs to get dressed. Everyone was so excited for a couple of reasons. Other than Mrs. Rowe and me, no one else had seen Maggie's dress, and per Maggie's request she had not seen the bridesmaids' dresses.

While Mrs. Rowe and Ally helped Maggie get dressed, the three of us bridesmaids went into the spare bedroom to put our dresses on. Maggie's only request was that the dresses we chose had to be plum—otherwise she didn't care. Alayna and I had spent many hours searching for the perfect dress for this country wedding. We'd decided on a simple knee-length dress with cap sleeves and a V-neck that stopped right below our cleavage. The back of the dress was what Alayna and I fell in love with. It had an open keyhole back. The fabric was plum-colored lace with taupe lining that subtly showed through. The color contrast made the little dress look rich and sexy yet simple as it lightly hugged our bodies.

We slipped into our dresses, zipped each other up, and then topped our outfits off with the one special part that made our ensemble country-chic. Alayna and I had tasked Amy with getting the four of us cowboy boots. We wanted ours to match, but we wanted Maggie's to be different. Lucky for Amy, shopping for us was pretty easy since Alayna, Maggie, and I all wore the same size. Maggie didn't know it yet, but we'd purposely left her silver heels at home. So she had no choice but to wear the boots as well. It was my idea and I swore I would accept the wrath of Maggie if she ended up pissed off with decision. My reasoning would be "how can you have a barn wedding and not have us in cowboy boots?"

Amy handed Alayna and I the boxes that held the boots. I knew nothing about cowboy boots. Amy rattled off that they were brown, full-grain leather, X-toe boots with a triad design, and a six-row stitch pattern design for the upper half. The only things I heard and understood were "brown" and "leather."

When we opened the boxes, there were pairs of plum socks to go with our boots. The three of us put on our socks and slid on the boots. Surprisingly, they were pretty comfortable.

We took turns in the full-length mirror twirling and checking ourselves out. We looked pretty good, not going to lie. In my mind I prayed that I looked a trillion times better then Jase's cunt. Let Jase's last memory of me be me looking like this, days before he got married. Bitter much? *Yup!*

I heard Maggie calling from the other room. "Hey, has anyone seen my shoes?" she yelled, sounding slightly frantic.

I looked at Alayna and Amy, who looked each other. I think they were slightly worried, and I'm not going to lie, I was a little worried myself.

Amy handed me the other box that contained Maggie's boots, but that box had an ivory organza ribbon tied around it in a bow. The two of them stepped aside to let me give Maggie the surprise that I prayed she would love.

I took a deep breath and said a silent prayer, hoping this wouldn't fuck up my best friend's wedding day. I went into Matt's bedroom, where Maggie was getting ready. I knocked and walked in with Alayna and Amy two steps behind me. Chickens.

First thing I noticed was Maggie's stuff scattered on the bed and her wedding dress hanging on the closet door. Her mom and Ally were looking all over for what were probably the shoes that were back in Jersey.

"Hey, did you call us?" I asked her.

Maggie stopped what she was doing and took notice of us in our dresses. "Holy shit! You guys look amazing. I love these dresses! Turn around," Maggie said, quite excited. "Oh. My. God. I love the cowboy boots!" she shouted and clapped her hands together.

This could totally work; maybe she won't be mad.

"Well, I'm glad you like the boots," I told her as I handed her the box with her boots in it.

"What's this?" she asked, puzzled as she tugged on the bow, untying it. She took the lid off the box and pulled out one of the cowboy boots.

Maggie's were different from ours. The leather was a lighter brown with white lace embroidery at the toe, heel, and at the top of the boot. They were really pretty. I was sure Amy could give Maggie the full rundown, but for now I just needed to know if she liked them.

"These are so pretty. Thank you guys," she said, not really understanding what they were for.

"They're to replace your heels," I said, pausing to let that sink in.

"Huh?" Maggie said in a questioning tone.

"It's a country wedding. You can't wear heels, so we got you these. And I purposely left your shoes at home," I confessed. "Hope you're not mad."

There was a longer pause then I expected. Then a smile crept across her face. "You guys are amazing and thoughtful and awesome..." she rambled on. Maggie took the boots and a pair of white socks that said "Just Married" and put them on. "They fit perfectly," Maggie told us, and I noticed Alayna and Amy had moved closer to me, since we didn't have a pissed off bride.

Mr. Rowe shouted from downstairs that the photographer had arrived.

"Time to get me dressed," Maggie said.

Mrs. Rowe grabbed the wedding dress from the closet door. Maggie stripped down to her underwear and new boots and we slipped her dress over her head. She looked stunning in the sleeveless, lace, sheath gown. It had an illusion neckline and a plunging back with scalloped lace around the neckline, back, and hem. The small train puddled on the floor. I watched as Maggie stared at herself in the mirror, admiring her own beauty.

The bride and her mom shared in a very sweet mother-daughter moment, both trying to hold back tears. Then Mrs. Rowe ticked off on her fingers the something borrowed and something blue, something old and something new. Maggie had accounted for all of them. All that was left was pictures and a wedding. We headed downstairs to see Mr. Rowe and Masen looking quite dapper in their tuxedos while chatting with the photographer. We took a slew of pictures and before we knew it, it was time to leave for the church. Alayna decided that one last toast was in order, so Masen popped open a bottle of champagne while Amy grabbed some toasting flutes.

Once the champagne was poured, Masen made a very sweet speech to his sister that left all of us with tears in our eyes. Maggie gave her little brother a big hug. She whispered something in his ear and they both laughed. After they had their moment, we gathered our things and headed outside to the waiting limo.

Matt had insisted on a "beefy" limo, so he'd booked a white Hummer H2 stretch limo. It looked obnoxious in his driveway and I loved it.

"Holy shit, who picked that out?" Maggie said, looking at me.

I laughed at her puzzled expression and answered her with, "Your future husband."

She rolled her eyes as she walked toward the beast on four wheels. We all climbed in while Masen and Ally followed us in his truck.

The church wasn't far from Matt's house. When we arrived at the church, there were a few people who were still walking in. After a couple minutes passed, we got out of the limo and headed into the church.

We stood in the entryway staring at the big wooden church doors that separated us from the waiting guests. It was nerve-racking and I wasn't even the one getting married. Looking over at the bride, I saw she was calm and smiling, anticipating the beginning of the rest of her life. I was so happy, but a piece of me was sad thinking how I might never find that for myself.

As we waited for our cue, Pachelbel's "Canon in D" began to play. We moved off to the side of the doors as they began to open. My stomach dropped knowing what was coming next: Jase, and not in the way that I wanted.

Once the doors opened, Amy took her position in the doorway, paused, and then began to slowly walk up the aisle to her designated spot. She looked great and walked with such grace. When she was halfway up the aisle, Alayna took her spot in front of the doorway. She mimicked Amy's stride, looking gorgeous as she walked. She seemed to have an attitude as she walked in her new cowboy boots. You would have thought it was fashion week in New York rather than a wedding out in east bumble-fuck. Once she was almost halfway up the aisle, I took my position in the doorway.

Before taking a step, I looked over at Maggie, who had her father's arm with her mom standing beside her. I gave her a big smile and mouthed, *I love you, Maggs.*

Turning my attention to the aisle before me, I took a step and began to walk. Instead of feeling nervous, I felt proud that my best friend had chosen me to be her maid of honor.

Not sure if it was the combination of the mimosas, champagne, and the high of being a part of my best friend's big day, but I felt brave and in charge of my being for once. I took this feeling and ran with it. I looked at Jase, and he looked gorgeous in his black tuxedo. I nearly creamed my panties right there in church. His face was cleanly shaven and his hair was neatly styled in a gentleman cut. I had a tight grip on my confidence as we kept our eyes locked on each other.

The look on Jase's face was priceless. First he looked happy, as I'm sure he was, since it was his brother's wedding. But as he watched me intently as I walked, step by step, his face changed. No longer smiling, he was glaring at me, and I didn't give two, three, or four fucks.

I couldn't help but give Jase a sly smile, hoping that the vision of me before him was seared into his memory. I prayed that he would daydream about me naked, only wearing my new cowboy boots and nothing else. Yes, I know—pretty shitty prayer, given the time and place. I dropped my eyes from his as I left the aisle, taking my spot next to my cousin.

The wooden doors closed and the music changed. All eyes were on the back doors for the introduction of the bride. The bridal march began to play for several seconds before the wooden doors opened in unison. There, standing in the doorway, was my best friend, looking beautiful as ever. On the one side was her father with her arm linked through his and on the other side was her mother holding her hand, just as they had rehearsed. They began to walk the aisle and I couldn't help the happy tears that began to swell in my eyes. I was overjoyed for them, and for their new beginning.

I stole a glance at Matt, who looked elated and proud that his bride would soon be joining him by his side. I also saw the familiar pale green eyes staring at me. Jase wasn't paying attention to the bride's procession up the aisle. He was watching me, straight-faced. I thought it was kind of rude, so I did the first thing that came to mind—well, the second thing that came to mind. The first thing would have been to give him the middle finger, but since we were in church, I decided to stick my tongue out at him instead. This made his eyes go wide in disbelief, and he probably thought it was quite childish of me but I didn't care. Fuck him.

I looked away from Jase as Maggie approached with her parents. She gave her mother a kiss on the cheek, and then her father, before she was handed off to Matt. Hand in hand they stood as we all listened to the words the priest spoke.

The ceremony was quick. Before I knew it they were exchanging rings. The priest pronounced them man and wife and Matt kissed his bride. Everyone cheered and clapped. They made an adorable couple. The music began to play and the bride and groom took that as their cue to leave. Hand in hand they quickly walked toward the entrance with big smiles on their faces.

I stepped out into the aisle, meeting Jase, linking my arm in his. This time I was willing, unlike the rehearsal. Except this time he didn't need to hold my hand on his arm as we walked, even though he did. His touch ignited something deep inside me. I started to feel the heat from his rough fingers on my hand.

Without looking at him I said, "No need to hold my hand," in a low voice out of the side of my mouth as we followed the bride and groom. I wasn't sure if he had heard me, but since his hold on my hand got tighter, that led me to believe the little shit heard me loud and clear.

I looked up at him through my long lashes, giving him an evil look. His pale green eyes were on me once again, but this time he wore that sly, panty-dropping smile that I loved so much, but my panties hated.

"Always so feisty," Jase said, winking at me.

What the fuck. I rolled my eyes at him, trying to show I didn't care about his words, but my body was on fire. I remembered him telling me that he really liked that I was feisty.

"Asshole," I said, a little louder then I should have.

When we reached Maggie and Matt, we stood next to them to start forming the receiving line. I pulled my hand from his, trying to shake the want that had built up inside me during that short walk. Jase stood closer to me than I would have liked him to. Well, that's a lie. I wanted him close to me. Behind me, even, naked and yanking my hair. My body craved him. Him on top of me would've been even better, but that wasn't going to happen. He was getting married in less than a week, and I needed to keep myself in check.

The guests said their praises and congratulations as they exited the church. Once the last of the guests left, I ducked out of my place next to Jase and headed toward Alayna and Amy. I definitely needed some distance from him. Unfortunately the distance was short-lived, because the photographer rounded us up for pictures. Jase tortured me with his nearness whenever he and I needed to stand next to each other.

Thankfully he didn't say anything more, but his eyes said a lot whenever he looked at me, which was too often. I was slightly worried at the story they were trying to tell me. I reminded myself, yet again, that he was getting married—so whatever the story, I wasn't interested. I was only interested in getting through this day. There was a light at the end of the tunnel and it had lounge chair and some fruity drink with an umbrella waiting for me almost five thousand miles away.

Chapter 28 | Country Reception

With the pictures and torture out of the way, we piled into the beefy limo and headed to the barn. I made sure that I had a buffer of bodies between Jase and me. I thought of my checklist, and it seemed my rules were not working so well for me.

The limo driver had bottles of champagne opened for us. The guys made sure we all had a glass. I think I had two glasses of champagne in the short drive. As we neared the barn, the sun was beginning to set. We approached the turn for the dirt road, which was lined with white luminary bags on either side, guiding the guests to their destination.

The limo pulled onto the dirt road, passing the flickering white bags before stopping. We stopped next to the barn and one by one we all got out of the limo. I was seriously done with getting in and out of that thing. I needed to unwind with a couple of drinks.

We waited outside the barn. We could hear the band playing, and I swore I could hear a banjo. The people inside were loud, but they sounded like they were having a good time. I kept up my buffer from Jase, but I knew it was only a matter of time before we would be walking in together.

The music began to quiet and I heard someone make an an-nouncement. The barn doors slid open and someone waved us over. This was it: we paired up once again. Amy was in front, her arms linked with Masen and her brother Casey. The person inside announced them and they began to walk in with the music. Everyone inside began to hoot and holler. It sounded like a fucking hoedown. Next was Alayna, who was quite preoccupied with Reid. The two had been pawing at each other since we'd gotten into the limo. She was being a shitty buffer. With her arms linked with the twins, Reid and Cole, they walked in when their names were announced.

Now it was my turn. *Five more minutes, Kenz, and this portion will be all over,* I had to tell myself. *No more touching or having to be near Jase.*

"You ready? We're up," he said close to my ear.

I didn't answer and I didn't wait for him either. I started walking in without holding his arm. This must have stumped him, because by the time he caught up to me I was already through the doorway of the barn. He tried to grab by hand but the Jersey girl in me fist pumped her way into the reception.

I stopped next to the others but I was taken aback by the barn all over again. With all the people, music, flowers, and lights, it was breathtaking. I looked around at all the detail, hoping to remember the scene before me. I was pulled out of my trance by Jase, who was talking to me.

"Did you hear me?" he asked.

"No," I told him, and I really didn't care to know what he had said.

He tried to speak again but was cut off by Matt and Maggie's names being announced as they entered the barn as husband and wife. We all shouted and cheered for them, and some threw confetti that rained down.

Hand in hand they walked to the center of the dance floor. Matt's hand moved to Maggie's lower back as he pulled her to him, taking her hand in his. The band began to play the melody of "Marry Me" by Train. The light in the barn dimmed, only leaving the three chandeliers lit. The new couple began to sway to the words as they were sung to them. Matt held Maggie close to him. They looked into each other's eyes as he quietly sang the words to the love of his life. It was so sweet.

Once the band was through the first chorus, they asked the rest of the wedding party to join the bride and groom. Without hesitation, Jase grabbed my hand tightly and pulled me to the dance floor. Cole and Casey opted out of the dance, leaving Alayna and Reid paired up as well as Masen and Amy.

I hoped the dance with Jase would be as simple and awkward as two twelve-year-olds trying to dance for the first time. I tried to put enough space between him and me as if there was an imaginary person between us. It seemed Jase wasn't having that. He pulled me closer, placing his rough hand in the middle of my back, which was open and exposed from my keyhole dress. I know, it sounds dirty, right? But dirty in a good way.

My mind and body were thinking crazy things. I tried to tell myself only a few minutes and the song would be over. I would be out of his embrace. My skin was on fire where his hand was. I felt the electricity we shared, and I swear by the way he was breathing he felt it too. Neither of us said a word, and I did my best not to look at him. I kept my head turned away, looking out over his shoulder, watching the faces that were staring back as we swayed to the song.

If looks could kill and if she had good aim, I would've been dead by the daggers Leah the Cunt was shooting me. I paid her no mind, though. I would have loved to give her the middle finger, but instead I played it cool, pretending like I didn't even notice her annoyance. I felt Jase's rough hand gently and slowly slide down the bare skin of my lower back. It made me think of the one night we'd shared so long ago. His hand stopped right where the fabric of my dress started. God, I loved keyhole dresses. This got my attention, catching me off guard.

Without realizing it, I peeked at Jase though my long lashes. I was fearful of what he would see, because my eyes were screaming "bend me over the nearest bale of hay and fuck me silly." Jase was looking down at me. He shifted his head to see what I was hiding.

The timing was perfect because the song came to an end. I took a quick step back from his embrace, exhaling a deep breath, not realizing I had been holding it in. Jase noticed and his pale green eyes darted to my mouth and then slowly met my eyes again.

Fuck.

I quickly turned on my heel and headed in the direction of the bar. I needed some liquid courage.

I wanted to look back and see if he was looking at me. But curiosity killed the cat, and even if I did look, what would that prove? Nothing. So I didn't look back, but out of the corner of my eye I saw the Cunt walking toward Jase. The quickness of her steps told me she was one pissed bitch, and I couldn't help but smile.

Ally was at the bar getting a beer. As the bartender handed it to her, I intercepted the beer and chugged it. Rude, I know, but I really needed a drink.

"Ooookay, you're welcome," Ally said. "I guess you needed a drink after *that* dance," she added, smiling at me shyly.

I looked at her wide-eyed, swallowing the last of the beer. "Thanks for letting me steal your drink," I told her.

"May I say something?" Ally asked.

I gave her the people's eyebrow, wondering what she had to say, considering she felt compelled to ask my permission.

"Go ahead," I told her, leery of what might follow.

"I listened when you explained what happened between you and Jase that night in the barn. From what I just saw, from what everyone probably saw, that isn't a man that doesn't want you," Ally pointed out.

"I don't know about that," I told her, trying to deflect her observations.

"Oh no? Then why does he look so guilty and she look so pissed?" Ally added.

I looked across the way to see Jase and Leah in what seemed to be a heated discussion. And yes, he looked guilty, and yes, she looked very pissed.

Masen joined us at the bar, as well as Alayna, Reid, and Amy.

"That was some dance," Alayna said, low enough that only I could hear.

I rolled my eyes, trying to downplay what she was suggesting.

"Do you remember what I told you last night?" I asked her.

"About what's happening next week?" Alayna replied.

"Yes, exactly. So the dance, it doesn't matter. None of it matters," I told her.

Alayna put her arm around my shoulders, giving me a good squeeze. "Kenz, it does matter. All of it matters, because it's clear that you matter to him," she told me.

"You do realize your words of wisdom aren't helping me right now," I told her.

"I know, and I'm sorry, but I'm not going to let it get you down. Let's celebrate," Alayna said, putting on a happy face for me.

Alayna ordered a round of shots for all of us. Shots cured all things. Even if only temporary, I would take it. It was time to let go and unwind for the night. The worst was past me, but I had a feeling these would be the longest hours of my life.

Chapter 29 | Words of Wisdom

The night was going great. The band was fantastic and we had all been dancing our asses off. While everyone was sitting down eating dinner, Jase stood from the table he was sharing with his family and tapped his glass of champagne to get everyone's attention. He walked over to the table that Maggie and Matt shared, carrying a microphone.

He tapped it to make sure it was on, which made a *poof, poof* sound come from the speakers.

"Hello, everyone. From what my mother has told me, it seems to be that time of the night were I get to embarrass my brother Matt," Jase said with a devilish grin, and people began to laugh. "Just kidding. I wanted to, believe me, but Mom swore she would disown me if I did. Love you, Mom," Jase added, being funny and light-hearted.

Leave it to Nancy to put limits on the speech.

Jase looked around at the guests and smiled before continuing. "I wanted to thank you all for being a part of this very special day. Matt, you chased your dream, went all in, and now you got her right next to you, looking beautiful as ever. It makes me hopeful. I, for one, am ecstatic that you both have found each other, so never let her go. To Matt and Maggie," he said as he raised his glass to the room and took a drink of champagne.

He then walked around the table, giving the bride and groom a hug.

"Wow," Alayna said, looking at me.

My thoughts exactly. What did he mean by "hopeful"? I hated reading between the lines.

"That shit had double meaning to it. It's like a homophone," Alayna added.

"What? Do you even know what a homophone is? That was not *like* a homophone, Alayna," I said, trying to school my cousin after one too many drinks.

"Of course it is," she argued back.

"It's not. Your thinking of double entendre, and yes, I heard his words, I was sitting right here," I told her, getting annoyed at the petty dispute.

"Oooh, you're right," Alayna realized.

I could only shake my head at her.

After Jase's speech, I stood up with my glass of champagne in hand and began to walk toward Maggie and Matt, who were talking with Jase.

"Where are you going?" Alayna questioned in a hushed voice, which really wasn't hushed. Alayna plus alcohol equaled no volume control.

I ignored my cousin and continued weaving through the tables.

When I reached Maggie and Matt, they were still chatting with Jase, who was still holding the microphone.

"Hey, I wanted to say a little something for you guys," I told them. They all seemed surprised—especially Maggie, because she knew how I loathed speaking in front of crowds.

I hadn't told anyone I was going to give a speech, just in case I chickened out.

"Jase, may I have the microphone, please?" I asked nicely, reaching toward him.

He handed me the microphone without looking at me, as if I didn't matter. He was like a fucking yo-yo, driving me crazy. Asshole. *See if I ever let him touch my keyhole again*, I thought to myself. It was funny to me and made me giggle.

Maggie, Matt, and Jase all looked at me like they had missed the joke. I turned without explaining my giggles. I switched the microphone on and blew into it to make sure it was on.

"Good evening, everyone. I'm Maggie's best friend and maid of honor. I wanted to say a little something as well," I told the guests.

K.A. MIHALICS

Everyone quieted and I thought I heard Alayna tell someone to put a sock in it. I hoped and prayed it was Reid. Last thing I needed was her involved in a barnyard brawl.

Looking at the bride and groom, I raised my glass of champagne to them before beginning my speech.

"To my best friend Maggie and her new husband Matt. We all know that the journey in life may not always be easy or joyful. Too many tequila shots have proven this true to us," I said, laughing.

"Amen to that one," Alayna shouted from the table as everyone chuckled.

I gave a quick nod of my head in the direction of Alayna.

"Says the girl who's usually pouring the shots," I said, placing the blame on my cousin. Everyone laughed again.

As the laughter subsided, I continued with my speech. "Life is about choices, good and bad, and how we navigate them. As your best friend, Maggie, this is what I hope for you and Matt. I hope your journey together is filled with more ups than downs, that the love and happiness that you both share will give you peace and a happily ever after without any regrets. And more importantly, I hope you both always believe in one another, never giving up on your dreams or the journey," I told them. "To Matt and Maggie."

A crying Maggie got up from her seat and gave me a big hug. "Thank you so much for your beautiful words and everything you've done for us and our wedding. I love you, Kenzie."

I began to cry too. So there we stood, hugging and crying. Matt finally ended our teary session, giving me a hug as well, but he told me he wouldn't say anything, fearing the waterworks would begin again. The three of us laughed.

I noticed Jase standing off to the side, watching me with conflict in his eyes. Maybe he was absorbing my words, given his secret nuptials were only days away. I knew I was still stuck on his "hopeful."

Nancy came over, interrupting our bonding to get the new couple to cut the cake. If Matt's mom was anything other than controlling, I would say she was punctual. The woman had a timeline and she stuck to it. She would have kicked ass and taken names in the corporate world. Not wanting to miss their moment, I decided nature called and it was time for me to take a port-a-potty break. I wasn't a fan of portable bathrooms that didn't flush. I had cringed at the port-a-potty idea when it was brought up, but I was told that they were really nice. Given the barn was in the middle of a field with no running water and no bathroom, there weren't many options.

I headed outside to the designated women's port-a-potties on the side of the barn. I chose one of the two that weren't occupied. To my surprise, it actually *was* nice. There was a sink with running water and flowers in a vase. After taking in the scenery, I quickly did my business, breaking the seal. After washing up and using some hand sanitizer, I unlocked the door.

I literally took a step out only to see Jase standing in front of me with both hands in his pockets. He startled me.

"The guys' bathroom is over there," I told him, pointing at the two potties about ten feet away, labeled *Men*.

"I was waiting for you," he said.

"Do you have some fascination with me in bathrooms?" I asked him, curious as to why he would be waiting for me.

"Seems that way, doesn't it?" he said with a small smile.

I looked up at the night sky, secretly asking the stars for strength or a sign. Something.

"They're bright tonight," Jase said.

I looked at him, puzzled. "Oh yes, the stars. They're much brighter up here in the boonies. So, did you need something?" I questioned, not wanting to hear his answer.

Jase took a step closer. "I wanted to tell you how beautiful you look," he said as he took his hand from his pocket, reached out, and touched a curl of my hair. He twirled it between his fingers. I was so jealous of my own hair. My heart began to pound, realizing how close he was to me, still twirling my hair.

"Thank you. You look pretty good yourself," I told him, trying not to stare at him all decked out, minus the tuxedo jacket. I took a step to the side. "I should probably get back in there. I don't want to miss the cake cutting," I said before walking away.

But then his words stopped me and crushed my heart.

"Do you hate me, Kenzie?" Jase asked in a curious tone.

I turned to look at him. His eyes and face were very serious.

"As much as I wish I could at times, I don't think I'm capable of hating you," I told him honestly before walking back inside. I picked up the pace, not wanting to answer any more questions.

When I walked back into the barn, I stood amongst the crowd of guests for the cake cutting. I watched as the bride and groom were trying to feed each other cake. You could see both Maggie and Matt were having an internal debate on whether to be nice. In the end they fed each carefully without making a mess of one another, and everyone clapped and cheered as they kissed with caked lips.

Someone nudged me from behind before speaking.

"I have to say a year and a half ago I would have never saw this coming, but I'm glad they gave it another shot. They're good together," the person said. I knew it was Jase. He was very close—so close that I could feel his shirt just so slightly graze the skin on my back. Did I mention I love keyhole dresses? It took everything in my body not to lean my back into him.

I felt dizzy with want. My body and mind wanted to give in, but I needed to keep my shit in check. I wanted to ask why he was doing this to me. Did he like the way I reacted to him? Was this a game? If so, it was cruel and I had started to get annoyed. I turned around, only to realize how close we truly were. My heart stammered. I knew by the look in his eyes that one of us had to be smart here, and it wasn't going to be him.

After blinking a couple times, trying to get my bearings, I began to speak. "They are good together," I told him, agreeing with his remark. "They realized the love they had for one another and went all in, like you said in your speech. Makes me also feel hopeful," I added as I smiled at him.

I'm not sure if my use of his words was a zing or a dare to him as we stood staring at each other, my brown eyes staring up at his pale green ones.

Tired of the game, I turned in to the crowd and joined Alayna and Maggie on the dance floor. I knew I had an at least an hour before the night was over. Even if I had to, I would hold off on using the bathroom again for fear of being surprised by Jase.

Chapter 30 | Game Over

Everyone sort of split up after the wedding. Some people left, but most ended up going back to Matt's parents' house. I definitely didn't want to go back to the Hainsworths' house, so when Masen said he was taking his parents and Ally back to Matt's, I jumped on the bandwagon. The last thing I needed or wanted was to be around Jase—especially if his cunt was with him.

Mr. and Mrs. Rowe were the first to go to bed. After Ally started dozing on the couch, it was only a matter of time before she and Masen went to bed too. Before I knew it, it was me and the fucking cricket that I swear was somewhere in the house.

Trying to ignore the cricket, I sat and thought about Maui and wondered if it would be everything I hoped and needed. I realized how nice it was to sit and think with no one around. Wanting to take advantage of the full moon and the bright stars, I grabbed a glass of wine and a throw blanket from the back of the couch and headed outside to the deck. With the blanket wrapped tightly around me, I sat on the deck steps in the cool, spring night air.

I watched the night sky hoping that, just maybe, I would see a shooting star.

"You warm enough?" a male voice asked, scaring the shit out of me.

I jumped up and spilled most of the wine from my glass on the blanket I had wrapped around me. I recognized that voice. "Holy fuck, Jase! Are you trying to give me a heart attack? Clear your throat, knock on something, warn a girl. Shit," I yelled at him.

Without me even realizing it, my hand was in a fist with my arm cocked back, like I was going to hit him.

"You gonna use that? Should I be scared?" Jase said sarcastically, referring to my arm.

"You're an asshole," I told him. Although my heart was still pounding, I relaxed my arm and tried to wipe off the wine I had spilled on myself. Ironic, I know. Thankfully it was white, not red.

I took my seat back on the steps, curious as to why he was there. I guess Jase took that as an invitation, because he took a seat next to me. It seemed I couldn't catch a fucking break that weekend when it came to him.

"Why are you here? What do you want?" I asked, annoyed.

"Why hello to you, too," he said, laughing a little.

I finished what was left of my wine and put the glass between Jase and me. I secretly thought that he and I both knew we couldn't cross that glass.

The way he looked at the glass and smiled, I think he understood the idea of its placement.

"You didn't come back to my parents' house," he said.

"Wow, you're quite observant aren't you?" I said, laying on the sarcasm extra thick.

"Do you wake up feisty, or is it only around me?" he asked, smiling his sly smile.

"I usually save my feistiness for dickheads like you," I quickly retorted, glaring at him.

He laughed so loud I swear someone inside Matt's house must have heard him.

"First I'm an asshole, now I'm a dickhead," he said, still laughing, which only annoyed me more.

"What do you want, Jase?" I asked through gritted teeth. He was ruining my quiet time.

"I wanted to know if you would dance with me," he asked sincerely.

"What? No. I don't know. No, definitely not," I said, debating with myself while also answering him.

"I'll take that as a yes," he said, grabbing my hand, but I pulled away from him. "It doesn't surprise me that you would be this difficult," he told me as he stood.

For a second I wished I would have just given in to him. But then Jase quickly grabbed my arm, pulling me up and tossing me over his shoulder.

"Jase fucking Hainsworth, put me down. Right now!" I demanded as I tried to wiggle out of his grasp. I pushed against his back as I tried to right myself. I could feel his muscles moving as he walked to wherever it was he was taking me. This was so caveman like, and it was totally hot.

I stopped fighting and quieted down, not wanting to wake anyone in the house. I also knew that it was pointless and that he would put me down wherever he wanted me to end up. My mind was hoping for his bed, but I fought off those thoughts, knowing it couldn't happen.

Jase put me down in the middle of Matt's big backyard, close to the pond. I could hear bullfrogs croaking nearby, and the moon made us look pale as we stood in front of each other. With my arms crossed, I briefly closed my eyes and took a deep breath before I spoke.

"There's no music," I said to him.

"Do *we* really need music, Kenzie?" he asked me, really stressing the "we."

I thought of us together and how in tune we were. He gently uncrossed my arms and I didn't fight it. Jase took my left hand and placed it on his shoulder, then took my other hand in his. He reached around my waist, fingers splayed on my bare skin, and pulled me close to him.

I wasn't sure how something could feel so awkward but so right at the same time. Tears pricked my eyes, because I knew this was the end before the beginning had even gotten a chance. I quickly blinked the tears away and looked up at him through my long lashes. We swayed back and forth to a tune that only we knew, as if we had heard it a million times before. We were so in sync.

If that moment was never-ending, I thought I would be okay with that, but I knew all good things had to come to an end. Jase must have known, too, as he leaned in toward me. Maybe this was him "all in," and I couldn't help but want to feel his lips one last time. His lips touched mine, parting them with his tongue. It was all so familiar and warm. My body was on fire, the kiss becoming fierce and more exciting.

Our hands were practically groping each other, not sure where to go or how long to stay in one spot, for fear it wouldn't be enough. Then an alarm went off far back in my brain. I wanted to ignore it, because I loved ignorance, but I knew I would hate myself.

I pulled away, taking a couple steps back from Jase, who was taking labored breaths.

"What am I doing?" I asked myself, swallowing hard and feeling my chest tighten from the pain of the heartbreak that was coming.

"I'm-I'm sorry, Kenzie," Jase stammered out.

"You fucking asshole! You're sorry? Are you fucking kidding me?" I yelled at him. "You're getting married next week and you kiss me!" I said, still shouting. "And I kissed you back! I'm a fucking moron. What was I thinking? What were *you* thinking, Jase? Am I a game to you? All fucking weekend you had to be near me, touching me when you shouldn't have, looking at me the way you do. Why, Jase?" I questioned.

I was so angry and hurt, tears began to spill from my eyes.

"You didn't want me, you said so, so why bother with me? Is this payback?" I demanded.

He didn't answer. He only looked at me wide-eyed.

I walked over to him, poking him the chest hard with my finger. "Answer me! I at least deserve that!" I shouted again. I was about five seconds from a tantrum.

"How did you know?" he asked in a low voice.

I shook my head and looked up at the night sky before I answered him. That was his answer to me?

"How did I know what? How do I know you're getting married next week? Your cunt of a fiancée told me, that's how I know. She also told me how amazing you are in bed, but I already knew that. Don't worry, I didn't share that detail with her," I told him in a clipped tone, but I didn't raise my voice again. "This, whatever it is," I said, pointing from him to me, "is done, I'm done," I confessed. "It's just bad timing on our parts and we have to accept that," I said with a weak smile, taking several steps away from him.

I turned toward the house and started to walk back, trying to keep the tears at bay. I hadn't heard his steps approach when he grabbed my arm to stop me. Either he was a fucking ninja or I needed to get my hearing checked.

"Kenzie, please, don't—" Jase said before I stopped him.

"No, Jase," I said as I shrugged out of his grasp. The pain and sadness in his eyes screamed at me to listen, but I couldn't.

Like a chicken, I ran the rest of the way back to the house, leaving the glass and blanket outside. I shut the door and locked it, making sure Jase couldn't follow. I leaned against the door, trying to process what had happened.

"Are you okay, Kenzie?" Ally asked.

I wasn't surprised that someone was waiting for me inside after I had lost my shit in Matt's backyard.

"Someday I'm sure I will be," I said to her as I wiped the tears from my face. "Is he still out there?" I asked her, because I wasn't sure if I had enough willpower to stay inside if he was.

She peeked out the window and shook her head, confirming he had left.

Ally stayed up with me for a little bit, and she let me vent and cry before she went back to bed. She told me two things that had me tossing and turning: she said maybe it wasn't a game Jase was playing, and maybe it wasn't over.

Chapter 31 | New Chapter

It was my fourth day in Maui, and it was truly a paradise that everyone should visit at some point in their lives. I already had a designated spot by the pool. I would get up early and run down to put my towel and book as a placeholder.

My days had been lazy while I laid out in my bikini. I soaked in the sun as it beamed down on my skin, recharging me. The light winds made it comfortable and relaxing. My two weeks there were free and clear. I had no plans and decided to take things hour by hour, or day by day.

It was day four of me relaxing poolside and working on my tan. Maybe the next day I would venture outside the hotel. It was very strange being there on that beautiful island alone, but I kept telling myself I needed it.

The night of the wedding, when Jase I had kissed, I barely slept. I had too much on my mind. The next morning when everyone in the house began to stir and pack up, I did the same. Maggie and Alayna were dragging ass and weren't planning on heading back just yet. So I got a ride with Masen, Ally, and his parents. The ride home was as torturous as my sleep. I was alone in my thoughts, and as much as I tried to think of someone other than Jase, my mind kept going back to him. I thought of our paths and how they continually crossed. I couldn't shake Ally's words and I wondered if I would ever know the truth.

In the end it didn't matter anymore. By now he might have already exchanged his *I do*s in front of an Elvis lookalike. That would be his new chapter and this is the beginning of mine, which I was thoroughly enjoying.

When the plane had landed, I'd called my mom, Alayna, and Maggie. I specifically told them I wouldn't have my phone on me all the time and the two weeks was me disconnecting from reality. That was my way of telling them not to bother me. I knew my mom and Maggie wouldn't be an issue, but I couldn't say the same about my cousin. Alayna and I were practically attached at the hip and did everything together. I figured she was probably going through withdrawals the minute my plane left the tarmac.

I was quite surprised when it took twenty-four hours for her to blow up my phone. After a day by the pool, I had gone back to my room to shower and get ready for dinner when I saw I had thirty-seven missed calls. I knew if it was a true emergency someone else would have also called, but all thirty-seven calls were from Alayna. I debated whether I should call her back or not, but I didn't want it to be a daily occurrence. So I gave in.

I didn't even think the phone had rung before she was cursing me out. Once she settled down, I figured I could probably get a word in.

"Hello to you, too. Are you done yelling at me? Do you feel better now?" I asked, laughing at my cousin.

"No, I'm still mad at you, but I have to tell you something!" Alayna told me, sounding not as angry as she had been just seconds before.

"What could possibly be so important that you needed to call me thirty-seven times?" I asked.

"Actually it was more, because I called your room as well," she said.

I looked over at the phone in my room, only to see the red light blinking for the message indicator.

I couldn't believe it—the bitch was crazy and she was my cousin. Lucky me.

"Are you sitting down?" Alayna asked, and I could sense whatever she needed to tell me was eating her up.

"Yes, actually, I am," I told her.

"Okay, here goes nothing," she mumbled before I heard her take a quick breath. "Reid told me that Jase and Leah got—" Alayna quickly tried to spit out before I cut her off.

Once I heard his name, I knew I didn't want to hear any more. "Stop, Alayna, just stop. I don't want to hear it," I told her, annoyed that she thought I would want to hear the gossip.

"But Kenzie," she tried again, but I was quicker this time.

"No, Alayna. I'm here to get away from all that bullshit. I don't want to hear about any Hainsworth-related topics. Understand?" I said, practically scolding her.

She paused before she answered. "Got it. I didn't mean... I'm sorry Kenzie," she apologized, sounding defeated.

I took a moment before saying anything more. "How is everything else? You miss me yet?" I asked, trying to sound upbeat. I wanted to change the topic and mood.

Everything was fine after that, and there was no more talk of anything Hainsworth-related. We both admitted we missed each other and I told Alayna I would call every couple of days.

Since it had been two days from when we last spoke, I decided to call Alayna. With the time difference, it was about eight o'clock at night in Jersey, so I began to pack up and head to my room. I got up from my lounge chair and slipped on my beach cover up. I grabbed my suntan lotion and saw a single white daisy lying on top of my book, which sat on the table next to me. I paused at first, just staring at the flower, which happened to be my favorite. I wasn't even sure if I should pick it up, but I did anyway.

I held it in my hand and stared at the petals. It was strangely coincidental. I wondered how it had gotten there on top of my book without me noticing. I looked around to see if anyone would claim the gesture, but not one face showed me anything. Maybe I was putting too much thought into it. Perhaps it was on the ground near my chair and someone had picked and placed it on my book just because.

Without giving it any more thought, I gathered the rest of my things and headed back to my room. When I got there, I checked my cell phone and there was only one text message from my mom, hoping I was having better weather than they were in Jersey. Apparently it had been raining on and off since I'd left. Strangely, not a single call or text message from Alayna. I gave her a quick call before jumping in the shower, but she didn't answer. I figured I would try calling her again later, so I didn't leave a message. I jumped in the shower to wash off the suntan lotion from my skin.

After getting out of the shower, I was drying off when I heard a knock at the door. I looked through the peephole to see a man standing there with his back to me.

"One second," I shouted at the door, so I could put some clothes on. I quickly threw on my beach cover-up. I opened the door and saw that the man was from the hotel staff, holding a silver ice bucket with a bottle of champagne and two champagne glasses.

"Yes?" I said, confused.

"Miss Shaw, your champagne," he said, stepping into my room.

"Ummm, there must be some mistake. I didn't order any champagne," I told him as he walked past me.

"There is no mistake, ma'am," he said, putting the bucket and glasses on the table before leaving without a tip.

"Hey, wait," I yelled after him as he walked out the door, closing it behind him. What the fuck had just happened?

Hoping to still catch him, I held my cover-up tightly to me as I quickly walked toward the door, remembering I had absolutely no underwear on. When I opened the door I couldn't believe who was standing there, leaning against the wall.

"What... the fuck... are you doing here?" I asked Alayna.

"It was dreary and rainy back home, so I decided to take a couple of days off and visit you. I figured we could celebrate my arrival with some champagne," she said, happily hugging me.

Alayna then strolled into my room, towing her rolling luggage past me. I was dumbfounded. Now the flower made sense, that little shit.

I closed the door behind her. "So you decided to crash my vacation. And I guess I should thank you for the daisy?" I asked her.

"What daisy?" she said, smiling at me. "I didn't leave you a daisy," she added, and I could tell she was lying. I wanted to be mad at her but I couldn't. I was kind of glad that she was there, even if it was only for a couple of days.

We popped open the bottle of champagne, pouring some into the glasses. I knew it was going to be a fun couple of days with Alayna there. She called and made reservations for six o'clock at one of the restaurants in the hotel. We talked a little about nothing in particular before we started to get ready. We modeled our potential dinner outfits for one another.

After several outfits and a whole bottle of champagne, Alayna and I settled on what to wear. I wore a burnt red, ruffled hi-lo wrap dress with my camel-colored sandals, and tied my hair up in a loose bun. Alayna wore a simple navy blue paisley maxi dress with cutout sandals, and put her long hair in braid. We were finally ready for dinner.

Chapter 32 | Dinner Date

We were a couple of minutes late for our reservations when we left my room, and were trying to hustle. Alayna and I were more than halfway there when she started to complain about her sandals. She wanted to go back and get her flip-flops instead. Not wanting to hear her complain all night, I gave her the extra key card for the room.

While she went back to the room, I headed to the restaurant, not wanting to lose our reservation. I was practically out of breath when I got there. Thankfully the maître d' was very nice and understanding. I let him know that Alayna was on her way. Rather than wait for her, he showed me to our table.

He walked me through the restaurant to the outside patio, where our table was. The tables looked like they were made from teak, and they sat on a stone patio that faded into the sand. The sun was setting in the distance, but the patio was lit with tiki torches that were strategically staged. The fronds on the palm trees gently swayed in the ocean breeze. We had such an amazing view from our table.

The maître d' pulled out my chair and I sat down at the table for two. He told me the server would be right over and walked away. I waited about fifteen minutes for Alayna, and I even tried to call her cell once, but she didn't answer. When the waiter came to the table a second time, I had to tell him to come back in a little bit.

Just then, someone placed a pink drink in front of me with a wedge of lime stuck on the glass.

"Kettle One and cranberry, if I remember correctly," a very familiar male voice said.

When I first looked up, I had to do a double take of the guy wearing khaki cargo shorts and an American Eagle T-shirt. I instantly felt the blood drain from my face.

My heart began to pound out of my chest and I was sure that if I didn't breathe soon I was probably going to be lying on the stone patio.

"I'm used to feisty, not speechless. This is a first for me," he said, smiling that sly smile that I loved.

Yup, it was Jase in the flesh, looking hot as ever. He looked like he hadn't shaved in a week, and I wanted to reach out and touch his face to feel the stubble.

Part of me felt like I might be hallucinating, and I thought I may have had too much sun. "You. Jase. What, what are you doing here?" I questioned, stumbling over my words. I was so confused. What the fuck was going on? *I swear if he is spending his honeymoon here, I will make those motherfuckers leave.* I'd be damned if they fucked up my vacation.

Jase laughed, and it was pretty clear that he was getting a kick out of this. "For you, of course," he said, staring down at me.

What did he just say? I was so confused. I noticed while looking at him that his pale green eyes looked clear with no conflict or confusion. They seemed free, and for the first time I felt hopeful.

Jase grabbed the other chair at the table, moving it next to me and taking a seat. With his rough hands he took mine in his, which I willingly gave. He looked over my face, smiling, before looking back into my eyes.

"Jase, why are you here? Why aren't you in Vegas? You're supposed to be getting married—or are already married," I said, sounding quite puzzled.

I realized that I was trembling, and I didn't think I could stop even if I tried.

"Kenzie," he said, and I loved when he said my name. "I don't know what to say really or how to explain it. All I can say is from the moment I met you at the farm market, it has always been you," Jase said, pausing before continuing.

"It sounds crazy, I know, and I never believed in that shit, but it's true. Not having you left a void inside me. The back-and-forth, the in and out of each other's life has been torture. It was like some cruel joke someone was playing on me. I did what I could, what I thought I should do, to move on, but you were always there. For a while I was pissed, but I realized the more pissed I got, the more I fought my feelings for you. I didn't know my head from my ass," he said, looking at our hands as he gently rubbed his thumbs over mine.

He looked back up at me before speaking.

"When you told me you knew about Leah and I eloping, hearing you actually say the words killed me. I knew then there was no way I could've gone through with marrying her. She's not who I want, because it's always been you. You're what I want and need, Kenz," Jase said as he caressed my face with the back of his hand.

My eyes felt the tears beginning to build, and before I knew it they spilled over, running down my face.

"I came here for another chance with you," Jase said, wiping my tears away. "I don't want to start over, because all the bullshit is part of our story, Kenzie. What I want is our next chapter," he said, still looking at me as I thought over his words. "So what do you say," he asked, sounding hopeful and smiling that sly smile of his.

Staring back at him, my heart still pounding, my body still trembling, I said, "I think I'm gonna love *our* next chapter," before jumping off my chair and into Jase's lap, taking his scruffy face in my hands and kissing him fiercely. In the distance I heard hoots and hollering from what had to be Alayna and Reid.

Jase and I did lots of talking and catching up. After dinner we took a walk along the beach outside the restaurant. We stopped to admire the stars. Jase pulled me close, holding me as we swayed back and forth dancing to the tune that only we knew. This was happiness, and even though I knew it would take time, my heart felt almost whole again.

As we swayed, I noticed a shooting star in the distance and silently made a wish. I wished for lasting love.

Acknowledgments

My biggest thank you goes to my husband, Rich. Having you by my side has made me feel like the luckiest girl in the world. One of the smartest things I did was say "Yes." The second was saying "I do." You're my soul mate and best friend. Without your encouraging words, confidence, love and support, this would only be a story in my mind and dreams, rather than on paper. You and our two beautiful children give me purpose. The life we've created is my fairytale and I wouldn't trade or change it for the world. I will always be the platter to your Gouda cheese. I look forward to many more lifetimes with you. I love you, always and forever.

To my beautiful children, Ryleigh and Logan, you both bring such happy chaos to my life. I'm blessed, grateful and honored to be to be your Mom. Your sweet souls make me so very proud. Never give up on yourselves or your dreams, and always be kind. Keep practicing guitar and remember I'll always be your number one fan. I love you to the moon and back.

Mom, thank you for all that you've done for me. You've given me such a great life and I couldn't have asked for more. Growing up, you allowed me to be my own person, but you were always right there if I needed you. Your love for family is admirable. You've kept me grounded and shaped me into the well-rounded but crazy, loving person I am today. I can only hope to be just as amazing and selfless as you are. You and George are such amazing parents and people. I appreciate all you both have done for me. I love you both very much.

Shana, what can I say that hasn't already been said? You're an amazing cousin and best friend. You're my sounding board, partner in crime and you've been my cheerleader throughout this whole process, page by page, chapter by chapter. Thank you for all you've done. I appreciate you more than you know. I love you my Sestra.

To the rest of my family, I couldn't be more proud to grow up and be a part of something so grand. I'm blessed to have such wonderful memories with each and every one of you. My life experiences are more like adventures that I will treasure forever. I'm grateful for so much, especially my family. I love you all.

To all my friends who played a part in my life and gave me fuel for my story, Thank You! You're all amazing and unique individuals. We've been through so much. We've laughed, cried and laughed some more. You've made my life interesting in one way or another. Our effortless friendships are hard to come by, and even though we may not see each other all the time, when we do, we pick up right where we left off. I'm proud to call each of you my best friend. Love you guys.

About the Author

K.A. Mihalics is an independent author and publisher. She was never one for reading until a few years ago when she binge read too many books to count. She currently lives in New Jersey with her husband, two children, two Dobermans and two Manx cats. She loves her family, their simple life and is a big fan of red wine, daisies and old pickup trucks.

One night she dreamt about a man and woman meeting at a farm market. After a couple of days and lots of thought elaborating on that dream, in her mind she gave it a beginning, middle and end. Curious at attempting to write a book, she confided in her husband and with his encouraging words, "Go for it," Cruel Joke came alive on paper.

Made in the USA
Middletown, DE
19 October 2016